KINGDOM OF FALLEN GODS

BARRY FOSTER

WOODS
PUBLISHING

*All of my stories are dedicated to my loving wife,
Marie Foster.*

CONTENTS

PART I
BRIANNE

CHAPTER 1

 irst Steps, 1286

BRIANNE PLAYED WITH HER TOYS WHILE PRETENDING not to hear the words exchanged on the other side of the rickety door that was filled with holes and missing a hinge. The whole house was the same; it was more likely to fall apart than be repaired and unfit for anyone to call home. The paladins abandoned it for nearly a decade and used it for storage until she arrived.

Brianne looked to be a small child, but given her lineage, she aged much slower than other children. Fifteen winters had passed since her birth, and most children would be preparing to start apprenticeships or entering their lifelong service to the Legion or other forms of service. As the daughter of Countess Elissar, she was expected to follow in her mother's footsteps and become an ambassador to the western reach. It was a thankless task—necessary to keep the regions of the kingdom from war, but one that kept her from spending much time in one place.

The amount of travel came with an unforeseen effect and drew more attention than they desired, but she wished to adventure. The idea of chatting with nobles and dining in banquet halls poisoned her thoughts and often left her bored and miserable. Her ambition, even at such a young age, was to follow in the footsteps of the greatest adventurer to ever live: Nishal Reduwar the Seventh, known for locating the ancient ruins of Castio Armpor and finding the goblins of Uligur in the southern peninsula. His accolades were so impressive that he retired and lived well while cataloging his many travels.

The yelling outside the room got louder, but she remained fixated on the toy horse and soldier she played with while Elissar labored away in negotiations; Brianne preferred it over being forced into joining. She built a fort of pillows and books, her soldier marched up the side, and in her mind, the great Dwarf Reduwar scaled the walls of the forgotten city of Ciro.

"It was said that you all would do what was needed. I have a target on my back. And where is the council? I cannot raise her any longer. Shaw, are you listening?"

She continued playing with her toys. In her mind, the small man stood alongside the wall and looked over the crystal spire and admired another momentous find. She pulled a notepad from her bag and started scribbling research notes of what would be found there.

"I hear your words, but what can I do?

Melissande entrusted us all with a task, and we all accepted the risk."

She wrote, pressing harder onto the page and even tearing it in some places. Her imagination faltered, and she returned to the moment. Hearing their words dragged her down, bringing tears to her eyes and causing her to let a soft sob slip. Wiping the tears away, she pushed back the negative emotions, shook her head, and returned to writing. She flipped to a new page and started again.

"You have to take her, Shaw. I am going away to Netoma for a summit in a week, and if she were discovered, it would put us all in the Lady's sights," she said.

There was a pause, followed by Shaw letting out a long-labored sigh. "I hear you, but what am I to do?"

"We swore an oath. It is your turn. Train her, and when it is time, send her to him. Maybe the old bastard will be more reliable than you." Her words stopped abruptly, followed by the sound of a set of bags landing on the ground and stomping down the path as she marched away from the cottage.

"Will you tell her goodbye? You raised her, after all," Shaw said.

Brianne's hands stopped. She turned to another page. Teardrops peppered the white canvas, and she fought to keep her eyes open. She wiped them away, but more came. She buried her head in her arms and muffled the sounds of her sobbing. The room around her fell silent, and she found it hard to breathe, but she managed to keep from making a sound and drawing attention to her pain.

"I cannot. Be kind to her. Farewell, Commander. May you fulfill your oath as I have," Elissar said.

Hoofbeats clattered up the path away from the cottage and faded into the distance. The door swung open, and rather than stay still, she climbed into the bed and covered her face, leaving only her feet visible from under the sad excuse for a blanket. Shaw sat on the edge of the mattress and placed a hand on her back. "You'll be staying with us for a time."

She pulled away and tucked the blanket tight. Refusing to look up, she imagined any place other than the broken down shack. Shaw stood and gave her another pat on the back. "I'll be outside when you feel like chatting. It is a rather beautiful day. Would be a shame to spend it inside." He got up and closed the door softly.

She threw the blanket off and looked over the room. Wind cut through the broken bits of glass still held in the window frames, and shafts of light cut through the dusty interior. The paint peeled in places, and the floors were rotted and broken. She was accustomed to luxurious inns and noble estates, but this brought her a sense of excitement and a myriad of fearful thoughts.

She peeked through the window to see Shaw sitting in an old rocking chair on the porch, his flashy armor glinting in the light of the midday sun. She used this moment to slip into a broken space in the floorboards and sneak out onto the grounds of the abbey. She ducked behind a shrub and waited until the guards were out of sight to climb the steps of the northern watchtower. About halfway up, she felt a pair of hands grab and lift her high into the air. Shaw raised her off the ground and placed her firmly on his shoulders. "You'll get a better view from up here."

He walked slowly to the top. He favored one side but tried his best to conceal it, with one foot landing harder than the other. Her focus remained glued to watching for any sign of her mother. At the top, she could see the dunes stretching into the distance and even the edge of the farmlands to the north, and between them was a dust trail scaling the farthest dune to the north.

He sat her down, and she pressed against the ledge and watched until it faded from sight. Her eyes were drawn to the floor again. She fought the urge to cry, but her age won over the years of etiquette training, and tears welled in her eyes. Shaw knelt and raised her chin. She noticed his pause when preparing to speak. He pulled her close and squeezed. Her head came to rest on his chest piece, and he cupped the back of her head while lifting her.

"It's fine to be afraid, but we must always look ahead."

She clutched the edges of his armor and sobbed. He fought the urge to join her but remained resolute. He struggled but managed to stand and carry her back to the cottage, placing her gently on the bed. She jumped when the ringing of the dinner bell started. He gave her a gentle pat and left, closing the door behind him. She poked out from under the covers and inspected the room again, but her imagination failed to bring her solace. Instead, she sat in the only space on the bed with nothing but a hollow feeling. She came to the edge of the bed and watched a beetle crawl back and forth across the hollow opening that once held a window.

"Ugh, I swear, humans are the worst," said a voice crawling under the building.

She crawled back and pulled the blanket up, cowering away from the approaching voice. She bundled up, her eyes barely poking over her knees as she watched as a small green lizardlike creature walk out of a hole in her closet.

"I know, I know, they aren't all bad but . . ." He tilted his head and looked on at her with dismay. "You're smaller and at the same time larger than I expected."

When she blinked, he vanished from view at the edge of the bed but hopped up over the side and landed on the blanket at her feet.

"What are you?" she asked.

Her toes curled, and she tucked away a bit farther.

"Oh, I see how it is. Don't like dragons?" he asked.

She perked up and leaned forward, and her eyes grew brighter. "You're a dragon? You don't look like a dragon. Aren't they big and menacing? And aren't they evil, breathing fire and eating people?"

He plopped down onto the bed and sat back on his legs and tail. He was covered in green scales that gave way to yellow as they reached his belly, and his eyes were a bright green with a golden ring at their center. With clawed hands and feet and a set of wings protruding from his back, he resembled a dragon, other than being small enough to fit in a person's hand.

"We aren't evil, don't care what the tomes say. And all dragons are different sizes, also you may be thinking of wyrms, the crazy cousins of dragons. We have different colors and shapes and. and some of us don't have wings or even tails."

He stretched out and rested his chin against his claws. "And then there is the Elder dragon, Emual, a guy or thing what would you call something that has no corporeal form? Anyway, Emual has tiny arms and legs in dragon form."

She laid down beside him and looked on with intrigue, "How many forms do dragons have?" She inched a bit closer and eyed his small form.

His eyes were closed, but he snickered a bit at her subtle attempt at a closer look. "Hmm, I have two forms. One is this majestic carapace you see now, and the other is as Alitherus, Dragon Watcher of the North, but I prefer this form. People don't hurl arrows at me when I am a dragonling. Well, they just try to stomp you for looking like a lizard."

With wide eyes, she marveled at the crème-colored crested ridges along his snout that ran the length of his body and the fanned tail covered in spikes. She reached out with a finger extended, but before the tip could touch his scales one eye opened, and he grabbed her hand and crawled up her arm. He came to rest on her shoulder and tucked himself into her long silver hair.

"Wonder why your hair is that color? Kind of like those from the far west across the ocean." He clawed at her hair a bit and swatted it back and forth.

She sat up and tried to pull him out, but he managed to hook his tail around her neck and drooped down. Doing this, he let go and landed in her lap.

"Why are you here?" she asked, using a comb to fix her hair as best she could.

He crawled his way back up after she put her long hair in a ponytail.

"I was—"

The heavy stomp of boots landed on the porch, and she grabbed Alit and shoved him under her pillow.

"Ugh, the smell is awful. Clean this thing, or I swear—"

She lifted the edge of the pillow and whispered to him, "Shhh, Shaw is back."

She placed it back over him and pulled a book from her bag at the foot of the bed. When the door opened, Shaw walked in carrying two plates with a waterskin attached to a string around his neck. Shaw had taken the time to change out of his armor and wore a cloth shirt and pants with leather shoes. He sat beside her and put a plate of food on her lap. The cut of meat offered more questions than could be answered, and it was accompanied by vegetables and two flaky biscuits. He took two metal cups from his pocket and filled them with water and placed them on the nightstand. She looked past him and saw Alit poking his head out while drooling at the sight of cooked meat. She grinned at Shaw and tossed her book on top of the pillow. He sat with his legs crossed and facing away from the headboard.

"Glad to see you've cheered up. Feeling better?" he asked. He kept slipping a small satchel that rested over his shoulder away before she could peek into it.

"Yes, sir." Her answer fit their relationship but seemed to strike a nerve in Shaw. "You don't have to call me sir when I'm out of the uniform."

She gave a nod and continued her attempt at looking into the bag. Best she saw was a stack of books, but nothing more could be made out from the angle, and he did well to keep it out of sight. He swung it behind his back and leaned to meet her eyes.

"Curious, are you? Do you like adventure stories?"

He plucked the last morsel of meat off his plate. He hardly chewed before swallowing it, and as quickly as possible, he moved his plate to the nightstand. Her interest in food faded, but she picked at it nevertheless, her eyes watching his every move before taking a last sip of water and sliding the plate and glass to him. Alit poked his head from under the pillow and eyed the meat sitting next to him on the plate. Brianne got Shaw's attention, buying time for Alit to snag the meat and slip under the pillow.

Shaw glanced back at the empty plate and raised an eyebrow. Scooting closer to Brianne, he stacked the plates and cups. "Rodents are getting bold, I guess. So, about this satchel . . ."

He pulled the satchel around and plopped it down between them. Inside were books from many different authors, but one stood out. *Reduwar, the Last Journal.* She heard of it but never thought it to exist. It told of his last whereabouts and how one could figure out his last riddle: finding the lost city of Ciro. Her eyes were big and gleaming for the first time since she arrived. He put them back inside and turned the satchel away from her.

"I'll give you these and a few more I have in my office, but first, you have to promise: no more sneaking off to climb the watchtowers," he said.

She grinned from ear to ear and nodded before snatching them away, spreading them across the bed and inspecting each cover.

Shaw gave her a pat on the head. "One last thing." He pulled a necklace from his pocket, and a symbol of Athys swung from it. "Every paladin needs to know the light. For now, this will be yours." He draped it around her neck and left with their empty plates, and he looked at the hole by the closet and then under the bed. After a bit of searching, he closed the door and left her to enjoy the books. She glanced out the window, watching his movement until he turned the corner and dropped from sight.

She pulled the pillow off Alit. He lay on his back with the chunk of meat on his stomach as he took slow methodical bites, savoring every bit. Using his other hand, he waved at her without turning his gaze from the mouthwatering meal.

"Were you hungry?" she asked.

He chewed for a moment and held a single claw up asking for her patience. "Well—mmm. so good—I haven't eaten in a few days. Is it days? Maybe longer."

She rolled her eyes and left him to look over the array of books before her. There were books on the oldest known ruins and even books speculating about the location of fabled cities and legendary items from the age of the Anian, but her eyes remained on the journal about Reduwar the Seventh and his intrepid group of adventurers. Elissar read them to her many times in their travels, and it brought a bit of familiarity to the bizarre moment.

The journal recounted the events around the fabled hunt for the city of Ciro. She spent the remainder of the day looking over the book and studying every word, while Alit remained cuddled up on the bed where he fell asleep after devouring every morsel. She placed some pillowcases into a box and carefully tucked him in, then she put a book over the edge, slid it under the bed, and piled books in front, blocking it from view.

She climbed into bed and looked out the window. The cracks blurred the image, but she made out Shaw walking up the path carrying another collection of books and a sack full of clothes. After a firm knock, he entered and placed them in a chair and placed a book and robe on the bed next to her. Every paladin wore the same clothes and carried the *Oath of the Paladin*. Before her were the blue-and-white paladin robes she would be wearing for the duration of her training.

"These are what you will wear when training. Tomorrow, you will begin lessons with Eandar and Falun," he said.

After straightening his shirt, he moved them to the bedside table and sat beside her, tucking her in and blowing out the candle beside her bed.

"I know it has been a busy day. Just rest, and tomorrow, we will—"

She sat up. "Did I do something wrong?" she asked.

Taken aback, he eased her back under the covers. With a hand on her shoulder, he comforted her and caressed her cheek. "No, no. You are fine, it is just that sometimes we must start a new journey. Elissar knew this, and now you're here with me."

Her eyes became heavy, and she looked away. The weight of her emotions came to rest once again on her shoulders, but in his company, she refused to cry. He leaned in and hugged her.

"You want to be an adventurer?" he asked.

She drew back, and through a clogged nose, she breathed through her mouth. "Yes!" she said with enthusiasm.

He grinned and spun a staff attached to a leather strap and twice her height and bigger around than her grip from his back. He placed it beside her on the bed.

"If you want to delve into dungeons and wade through murky water to find the relics of old, you'll need to protect yourself." He stepped away and clutched the door handle. "Go on and get some sleep. We'll train tomorrow." Before closing the door, he poked back in. "Goodnight, Blue. Sleep well."

She pulled the staff close and fell asleep to dream of wondrous discoveries and epic battles with her new dragon companion at her side.

CHAPTER 2

*S*teady Hands

BRIANNE WATCHED MORRIS THROUGH A SMALL SEAM in the wardrobe. He moved swiftly for a man of his age; he was not withered, but between his salt-and-pepper hair and the deep lines on his face, one could tell that he no longer enjoyed the luxury of being a young man. He was the oldest soldier under Shaw's command and had been trusted with keeping watch over the young girl until Shaw's daily tasks were concluded.

"Brianne, I know you're in here," he said.

He pulled the door open, and she popped out, slamming his toe with her staff and sprinting toward the door.

"Not fair! We agreed no weapons!"

She slipped through a few crates blocking the path, forcing Morris to go around. She slammed the door, laughing as she raced down the corridor. She slowed as she reached a pair of ornate locked doors, and within, she heard the distinctive sound of a highly agitated Shaw arguing with nobles from Oncier and Mourningstar. She froze and listened. He shouted at the top of his lungs, and the nobles were gasping at his outbursts.

She could hear the loud footsteps of Morris trying to sneak up behind her. Being sly, she ducked him and darted down a small path leading into the larder and ducked through a storage door. Coming out next to the entrance to the crypts, she could hear chanting, and an eerie light came from the windows. Someone had passed their trials, but she didn't care for their odd rituals and made haste in her effort. She raced toward the northern tower, but Morris stepped out into her path.

"I got you now."

She smiled at him and dodged his lazy attempt at catching her and caught the back of his knee with her staff and sent him tumbling into a thorny shrub.

"Too slow, oldie!"

She reached a full sprint up the stairs, but near the top, her foot slipped on the loose stone from the crumbled upper floors, and she lost her balance. Sliding over the side, she grabbed hold of a bundle of twine wrapped around one of the boards. Morris came to the top and looked over the broken cap of the tower. She could see his feet through the spaces in the boards.

"Brianne, where did you go? If I catch you this time, we will play a game that doesn't require me to chase you all over the abbey. Maybe something that allows me a nap or time to speak with Brena."

"Morris!" Her panicked scream drew him to her hanging over the two-hundred-foot drop, and he reached down and pulled her from the edge. Squeezing his neck, she latched on to him, refusing to let go. Her eyes were closed, and her face was pressed against his shoulder. Blood ran down her leg, with a nasty laceration on her right thigh. He took a rag from his pocket and pressed it to the wound to reduce the bleeding and with his other, he cupped under her leg and carried her down the tower.

"Oh dear, we will need to get you to Shaw's office. He's not going to like this," he said.

Burying her face into his beard, she kept from looking at the blood-soaked cloth. She wiped the tears and snot on his tunic and heard him step off the cobblestone path and onto the hardwood floors of the interior hallway. The aroma of expensive perfume choked the air from the room, and the voices of condescension echoed the halls. Shaw's voice carried over the rest, not fanciful nor well-read but authoritative. He commanded the respect of those around him, and for Brianne, he could offer a blistering punishment using only the look in his eyes. He took Brianne from Morris's arms and carried her into his office.

"ANOTHER SCRAPE?" SHAW ASKED.

She pulled back tears and drew a snot-filled breath through her nose. "Yes, we were playing, and I slipped."

When he removed the cloth, she turned away, avoiding the sight and biting her lip to compensate for the pain. "Brianne, look at it. How can you ever grow into a paladin if you're afraid of a little blood?"

She looked at the blood seeping from the wound

and how he calmly opened a small bag from beside his desk and pulled out a bottle of expensive whiskey. "This will hurt, but pain is a teacher we can never argue with."

He poured it over the wound, and she let out a whelp. Taking a needle and thread from his desk, he took a few pieces of clean cloth from his pocket and prepared to work. Holding the needle over the fire, he smiled at her. "Crying is natural, but you must learn to divorce your feelings from what is happening."

He quenched the red-hot needle with some whiskey and pulled the two pieces of skin together. "Today, you will learn how to suture a wound." He started the needle through the folds of skin, and she winced with each pass. halfway down, he stopped. "Take the needle. I'll make sure it doesn't pull apart."

With her hands trembling, she grasped the needle and closed her eyes for the first pass, then the second. "You must see what needs stitching. Open your eyes, and remember: pain is temporary."

She opened her eyes and made the last few loops before he took the thread and tied it, cutting the end with his knife and pouring more whiskey over the wound before using a clean bandage and wrapping it tight.

"Good as new. You'll need to rest, and maybe in a few days, you'll be able to run and play without concern of the stitches bursting," Shaw said.

Morris stood by the door, waiting with his eyes fixed on the wall as he stood at attention for the duration. "Morris, I'm taking her home. See to the nobles and remind them that tomorrow we will continue our. discussion."

"Yes, sir." Morris vanished into the crowd, and

the door slammed. His withered voice called for silence, and they exited the building.

"Okay, Blue. What do you say we take the long way home?" Shaw asked.

"Can we stop at the bakery?" she asked in retort.

"Only if you can follow a simple instruction for once. Deal?"

She squirmed a bit and rolled her eyes. "Fine, what do you want me to do?"

He raised her up and placed her on his shoulders. "I want you to stop giving Morris such a hard time. He is an old man and would fall apart if something really happened to you."

She ducked under the overhang and grinned ear to ear at the nobles as she passed through the crowd with her most comfortable of perches.

"Why are the nobles here? Elissar always said that they would rather dine on slop in someone else's hold than eat like kings at home," Brianne said.

He gripped her knee and dug his finger and thumb in to make her giggle. "Because they have a hand in everything, where you can pray to what statue is worthy of our affection. I'll be honest, I don't know what will happen if they deny the sacred charge and denounce the paladins," he said.

They reached the city gate, and Shaw gave the guards a nod and passed through without question.

"Blue, can I ask you something?"

"Sure," she said.

He stopped at a bench and sat her down, taking a seat alongside her and putting an arm over the back.

"How much do you know about Elissar?"

He looked at her with a grin and squeezed the back of her neck. She ducked away, and her blue eyes followed the cracks in the road. "She had two daughters—younger than me, but they looked older. We used to play. Running around the estate in Mourningstar, we would spend our days hiding from her and avoiding the smelly nobles."

"You know she wasn't your real mother, don't you?" Shaw asked.

"That's what they said. Didn't matter. Felt real enough to me," she said.

He pulled her against his chest and shook her upper body. "You're right, just wondering if you ever knew your real mother? Ready for a strawberry pastry?"

The glow in her eyes shined bright with a warm excitement as she bounced off the bench. "Can we get some jerky? I really like jerky too."

He messed up her hair and walked ahead. "Sure, but if you wait around, I'm not sure how many pastries will be left. It is almost time for closing, after all," he said.

One of the townsfolk stopped in their tracks at the rumble of thunder over the sea. Clouds were rolling in, and the shouting started. Bells were rung, and the gates were drawn.

"What's going on?" she asked.

Shaw placed her back on his shoulders and made his way to the bakery. "A storm is rolling in—a nasty one, from the sounds of it. Doesn't matter much to us though."

They reached the town square, and people gathered with spears and torches. They massed at the magistrate's office, and each signed a piece of paper before exiting, the single door still open.

"What are they doing?" she asked.

"Ah, those are fools." He spoke loud enough so anyone in earshot could listen. "They plan on hunting one of the ever-elusive Prowlers, thick hides and claws like short swords, and they blend in with the sand. But like I said, fools."

She raised an eyebrow and looked at him. "In the storm?"

He smiled at her and gave a pat on her knee as they approached the bakery, he placed their order, and they waited for the last set of baked goods to be placed on the awning by the window.

"Prowlers only come out during the heavy rains. Those fools are chasing wealth and glory." He sat her on the awning and adjusted his chest piece. "I had the displeasure of encountering one many years ago. Wasn't a good experience, and that is putting it lightly."

She climbed back on his shoulders and promptly took their food from the baker. The sky darkened, and the rumble of thunder shook the ground. She scarfed down every bite and tucked the jerky in her pocket. "So, what happened? Killing something like that had to be a great story."

He laughed and shook his head. "No, honestly, it is a boring story."

She started drumming on his head. "Tell me, tell me! Please tell me?"

He let out a long and exaggerated sigh before looking up at her. The bright grin on her face and cheerful laugh nearly broke through his hardened exterior, but he remained composed.

"It was before I joined the Order. Morris told me about a recruit. Eandar, if you must know."

Hearing this, she stuck out her tongue and pinched her nose.

"Well, he wasn't always so hard on recruits. I traveled to a farm town on the coast, Atora, Kor. something like that. A storm had set in, and I needed to make it to Sarntheris, so I ignored the pleas of the townsfolk and trekked into the wilds. It wasn't long, and I heard the beast lurking in the dunes, then a howl followed by cries, and then silence. I knew my only chance was the shore."

She locked onto every word, listening to his story and ignoring the bright flashes of lightning and rolling thunder.

"I found several young Catha stalks, sharpened them, and made a path narrow enough for it to come down and wide enough for me to reposition, if necessary. I stood against a twenty-foot-tall embankment and waited for it."

They reached the cottage, and the sky turned as black as night by the storm and lightning rippled across the sky. The city went silent, and the rain started to fall. He ducked into the small shack and sat in a chair by her bed. The windows still needed to be replaced, but the holes in the roof were patched.

"Did you kill it?" She sat on the edge, staring at him wide-eyed and ready to hear more.

"Yes, I could see it lurking down by the waves. It waited until my fire burned out to make a move, but I was ready." He pointed to the middle of his chest. "Their scales meet here," he said, tapping his breastbone. "I could see it during each lightning strike, and when it jumped, I put a spear through its chest. My armor protected me from its claws. One of the good things about wearing thick plate armor; might not be able to move as quickly, but it can protect from attacks."

He picked her up and slammed her onto the mattress, and she let out an adorable giggle while he gave her a slight tickle and tucked her in for the night.

"I waited until morning to travel to Sarntheris, and as you have seen, Eandar is here and a joy for all to admire, but those men that are wandering the desert tonight, they are fools, tempting fate for a handful of gold. And gold is no reason to throw away one's life." He kissed her forehead and blew out the candles but noticed the pouch of jerky sat on the chair at the foot of her bed—empty, yet he did not remember her taking a single bite.

"Night, Blue. Will you promise not to slip out again?" he asked.

With a nod, she rolled over, and he stepped out the door and sat on the porch. She opened her eyes, and Alit lay on the pillow beside her. He licked his fingertips and scratched his belly.

"You really should thank the butcher. He has a way with meats," Alit said.

She poked his belly. Being full caused him to be sluggish, and he failed to swat her hand.

"Come on, I don't go poking your scrawny frame. What do they feed you, grass? Or is it just water?" Alit asked.

"I eat, just never gained any weight. What about you? Maybe you shouldn't be snacking so much." She poked his bulging belly again.

"Now let's not get too carried away. Dragons can

eat their body weight in food! Just because I'm in this form doesn't mean I'm any more or less a dragon."

She nestled up against him. "Don't you think being a dragon of any size will get in the way when I'm traveling the world?"

"Ha, that is where you are wrong." He struggled a bit but managed to roll over. "I can do this." He took the form of a black cat, fat gut and all. "Now I can travel with you."

She wrapped her arms around him and snuggled her face into his fur, and he folded his paws over and rested his chin on her arm.

"Fine, we can cuddle this once." He turned toward her. "Never again. Understood?"

She smiled and scratched under his chin. The rattling rain on the roof sang her to sleep.

CHAPTER 3

ind Words, 1297

BRIANNE'S TIME IN THE ABBEY FELT SHORT, EVEN
with several years passing—hardly time wasted with
hours of training and education taking up much of her
days. She often didn't finish her day's work before a
new day started. She only aged a few years but often
struggled with her physical age not matching her
appearance or development—too wise for her age but
foolish as one matching her size. Her hair reached
down below her waist, and she wore initiate's garb: a
blue- andwhite set of thin plate armor with white
robes draped over top. Her sandals were old and
ragged, as she had worn them for many years and
would need a new pair before she grew enough to no
longer need them.

She watched merchants set up their stalls and the
shops open their doors as the morning sun crested the
outer walls. Early for most, but Shaw preferred an
early start and moving about during the early

morning hours, and training directly with him, he required Brianne to join in these morning activities no matter how late she stayed up sifting through old tomes she secretly ordered with money she slipped from Shaw's desk while studying.

She wiped the sleep from her eyes once more and fantasized about another of Reduwar's adventures. After searching for months, she finally found an earlier journal that told the story of his search for the forgotten city of Isduin, the lost Dwarven capital and original seat of the pantheon. The fabled city lived in memory, considered to most a story and nothing more, but to Brianne, every snippet of text and primitive engraving held a clue that she needed to make note of in her pursuit of secrets needing to be revealed.

Alit followed along and preferred the guise of a cat over the many different animals he attempted to be over the years, one of his more successful attempts at the illusion. His body was formed of mostly fluff than anything else, and his eyes were a sharp green, much like his scales in dragon form.

Brushing against Brianne's leg, Alit caught her eye. "Now isn't the best time for that. He already said if you daydream again while making rounds, he will send you to clean rooms with Brena. Maybe let's not tempt fate?"

He lay down under her legs and used the steps to block Shaw's view when he threw the doors open and stormed out.

"Damned fools. Let's go, Brianne. They would rather care for tradition than making sure those in the field are properly supplied. War rages in the west, and all they care for is whether their tithes are paid. If no one answers the call, it will spill over into Empryss soon enough," Shaw said.

He held out his arm for her before crossing the street into the city proper. She latched on to his elbow, and they ventured to their next destination. Most of the buildings were older than the abbey, and the bricks were a reddish color with a white mortar holding them together. They traveled the city until they reached the regent lord's office, Haviland Soptmire the Twelfth. The last of his line feared the God Queen's overreach and had been at war with the north for as long as his family had held power in the region. The pointless effort tainted the family legacy and the God Queen in Mourningstar hardly noticed the conflict because they abandoned the southern outposts to save on resources. Under his leadership, they sustained losses to the farmers, leaving only the paladins to protect the city from all threats from abroad.

"Brianne, do not speak of the war. It is a sensitive subject, and a man like him needs his ego stroked. Smile and nod. Just let me handle the speaking." Shaw's shoulders shuddered a bit, but he managed to keep his stoic expression. "On second thought, I think you should go to the shops and buy yourself something." He pulled a few gold coins from his vest and placed them into her hand. Folding her fingers over, he locked eyes with her. "Buy us something to snack on, stay in the square, and I'll be along shortly. And please don't make any messes; you have a way with things, Blue, so please do as I ask."

He straightened his breastplate and walked through the garishly decorated doors into the main hall of the lord's estate. Through the door, Brianne could see gold and silver attached to everything and priceless relics hanging from every wall. Curling her nose at the sight, she skipped down toward the baker's window. With the morning sun, each vendor prepared for their day—none more desired than that of the bakery—and from the corner, she could see pastries hanging on the sill. Dozens of fruit pasties waited for her, and at the end, the strawberry tarts. She could taste them long before the smell reached her nose, but Alit stopped in her path.

"Wait," he said.

A group of guards stormed past, their sights fixed on the old man lurching through the square. He wore tattered clothes and pushed a cart of junk—odds and ends, but nothing of any value to anyone but him. They encircled his cart and picked through his things.

"Damned fool! This is a place where they sell goods, not useless junk." The guards knocked over his cart and shoved the old man down. His eerie green eyes glared back at them while holding on to his cane. The sleek ivory bore no markings and was adorned with a silver grip with a strange stamp on the pommel.

"Why do you trouble an old man? Do you have no kindness nor love?" he asked.

The men laughed and scattered his belongings, dumping everything onto the ground before they marched back toward the gate. "Clean this mess, or we will be forced to remove you from the city!" the captain shouted as they left him to gather his things.

Alit moved toward the baker's window, but Brianne froze. She watched the old man right his cart and slowly collect what he could, one piece at a time. His frail hands shook as he gathered each item, pausing to catch his breath before returning to his task.

"No. He is a stranger, and we should avoid him. Brianne, he could be dangerous, and worst of all, it could be the kind of thing Shaw said not to do." Alit arched his back and rubbed against her leg.

She shrugged it off and picked up a few of the old man's things, placing them on the cart and giving him a warm smile, causing him to pause and admire her kindness. He leaned forward and offered her his hand. His eyes were mesmerizing; they were far more distinctive up close and held a faint light deep within.

"Thank you, child, but you mustn't give them a reason to bother you as well." He gave her a pat on her head and returned to gathering items one by one. She, on the other hand, collected as much as she could, piling everything up and smiling at him when she finished. He blocked the view of his face with a shawl, but his eyes softened, and his shoulders slumped.

"You honor me, young one. How might I thank such kindness?" he asked.

"I'm a paladin. We help those in need. What would I be if someone in need was left abandoned? And no thanks required. It was an honor to help you today." She leaned in close and whispered, "Are you selling that?" Her finger was fixed on a journal from the famed adventurer Reduwar. "If so, I would like to buy it."

He smiled. "I am Thealen, collector of strange and peculiar items. I travel about the sands, bargaining for the greatest wealth a person can have." He lifted it and placed it into her hands. "Come, we can talk payment." He walked into an alcove and set up his shop. A small sign and randomly assorted things were scattered on the table before him. Every morning, she'd watched him enter and set out his things, never speaking before this day.

"I do not barter in gold nor silver. I barter in knowledge. You can have it for a small piece of information. Deal?" he asked.

She gave a nod but no longer focused on him. The pages of the journal pulled her in, and she could do nothing but daydream about what waited to be gleaned from its pages.

"What is your name?" he asked.

"Brianne, but everyone calls me Blue." She looked up at him and blinked a few times. "It's because of my eyes, see?" The light from her eyes glowed a deep blue and followed her pupils. Like all elves, her eyes offered a glow, but unlike woodland elves and mountain elves—whose eyes are green—her eyes were blue, and with silver hair, she stood out as different among the elves.

"Quite beautiful, if I might say, but I will call you Brianne. Have you stayed long within the city?" he asked.

"No, I live in the abbey." She pointed to the cathedral and dilapidated towers beyond the northern wall. "I study to be a brave defender of the light. I'll stop evil in its tracks and vanquish our enemies, and when I'm done saving the world, I'm going adventuring. Lots of lost cities just waiting for me to find them."

He chuckled but stopped due to a raspy cough that caused his body to tremble and wheeze. He took a breath and corrected his posture. "Evil will certainly face its match in you. Have you trained long?"

"Yes. They said when I grow a bit more, I can do the trials and be a full paladin." Her eyes rolled, and she leaned forcefully against the building beside them. "Right now, I'm just an initiate. They said I'm too small to complete the journey." She kicked a few pebbles across the ground. "I think I'm ready. I am faster and stronger than the other students. I might not be as tall, but I deserve a chance. Don't I?"

He gave a gentle pat on her back. "It is alright to wait. Some of us spend a bit too long waiting for our trials, and others experience trials from birth. Last question. What would you wish for among all others? What desire would you grasp should you be given the chance?"

She looked out to the docks only to be pulled back by the sound of several sets of footsteps walking in unison. The guards had returned, and with them were the magistrate and his scribe. They pulled Thealen from his stall and shoved Brianne against the wall.

"By order of law, it has been decided you must be removed for disturbing our beloved city and defiling it with your presence, under code seventy-two A." The magistrate looked over the note held by his scribe. "You are hereby banished from Sarntheris and required to forfeit all of your belongings."

The magistrate wasted no time and spun on his heel, kicking up dust as he and the scribe left the guards to their business. Brianne pulled her staff loose and smacked the shin of the guard holding her. She came up with the other end and caught his jaw. The guard collapsed to the ground, and she swung at the next one, but having seen his companion's fate, he grabbed the weapon and restrained her.

"Looks like we got a sympathizer. You want to join him among the dunes?" The guard leaned in and curled his lip at seeing her eyes. "Damned elf. Thought they were all extinct?" He raised a hand to slap her, only to be stopped by an armored hand grasping his forearm. Shaw stood beside him, his sword against the other guard's neck.

"Unhand the child, or I paint the courtyard with your blood," he said.

The magistrate rushed back over shouting, "Criminal! Criminal, we'll have you hanged for interfering in the Divine's work!"

Shaw released the guard and shoved him into the wall. Once in range, Shaw grabbed the magistrate by the throat. "What crime has been committed that a coward can claim over a man of the Order?" Shaw asked. "The old man has been in the market for years peddling his wares, and you decide today that you wish to remove him." He lifted the magistrate against the wall. "Again, I ask what crime will you hold against me that you stand so brazenly and shout out to the masses?"

"My apologies, sir," the magistrate said through the tight grip on his throat. "It was not to take offense, but our city has become unclean, and it would be best if his kind were removed to where they belong. If you vouch for him, I will make a note, and he will—"

The magistrate's voice cut out as Shaw tightened his grip. "I entertain your lord's whim only because it is tradition, but should your guards raise a hand to my daughter again, I will take it as an act of aggression."

He slammed him into the wall, his eyes bulging from his airway being cut off. "Do I make myself clear?"

The magistrate nodded, and Shaw dropped him into the dirt. He scrambled to his feet and gasped for air while yelling orders at his scribe while they ran back to his office.

"Come on, Blue, let's get those pastries," Shaw said.

The guards dragged their unconscious companion away while she took Shaw's hand joined him and walked to the baker's.

"Thank you little one," Thealen said, handing Brianne the journal.

She smiled and waved as she left him to his stall.

The city filled with people, and a line formed as some waited for pastries. Shaw looked down once out of sight. "Does trouble always follow you?" He knelt and wiped a bit of dirt from her cheek and smiled at her. "Let's get our breakfast and return to the abbey. Eandar will be waiting for your lesson and will be delighted to know you are still beating up the city guards."

She smiled and grabbed a few strawberry tarts with the journal tucked under her arm. Cramming as many as she could into her mouth at a time, she waved to Thealen as they pushed their way through the city gate.

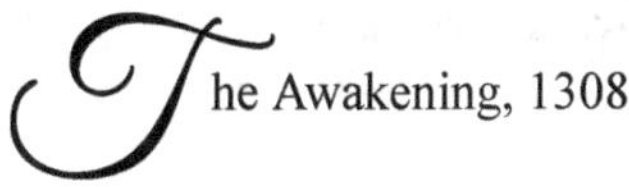

he Awakening, 1308

ELEVEN YEARS PASSED, AND BRIANNE FOUND herself among a pile of books. She leafed through each pile and shoved them off the bed. Alit rested peacefully on the windowsill, taking the form of an orange cat and ignoring her annoyed groaning as the sun set over the far wall.

"Do all adventurers have to read so much?" she asked.

Alit continued to sleep, only moving when the cool evening chill slipped through the seams of the window frame. He stretched and shivered before climbing under her blanket. Crinkling her nose, she returned to the pile of notes she took on Dwarven etiquette. With the sun gone, she used a glowstone to finish what she needed to turn in the following day.

"Ugh, being a paladin is stupid," she said.

From under the cover, Alit spoke, "Be careful.

Shaw will hear you and come running to make sure the lessons of the ancestors are taken into account." His head poked out, and he gave her a concerned stare.

Brianne gave him a pat on the head and sprung from her bed, books scattering about the floor as she pulled a wooden practice sword from its scabbard. She hung from the bedpost, her focus drifting to swinging it about and fighting imaginary monsters.

"I should be delving into the mines of Iskal or searching for relics in the lost city of Ciro, not spending every day watching Eandar get a few years older. Do you think he is getting shorter with each lesson?" she asked.

"Watch it. Thinking like that could bring another boredom-inducing lecture from Shaw. Do you think Brena can sneak us some more of that jerky? Stuff is tasty," Alit said.

Brianne paused and stared longingly out the window. Floating sparks of multicolored light drifted through the air. The laughter of children filled the abbey and the city beyond, and even the adults were joining in the fun. She opened the window and looked out to the twin moons rising. They were both full, and their auras bonded into a single resplendent light. Each floating spark became a swirl of light upon reaching the sky, putting on a display that left many in awe.

"Do you ever wish we could be out there? Not watching from a window, but a part of these things. I wish I could leave this place behind, the abbey, Shaw, and the forsaken desert. I just want to do something other than waste away in this—"

"I dreamed of those things too, and every time I

see the awakening, I'm reminded of why I'm here and not out there chasing some fantasy." Shaw cut her off, leaning against the outside wall. He spun the corner and leaned his back on the windowsill. Brianne's head poked out, and she sat on the pile of books stacked in a chair so she could see comfortably.

"I was young once," he said.

She rolled her eyes, snickered, and covered her mouth before eyeing him again.

"Funny, I wasn't always old. Several years before you came, I was following an old friend on an adventure into the northern reach. She had a fiery spirit and would drag me almost anywhere." A warm smile rolled over his otherwise bitter face. "Didn't find anything but a few old gems and a book describing what we were after. When we left, the awakening had started, and we both watched with joy."

Brianne rested her chin on her hands and hung on his every word, allowing her mind to run wild with imagining what life would be like if her dreams became reality.

"A good foot or so of snow covered the hills east of Iskal, and we dredged through, but under skies like this, we found ourselves being hunted by a handful of Order goons. Coren wanted what we found and had his heart set on getting it. Never understood what was so great about the book, but my friend or not, a paladin stands firm." The smile faded, and he took a moment before shaking his head and launching into the next part of his story.

"We were trapped over the Idris River. Behind us were the goons, and ahead was a forty-foot drop. We hid behind some rocks and ambushed them. I took an arrow through my thigh, and we fought for a good while and took down the lot of them."

A tear formed in his eye, but he pulled back and smiled again while looking at the floating sparks of arcana. His eyes turned to Brianne, and he put a hand on her shoulder. "We stayed up until dawn watching them fade into the sky. Not long after, I returned home, and due to my injury, they gave me the task of handling our newest recruits."

"Where is she now?" Brianne asked.

Shaw took a breath and smiled. "Returned to her people in Oncier. An old adventurer must hang up their gear someday. Before I fully recovered, you came along, and I found a new purpose: keeping you out of trouble and making sure Eandar doesn't put you in the stockade for the constant sneaking off abbey grounds." He smiled and punched her shoulder lightly. "Do you really hate it here? Or is it the studying that has you flustered?"

She sank and winced as if expecting something painful. "You heard all of that?"

He lowered to look her in the eye. "Yep. Well, the important bits, mostly, and you are still a child. What would you do if a group of bandits were chasing you? Or what would you do if the Order had you cornered?"

"I can fight. Eandar told me if I don't hold back, they will have to get an adult to be my sparring partner," she said.

"Is that right?" He grabbed her by the back of her pants and pulled her out the window, the wooden sword still in her hand. He raised the walking stick he carved himself and swatted the tip of her sword.

"Show me what you got. Beat me, and we'll go on an adventure." He placed the tip against her shoulder and grinned. "If I win you will help Brena with the housekeeping. deal?"

She smiled and gave a nod. "What are we calling a win?" she asked, tossing the sword up a bit and twirling it before catching it again.

"First to tag the other's chest wins," he said.

They squared off and gave a few test strikes, both meeting each other's advance. She weighed a hundred pounds soaking wet, and he weighed a solid hundred more than her and stood at least a foot taller than her. She didn't care. Using her training and a bit of guile to avoid his heavier attacks and stay out of reach until she wanted to attack, she moved quickly but staggered a bit each time he got in range to swing at her.

"Trying to wear me out? Will take a bit more than you hiding behind trees and shrubs to avoid a day of housekeeping," he said.

She remained silent and lashed at him with a few quick strikes before slipping out of range of his lumbering attacks. "I can do more than run away." She slipped in close and struck at his chest but missed and nearly took a blow from his walking stick, managing to deflect it and stumble back from the force of his backhand.

Alit crawled up onto the window and eyed Shaw's back. They weren't on good terms, and Alit remained under threat that he would be ditched in the dunes if Brianne did not follow the rules.

Brianne watched him and locked her eyes on Shaw. "So, what adventure might we go on if I win?

Did you think that far, or are you so foolish to think I couldn't win?"

He smiled, his wrinkled skin and the shadows cast by the eerie moonlight were a bit frightening, but she wasn't fazed and went in for another attack. She sidestepped his overhand swing and slashed at his leg, which drew his walking stick to cover for the blow, and just before he could recover, Alit sprang into action. He pounced onto Shaw's back and latched on, opening his chest for a clean attack for Brianne. With a soft tap, she poked his chest and started laughing.

"Haha! What do you always say? Watch your surroundings!" She leaned on the hilt of her sword and watched him with a smile. Alit let go and slipped under the cottage before Shaw could do anything to the ferocious feline.

"A deal is a deal after all. Tomorrow morning, Magister Carsis will be coming to train you to use magic. Apparently the council believes an elf, paladin or not, should learn to control the arcana within them," he said.

She raised an eyebrow and sneered at him. "What about my adventure? I think—"

"Hey, I was getting to that, calm down a bit. Falun and I are traveling to the southern dunes, and Kindri is coming too. Figured you would enjoy a day of fun before training with Carsis."

"When?" she asked.

"Do you ever just take something for what it is?" he asked.

She crossed her arms and scrunched her face while giving an exaggerated eye roll.

"Tomorrow, before the magister comes. Is that good enough?" he asked.

She smiled and hugged him, squeezing tightly and giggling. They embraced for a moment before Shaw pulled away and gave her a pat on the head. The bells started ringing, and everyone other than the night watch was under curfew, required to be inside during the late-night hours. He picked her up and plopped her back down in the window before making his way down the path to his office.

"Night!" she yelled as loud as she could, her voice echoing through the empty courtyard.

"Get some sleep, Blue. We have a long day tomorrow!" he said loudly.

She closed the window, and her reflection revealed her blue eyes were a gold color. When she pulled away from the moonlight, they were once again shining a deep blue. She went to the window again and held a hand over her face, and the light on her hands radiated a golden hue. She held the glowstone to the moonlight, and it held the same glow, just a bit dull from the brightness of the moons.

"Alit. Alit!" she yelled.

He poked his head through the crawlspace and climbed out onto the rug at the foot of her bed. "Yes? What would you require of your savior?" he asked, puffing out his chest and digging his claws into the wooden bed frame.

"Why are my eyes doing this?" she asked.

The blue color faded when she leaned out into the moonlight.

He shrugged and rolled his eyes. "How should I know? You're an elf. Known a whole bunch, but never looked at their eyes much, you know?"

She stumbled over the spread of books on the floor and crashed face-first onto her mattress. "How would I know? The only other elf I've met was Elissar, but she was always too busy to talk about our people—or anything, for that matter. Just figured you'd know since you were the Great Dragon."

The night dragged on, but she still needed to work, and now she faced a busy day that would keep her from finishing even more work. She sprung up again and threw open her closet. Clothes were scattered on hangers and the floor, and others were stuffed into crates and shelves. She tossed things about and pulled out the brown leather chest piece and off-white tunic, gathering the different items for her outfit and tossing them onto the bed. She looked over the worn-out and dingy items she wore a dozen times without washing. There were stains on every piece, and the pants were missing one of the pockets.

"When Shaw returns, I need to have everything ready. Kindri and I are slipping out to see the midnight aura. Heard it is amazing."

Alit swiped her with his claws, drawing a bit of blood and causing her to give him her full attention. "Have you gone mad? Sneaking out again could get you in so much trouble. If you get caught, there isn't anything I can do to help—unless I can jump on their backs too?"

Nursing the scratches, she turned to him with an angry look. "Fine. San I smile, or will that cause the world to end?"

"Brianne, I was told to protect you. I cannot do that if you are constantly sneaking out and causing trouble." He climbed up on the bed and put his paws on her leg. "Help me out here. The last time you snuck out, the east tower lost its top three floors. Maybe sneaking out at night isn't something you should be doing?"

She gathered the outfit, folding and stacking each piece before climbing onto the bed and focusing on her studies again. She flipped through each paper and scribbled what answers she knew, leaving blank anything that required thought or she lacked the understanding of. She would peer out the window at times to marvel at the brightness of the twin moons. The midday sun looked dim in comparison, and she could see the echo of Illi'ath, the great celestial. A streak of golden stars stretched between the moons and became visible during the awakening.

As she finished, she moved everything off the bed and stacked the papers on her nightstand, taking the time to get dressed and leaving the chest armor and shoulder guards under the side of the bed. Her arm went around Alit as she pulled him against her hip. "What was the story of Illi'ath again?" she asked.

"Are you going to make me tell this story every night?" he asked, only to receive a yawn and nod before she closed her eyes. Alit sighed and started, "Eons ago, before the lands were formed and the seas were connected, Illi'ath helped to order the world. The hearth gods were pushed into their realms, but the great hound followed her. Their fight lasted for ten thousand years. Almost defeated, she tried to tap into the world's arcana, causing the world to shutter. She feared what would happen to the young races of the world, so she called to the elders, beings from a time before the ordering, the Baeothen. She instructed them to watch over the world in her stead, and with their promise, she sacrificed herself, using the moons and her light to trap the great hound and protect the world from its insatiable hunger."

Brianne slipped the glowstone under her pillow and curled on her side, waiting for Shaw to return for his last check-in for the night.

he Shattered City

BRIANNE LAY TUCKED IN HER BED, HER EYES CLOSED tight and a faint whistle each time she breathed. She knew that the guards were instructed to stay close until she fell asleep, and she used this to her advantage. When the heavy steps of the guards' old and ragged boots moved far enough away that she could no longer hear the clasps rattle, she sprung from the bed, wearing her special attire for adventuring. She had snuck the final pieces of gear on after Shaw left.

She stuffed everything she could in the bag and left out the crawlspace, tying the bag around her ankle and dragging it. At the edge of the porch, she was cut off by a guard sleeping in a chair propped against the outer wall. Being as silent as possible, she ducked into a bush on the far side of the path from her cottage. The guard grumbled a bit but never opened his eyes and stayed fast asleep. Through the window, she could see the mound of junk she piled on the bed and covered with a few blankets, hoping to fool the guards long enough to enjoy a small adventure before having to go back inside.

When Morris made his way back up the path, Brianne made her move, diving over the hedges and making her way carefully through the abbey. Each row of hedges had a small place she hollowed out through her many attempts of sneaking out over the years. After a few close calls, she arrived at Kindri's window. Noticing the lack of light when his house came into view, she hoped he remembered that tonight they would go off on their grand adventure. Hoping he remembered, she tapped on the window. Nothing. She tapped again, but this time, a bit louder.

Alit followed her and remained quiet until now. "Do you think it's a good idea to sneak out like this? I mean, Shaw would ground you for a month."

She patted him and slipped a piece of meat to him. "Would you stay inside? I really want to hang out with Kindri alone."

Alit shrugged and started down the path toward her cottage. "If you aren't back soon, I will come searching. Why do I bother with these children?" he continued to mumble to himself as he sauntered down the path.

Brianne smiled at his reaction and climbed in the window and snuck up on Kindri's bed, pulling the covers back to reveal he did the same as her and left random items scattered across the bed and covered them in blankets.

She heard a chuckle from the corner and turned to find him leaning against the wall. She walked to him and punched his arm. "What if I would have screamed?" She placed both hands on her hips and stared at him, waiting for whatever unsatisfying answer he could give.

He replied by giving her a hug and a gentle pat on her cheek before diving out the open window. Poking his head back through, he said, "Want to hurry up, or were we just hanging out here all night?"

She scrunched her nose and growled at him, causing him to chuckle again while helping her out the window. In the weeks since she last snuck out, the guards weren't where they should be, and she wasn't in time with the patrols and mistimed their approach.

Morris made his way to this corner of the abbey and close to where they were hiding. Kindri had forgotten to close the window, and it didn't go unnoticed by Morris. He clamored over and peered inside, but with his awful eyesight, he likely figured the lumps on the bed were Kindri and closed the window before returning to his patrol. He stopped a few feet from where Kindri hid, and Brianne made it to the opposite end of the street while Kindri froze behind the few gnarled trees beside his house.

Brianne acted quickly, and without thinking, she grabbed a rock and threw it across the square. With a loud crash, it shattered the front window of the washhouse, followed by loud yelling from the people working inside.

Morris ran to inspect the commotion, leaving them on the adventure they planned. Using the distraction, they slipped through the courtyard and into the pasture on the eastern end of the abbey. Once out of earshot, Brianne burst into laughter.

Fearful Kindri panicked over the situation. "What

if someone finds out? Eandar will have us running laps until our legs fall off," he said.

Brianne put an arm around him and tugged him toward the outer fence. "If we are getting punished, shouldn't it be for something worthwhile?" she asked, pointing toward the dunes in the direction of the crumbled city fort of Bruin. Once the shining star of the Southlands but now an abandoned relic of the first age, it sank into the sand to be forgotten by the world. Its broken towers and walls scraped the sky above like fingers reaching from beneath the earth.

"No, it's forbidden. They said it was a part of the collapse of the Olian empire. I'm not going, Brianne!" Kindri crossed his arms and looked away. "Also, I heard the place is haunted."

She shoved him. "Guess I'll go alone. Would be a shame if someday we meet the great Reduwar and have to tell him you were afraid of a little adventure." She squeezed through the spaces in the fence and smiled at him before dropping down to the pile of sand below. "Have fun with the books! Maybe you'll read mine someday," she said.

He followed suit and landed beside her. "Fine, but when we get caught, I'm saying it was all your idea. So, how do you plan on getting over the dunes before Marcus sees us?"

"Hear that?" she asked.

Shouting and grumbling could be heard from the tower and across most of the abbey, followed by silence and then another outburst of yelling.

"They play cards, and pretty soon, they will be so drunk, we'll hear them snoring from here."

She plopped down in the sand, and he sat beside her. His eyes wandered, and his hand moved to the small of her back. He closed his eyes and leaned in for a kiss, but she spurned his advance and smiled at him.

"I think they are ready." Her heart raced. Unprepared, she pushed the feeling down and returned to her task.

The short distance across the dunes made for a nice walk, taking less than an hour to drop out of the watch tower's sightline. The only company was the howling winds across the sand. The moons fell behind the clouds rolling in from the bay. With less light, she pulled a recently obtained glowstone from her bag and held it aloft while they traversed the dilapidated stone path leading toward the city.

They reached the old road and found it was still intact—buried in a foot of sand in places, but still in pristine condition. The statues leading to the enormous steel gates were stolen by looters many centuries ago, and the exterior walls and towers were still standing firm. Through the gates, they could see the chasm that was slowly swallowing the city. From a distance, they watched the strange substance that pooled around the area. It held the same appearance of a star-filled sky and moved like water, pooling in holes and dips in the sand.

Brianne stepped to the edge of the first pool and peered inside, while Kindri stayed back, preferring to wait at a safe distance from anything potentially harmful. She sneered at him and rolled her eyes.

An unreal scene played out before her eyes. The dead city came to life. Hundreds of people were doing business around the gate, and inside, a bustling market of elves and humans alike rose from the sand. The aroma of freshly baked bread and cured meats rolled in with a breeze that wafted across the pool, and the warm breeze carried a cool tinge, but a stinging pain crawled up her spine. She looked up and saw a young human woman standing on the surface of the pool. Her black hair held the same star-like appearance, with pale skin and a flat expression. Following down her body, Brianne noticed her feet were still submerged in the pool.

"Welcome," the woman said. She walked toward them, but her feet did not lift from the water—rather, they tugged at the surface as she moved closer. "Have you come for the party?" she asked.

Brianne stumbled back and bumped into Kindri. Both were startled by the woman and stepped back toward the dunes.

He pulled at Brianne, but she felt the need to investigate the woman as closely as the situation would allow. He managed to move her back and put space between them and the woman. They watched as her eyes seemed to drift apart, and her body changed direction without moving. The pool moved closer to them and forced them back, but the woman reached out a hand and beckoned them.

"We aren't evil; there's no need to hide from us," the woman said.

"We?" Brianne asked.

"Sorry, we haven't had a visitor in some time. Welcome to Bruin. You are the honored guest of Galen, king of Imithia. Join us and enjoy our hospitality," the woman said.

"Who are you?" Brianne asked, ignoring the bells ringing in the distance and pressing for more answers.

"This body belonged to a simple peasant. She

dreamed of living a better life, and we allowed that to happen. She enjoys lavish parties and rubbing elbows with nobles. What do you desire?"

Brianne stepped back tugging at Kindri's sleeve, "You didn't say your name!"

The woman smiled and looked at Kindri. "You know our name. You've heard our call for as long as you can remember. Come join us. Be free from her constant control and nagging voice. A mother should never hold her children back."

Kindri walked toward the woman, his arm reaching for her hand as Brianne fought against him. She slapped him and fought his every step until she almost fell into the pool herself. Enthralled, he took the woman's hand, and Brianne watched the two become one as his voice faded, making only a faint yelp. He turned to her, half melded with the woman standing before them, his face contorted and eyes filled with a swirling black ichor. His mouth was agape with the sound of a thousand screams rippling from his throat. His new twisted form writhed and moaned, being pulled and torn until he became nothing more than flesh bereft of form and his bones were moving independently, forcing his body to take different shapes.

Brianne closed her eyes while she stumbled back and lost her balance to a crumbled stone pillar under her feet. A pile of sand at its base broke her fall, and his screams ceased, the voice of the woman called to her.

"You can join us too. Imagine the happiness you will find."

When she opened her eyes again, Kindri and the woman were gone. The howling wind returned, and she felt cold again. The flapping of wings grew louder, but she scrambled to her feet, and through her concern for Kindri, she returned to the pool, but when she peered within, Kindri walked arm in arm with the woman. Both looked back at her and held out a hand, beckoning her to join them. She knelt and cried.

"Kindri come back! Please, don't follow her. W-what have I done?"

They vanished within the pool, leaving Brianne to scream alone among the ruins. A clawed hand gripped her shoulder and pulled her back.

"He's gone. You shouldn't have come here. This place is shrouded in corruption. We must go, the whole abbey is searching for you." Alit stood over her in his true form, taller than the city gates, and he clutched her in his hand.

"Wait, why would you leave us? We thought you were our friend!" Kindri and the pale woman stood before them. He shared the same pale appearance of the woman, and his eyes were devoid of color. His hands reached for Brianne's, but she pulled away.

Alit reared back and bathed the figure in flame. "Be gone, creature of the deep! Brianne, we must go. Kindri is no more."

"Pitiful. You fight our love. You have been abandoned by everyone. We would never withhold our love. Do not listen to this creature of ruin!" Kindri reformed and stood among the flames. "The dragons failed their singular task and claw like rabid animals in their vain attempt to reclaim power," they said.

The creature's words enraged Alit, causing him to swat it with his tail, only for it to reform within the pool.

"Are we lying?" they asked.

"You only lie, Dhral. You burrow into the minds of the desperate and play with their doubts. Set your sights on another meal! She is not a prize to be won!" Alit said.

"You're Dhral?" Brianne asked.

Alit sent another torrent of flames, melting the visage and leaving a pool of melted flesh and bone. It reformed as Kindri again. "Brianne, the name is meaningless. We can go anywhere in the world! We can—"

Alit burned the creature away again, but it returned immediately, and with each attempt, it drew closer to where she stood. "Think of all we could do. We would be together forever. No more hiding, no more concealing your feelings."

Alit lifted her into the sky, and his eyes turned a bright green as fire rained from the sky, and he unleashed a final torrent of flame, not letting up until the gate and walls were reduced to rubble, causing the sand to turn into glass. The visage of Dhral did not reform, giving Alit a chance to fly them away. Reaching the outer wall of the abbey, he sat her down.

"You mustn't speak of this to anyone. I fear his corruption runs deeper than I realized," Alit said.

"Is he really gone? Is there truly nothing we can do?" she asked.

Alit used his massive claw to wipe away a tear from her cheek. "The moment he accepted Dhral's bargain, nothing of Kindri remained. He joined the chorus of the deep and will be tormented until the world ends and all is ruined. So the tale says, no matter the truth. He is gone, Brianne. Another victim of a pointless war."

"But why?"

Guards were closing in on their position, forcing Alit to take his feline form and climb onto a fence post. "Because of you. They want you, the strength that you hold. To be honest, it surprises me that none have come until now. But I fear that what has happened here will have repercussions affecting more than just poor Kindri's soul."

She followed him up the railings and through the opening in the eastern wall, leading into the pasture. They waited among the cows and mules for the guards to move away from her cottage.

"Am I cursed?" She took a seat on a pile of hay, sobbing with her head cupped in her hands.

"No. You were born like any other, but some are gifted in many ways that others covet." He hopped into her lap and nestled against her chin. "It is alright to grieve; it's healthy for you. But remember, speaking of what happened tonight could draw more attention than we want. Best to not let them know everything."

The guards moved away and searched the northern wall and area near the washhouse. She wiped the tears away and snuck to the entrance to her secret tunnel. Taking a deep breath, she climbed through. She returned without her gear, leaving it to be swallowed by the sands. She opened the trap door and pulled herself up. The dark room felt cold and empty, and she sat with her feet dangling. From the bed, Shaw's voice broke the silence.

"They didn't know about you slipping out. Guessing Kindri was with you?" he asked.

She refused to turn. "No, I went to the old tower and watched the stars like I always do."

"You sure?" he asked.

"Yep. I just watched them until the moons fell behind the clouds. Like I do most nights."

He grunted and slammed the door, leaving her in the darkened room alone. She curled up in bed and completely covered herself with the blanket. As sleep took hold, Kindri's face—twisting and pleading for mercy before being subsumed by the corruption—haunted her thoughts. Just before she drifted off, Kindri's voice rolled with a breeze outside her cottage.

Soon. Soon, we will be together.

Tears streaked her face, but her sobbing ceased when Alit curled into a ball at the small of her back.

CHAPTER 6

Morning Routine, 1313

BRIANNE WOKE TO ALIT HOLDING HER EYELID OPEN. "Brena is going to kill you."

She stretched and smiled at him, and her eyes drifted to the window and the speck of light at the top of the crumbled tower. Her eyes widened as she bounced from bed, late again for the start of her day. Brena likely waited for her by the storehouse, already hard at work, not the type to fuss or complain when it came to the little things or big things. She would often just shrug and smile before returning to her duties, but for Brianne, it held importance not to let the old woman down again. She did so with such regularity that guards were taking bets on whether she would make it to the cart before Brena had already made her way to the barracks.

She tossed her nightgown in a pile with the others she had worn over the past week. Forgetting to wash her own clothes had become a common issue, but she would worry about that later. She put on a pair of dirty clothes she wore three days in a row. Each morning, she fought with her clothes. They had always been ill-fitting, but since she had become a young woman, it exacerbated the issue.

"You should ask for new clothes," Alit said as Brianne struggled with the straps on her blouse.

"It's fine, just need to suck in a bit," she said. Lying on the bed, she pulled them as tight as possible, but again, the straps pulled loose. "Gods, why? Guess I'll speak with Shaw. Maybe it will go better than last time."

Alit sprawled out on the bed, digging his claws into the mattress and stretching his back. He kept the form of a cat for so long that it became his preferred form when wandering the abbey.

"I doubt he's still mad. Well, maybe a little mad," he said.

She took another outfit from her closet and hastily threw it on. Stains dotted the front, and it was littered with stray threads and tears. The apron that went with the outfit sat on the old half-broken chair, and she froze while standing over it. Her hand ran up the side, pressing her thumb into a splotch of dried soup. Five years came and went, but she remained rebellious and refused to stop sneaking out to speak with Thealen, and because of her continued attempts to break the rules, they removed her from training and relegated her to the position of maid, no longer allowed to train and left to clean rooms beside an old lady each day. It was a punishment she felt was harsh and undeserved, but the council made their decision and ended her training.

She lifted it, knocked the dried chunks of

questionable material loose, and draped it over her chest. She hastily tied the straps and left them partially undone. Looking at herself in the mirror, her eyes drifted to the floor, and she slumped down on the bed.

"Is this my life now? To be stuck here forgotten by everyone, waking up every morning to clean rooms with an old lady for the rest of my life?" She fumbled with her shoes, and with her eyes elsewhere, she put each on the wrong foot and started over.

Alit scoffed. "They can't really be that upset about a few rules, right? I mean, you did desecrate a grave. Also, didn't you cause the chapel to burst into flames while training with Carsis? Oh, and what about that time you—"

He stopped after noticing her hands slide up to cover her face before letting out a labored sigh. "Don't remind me. I wanted to do the trials before Timul. Now he is off having fun, and I get to watch the sand get blown from one dune to the next."

"Come on, it isn't all bad. He does look striking in that armor, like a brave hero, and you have the innate ability to cause any glowstone within one hundred feet to explode. I call that skill."

She shoved him off the bed and stood up, patting down her pockets to make sure she gathered everything. With a knife to cut twine and rags in each of her apron pockets, she pulled a small box from under the bed. Filled with gold pieces and jewelry from her time with Elissar, she took a pendant from a flap under the main compartment. It bore the symbols of Athys and Balessa intertwined. She slipped it into her shirt pocket and smiled as she put the box back into its hiding spot.

"I think I'm ready. He comes back today, and when he comes through those gates, I'm giving him this and telling him I love . . . Ugh!" She slapped the pillow off the bed. "Why is this so hard? It's just simple words. He said it to me, and I should feel the same, right?"

Alit's eyes shot to the floor, and he pointed to a cracked board. "You'll need to get that fixed. It could really be a problem later." He avoided making eye contact and kept looking for other things of note. "I do think you should clean the windows. Kind of dirty if you ask me. Really affects the amount of light this room gets."

She lowered down into his field of view. "Am I thinking about this too much?" Her eyes were crazed and erratic, and she forced a smile.

"Umm, I don't have much experience with love. Dragons don't get married, and we don't sit around worried about words," Alit said.

"What do dragons do to show love?" she asked.

"Set each other on fire. Our scales glow when exposed to our mate's flames. Hurts a bit, but I'm not sure it will work with him," he said.

A sparkle of light caught her eye. The sunlight reached the first window on the tower, and the gates would open soon. She snatched a waterskin and ran out the door, slamming it in Alit's face. She winced and bit her lip as the door swung open and his body was laid out on the floor. His feet twitched, and his tail fell flat. She rolled her eyes and tapped his stomach with her foot.

"Stop playing around. We're already late, and if we don't hurry, we'll have to hear it from Morris about how we keep standing up Brena."

"Oof, I could have really been hurt. Cats are quite soft and easy to peel. I mean harm! No one skins cats. Do they?" he asked.

She rolled her eyes again and started down the path. He followed behind, his little legs racing to keep pace with hers. He took the form of a fluffy, plump cat with dense fur. He would keep a form for as long as it would hold together and would require changing soon, as evidenced by his missing patches of fur to the sores developing on his stomach.

"How do you get a new appearance?" she asked.

"Not a big deal. I'll tell you someday. Might be a lot worse now that I think about it," he said.

They arrived at the crossroads. Guards were off preparing the main gate for the arriving soldiers. Two hundred traveled to Oncier and would arrive home later that day. She watched the banners being hung over the main gate and the bouquets of flowers placed for each that were to return. "Do you think Sprine's service will keep Shaw busy today?"

She could hear the grumbling from the houses as people readied for the long day of celebration.

Alit swiped a paw at the staff affixed to her back. "Not busy enough to not notice what you're wearing. What did he call it? A child's weapon?"

"He isn't one to talk. Have you seen his shield? Splintered edges and a hole near the grips; not worth using in its state." She adjusted the staff, returning it to its normal position. "Wait. what if they say I can do the trials? By the light, I need no bargain! And that stuff? Wonder if it is a test where I recite the tenants and pray a bit?"

"How do you not know? Isn't that the whole deal of a paladin?" He changed the tone of his voice to be an exaggerated noble tone. "By the light, we passed the god's trials and prevailed. Blah blah. Self-righteous nonsense."

"Hey. I'm not the dragon? Why choose me and think my choice of service to the light is nonsense?" she asked.

"There was no choice. Emuel said 'Follow that one. She will be important in what is to come.' Uhh, and here I am. The great Alitherus, defender of the last Anian, shadow of the frozen winds and light of Aud Nua. Diminished to follow you around like a pet."

He shivered, and through his feline mouth, he spat a hunk of burning metal. "I long to be carried on the winds over Iskal, to watch the sunset while enjoying the waves on the western ocean, but here we are. A daydreaming elf and a cat cleaning rooms, removed from all the enjoyment and fun."

"I'm sorry." She stormed off, leaving him to roll his eyes before chasing after her.

"Brianne, wait, I didn't mean it like that. Okay, maybe I did, but this is good in its own way. I get lots of jerky. Stop!"

He stepped in her way and tripped her as she tried to avoid stepping on him. She landed on the ground with a thud and scraped the palm of her hand.

He placed a paw on her shoulder. "I shouldn't have said that you'd think a thousand-year-old dragon would be above this. I'm just tired of having to wait endlessly."

She turned away from him and wiped the spots of blood from her hand and dusted the gravel from her knees. Her eyes narrowed as she stared him down. "Fine, but I'm not giving you any of my food today."

His eyes softened, and he raised his paws to beg. "Okay, maybe the stuff I don't like, but nothing else."

Following her, he laughed and bounced a bit with each step.

She turned to leave but bumped into an older man wearing a guard's uniform and carrying a bouquet. His weapon offered no real use, blunted and hung from a sheath on his back—inaccessible but more for show than anything else.

"Oh. Brianne. Sorry, my old eyes aren't what they once were," Morris said. His raspy voice barely carried over the sound of his breathing. He fumbled around with the few things he carried and hugged Brianne like he did every morning. "I can still sneak up on you young ones, though; the old man's still got it."

"Sorry, Morris. I should have been watching my step."

Alit rubbed against his leg and purred loud enough to be heard over the commotion in the courtyard.

"What a nice cat. Ugly but sweet. Where are ya headed so early, girl?" he asked.

"Brena is waiting for me by the storehouse. Those rooms won't clean themselves," she said.

He scratched the tuft of white hair on his chin and raised an eyebrow at what she said. "That beautiful woman. Quite a minx, if you ask me. Gave me this note and told me to give it to the blue-eyed girl, something about her back." He held the note between two fingers in the same hand as the bouquet and a torch in his other hand, and seeing the sun rising, he walked to the corner of the barracks and dropped the torch into a bucket of water. He gave a bow to

Brianne and then gave Alit a piece of cured meat from his coat pocket. "Good day, Brianne. Be sure to leave an extra pillowcase by my bed. I sweat a lot at night, as you know."

"Thank you again, Morris. Hope to see you at the celebration," she said.

He huffed and gave a slight grin before slipping inside the barracks. She would have to return with all the supplies, and the others were up for morning drills. She picked up the pace and cleared the courtyard before everyone arrived to set out things for the celebration. She stopped at the partially broken sewer grate and stuffed her pack inside, just far enough in that no one would notice it, and started down the path toward the washhouse.

hree Words

BRIANNE WALKED EXPEDIENTLY ALONG THE WORN cobblestone path, nearing the washhouse. She needed to catch up with Brena before the old woman left to make her rounds cleaning. She hadn't read the note that Morris gave her, but she would just have Brena tell her when they were cleaning.

The early morning breeze caused her to shiver, but time did not allow her to care about comfort. With the sound of hoofbeats nearing the main gate, she would have a few hours to clean before the arriving soldiers would want to rest. She saw the horizon brimming with light, and soon, the sun would bring the oppressive heat, but for now, it was cool with the smell of spring rain carried from the storms rumbling in the distant farmlands to the north.

Walking along the darkened path in the narrow spaces tucked away from the rest of the abbey, she slipped through a shortcut. She didn't care about the dark as she walked past the broken lampposts and those missing their glowstones, most burned out and just removed or ignored.

Alit followed just to her left and slightly behind, but kept pace. She arrived at the washhouse to a distinct lack of Brena. The cart remained stowed away, and the mules were still eating their morning meal of grain. She opened the note, and all it said was Brena injured her back and would need to remain in bed for the next few days. Brianne rolled her eyes and sat on the edge of the rickety cart.

"How am I going to get this all done?" she asked.

Not receiving an answer from her companion, she moved things around and flipped through the keys until she found the right one.

She fumbled with the locks and opened the storeroom, gathering supplies. She fought to get caught up as the sun rose over the walls. The temperature started to rise, and she would be stuck cleaning the entire abbey alone. It wouldn't be the first time, but she managed to fill the cart and prepare it for the day.

An hour passed, and the festivities were in full swing. Singing and dancing echoed through the pathways and streets. She could smell the array of foods that were set out for their feast, and elaborate decorations were being hung. She hopped over the fence and stalked the best-looking mule for the task at hand. With a bag of apples and several carrots, she tried everything possible to get one of the young, strong mules, even going so far as trying to corner one, but she only managed to get herself covered in manure and more dirt than usual.

"Maybe Timul could help you catch one?" Alit asked.

She turned and growled at him, rolling her eyes. She threw a carrot at the mule she chased and dusted herself off. "Funny!"

After a solid fifteen minutes of chasing them around, she threw the full sack of apples into the dirt and stomped over to Topper. He stood peacefully at the gate, his head and ears drooped, and his eyes were heavy, but he willingly let her put the halter on and lead him to the cart, only stopping a few times along the way to eat the green sprouts outside the fence.

When she finally got him in place, she could hear Shaw's voice. Her stomach turned, and she hurried, tying the knots and trying to get Topper to move.

Alit rubbed against her leg and drew her eyes to him. "Maybe he has good news," he said. "Stop thinking he will come just to be mean. You only made the glowstones in the washhouse explode. And you shattered all the windows in the mess hall. And . . . Oh, you could be right."

Brianne brushed him off and returned to her task. After adjusting the harness properly, she picked up Alit and placed him on the front of the cart. "And I was trying to fix them. They let those things drain, and I could hardly see." She gave him a pat on the head before grabbing Topper's reins.

"You broke all the windows, and you embedded shards into the walls. If we hadn't been alone, someone could have been hurt," Alit said.

"You make it sound worse than it was. Carsis taught me to charge several at a time, so I figured, why not?" she said.

Alit sat up and walked up the harness to sit on Topper's back. "You have never charged one successfully. Why would you think charging eight while they were still in their sconces would work?"

"Please, I saw him do it. I practiced, and those last few almost didn't shatter. Why can't I—? Ugh, Topper, move." She pulled against him, but the old mule stood firm and chewed the mouthful of grass he snatched on his way to the cart. His face relaxed, and he almost smiled at the joy his meal brought. She pulled and pushed, trying to bribe him, but carrots and apples did nothing, and she found herself standing in the middle of the path as Timul snuck up behind her. Brianne leaned against Topper, burying her head into his thick neck. "Why do I always get stuck with you?" she asked.

Not wasting the moment, Timul leaned in and whispered into her ear, "Figured you would be happy to see me."

Startled, she jumped and spun around, slapping him with more force than necessary, knocking his helmet off and causing him to stagger for a moment. Shaken, he gathered himself and collected his belongings that scattered during the attack.

"Guess I deserved that. Also, you still hit really hard." He wiggled his jaw around before putting an arm around her. "Do I get a kiss from my lovely lady?"

She leaned in, and just before her lips touched his, she kneed him in the crotch before gathering a few of her supplies and walking toward the first building she needed to clean. He followed behind, taking a few bites of an apple he got off the cart.

"I deserved that too. You know, Shaw is back. Maybe you can talk to him about his meeting—"

She caught him again, landing a blow on his stomach, this time with her staff, lifting him slightly off the ground before she returned to the task at hand. They traveled through a narrow path that led between the different buildings she would need to clean. Timul sat down and waited until the pain subsided before following.

"This form gets on my nerves," Alit said.

He tugged at his fur and growled. Small insects gathered on his skin and were biting. "Wait!" he yelled.

They were standing in a secluded spot where no one could see either of them. He changed into his normal form. The husk of his feline form flopped with a wet thud on the ground, and he leaped, using his wings to glide forward a bit and land ahead of her. "That is so much better. I don't know how you soft skins do it. Things biting me just doesn't sit well."

He raised his hands in the air and called to Emual the Great Dragon. His eyes glowed brightly with a fiery green hue, and he became a cat once more, taking the form of a black cat with a few white spots —and not fluffy like before, but sleek and youthful, full of energy. He ran a few circles around her.

"Much better. I held that form too long," he said.

Brianne leaned against a cracked brick wall and stared at him. "What are your illusions? Are they real?" she asked as the husk just sat festering like a pustule in the sand.

"No, they aren't. Okay, so, they are kind of real, but only like they are part of my skin." He tugged at his tail. "If it was just an illusion, someone could touch my fur and feel scales. Nope. This is conjuration and illusion with a bit of other stuff mixed in." He followed her eyes and saw her staring at the old husk. "It will be gone in a day or two. I think."

She shrugged and squeezed her way up the path. The residents were stirring in their homes before making the short walk to the city of Sarntheris. In years past, she would be making her way with Shaw into the city at this time, but things changed, and they hadn't spoken much over the past few years.

In recent years, the city had become a cesspool. It smelled awful year-round, and each day, while eating lunch, she could see people shuffling about the refuse-littered streets. Bustling with life, the harbor never slept, and business ran all night and day. She would often daydream of sneaking onto a ship and going where the winds might take her. But such idle daydreams were a luxury when she worked alone.

The putrid stench of the city crawled up her nose as she passed an access tunnel leading into a closed-off section of the city's sewers. Brianne gave the half-broken grate a wide birth. The aroma aside, she knew how often thieves would wait in the shadows and attempt to rob anyone foolish enough to stray too close to the sewer.

"Do you think we can dodge the watch commander?" she asked, but Alit did not reply. He sat quietly on the path, cleaning himself like a real cat. She kicked a bit of dust at him, but he just sneered and continued cleaning his new body.

A shadow popped out behind her, and without hesitation, she pulled the broom from her sling and let it crack over the head of her stalker. Shards of flimsy wood were sent flying, and she held a broken handle with the bristles flying against the wall of the neighboring house.

"Ouch! Why do you always hit me?" Timul asked.

He rubbed his head fervently, and he squinted at her as he moaned in pain. She stepped closer and moved his hand. A reddish bump formed, but there were no lacerations, and he seemed alert. With nothing broken, she rubbed a bit of ointment she tucked into one of her pockets on the sore and gave him a peck on the cheek.

"Why do you always try to sneak up on me?" she asked. Her eyes surveyed the scene, and she noticed a bundle of white lilies—her favorite flower—in his right hand, and a small wooden box that fell from his hand.

"Figured since you were having such a rough morning, I'd get you something special." He handed her the flowers and collected the box. "Hope you don't mind, but I heard you say that you were a fan of Reduwar. Umm, the adventurer?" He didn't sound confident in his assertion, but Brianne looked past it and leaned closer.

"So, I was at the bazaar in Oncier and saw this." He opened the box, and inside was a real and very well-maintained lockpicking set, engraved with the seal of the Order. Brianne's eyes softened and grew large, a smile washed over her face, and she grabbed him with both arms, laying a kiss on his lips and snatching the box from his hand.

"Do you like it?" he asked.

"No, I just hate it." She giggled and pressed her head against his neck. "How did you afford these?

It's nothing like those old sets people try to sell in Sarn!"

He kissed her forehead and smiled. "I used my savings because I figured you needed something to cheer you up. Shaw didn't seem so happy with what the council said, so I wanted to surprise you with something." Tossing his arm over her shoulder and taking the dropped sack of linens, he walked to her first destination. "Can we have lunch together?" he asked.

She put the box in her pocket and organized her supplies. "Umm, I, uh, sure?" Her hand grazed the box with the pendant, and her heart sank. She would need to sneak into the city and get a new chain from Thealen before lunch.

He caressed her cheek. "Are you okay?"

She smiled back at him. "Yeah, I'm fine, just have a lot to do today, and lunch is so far off." She pulled the sack from his hand and tossed it by the door. "Shaw is back, so I might have to spend it with him. But if that is so, I can meet you in the old tower after?"

Timul grinned and kissed her cheek. "See you then."

Brianne's heart fluttered a bit, and she tried unconvincingly to hide her smile.

He gave Alit a firm pat and sauntered off toward the barracks.

"You could do worse," Alit said, climbing up onto the fence post. "He has good hair. maybe most of his teeth. Can check that later if you like. Oh, and Shaw thinks a lot of him."

Brianne waited until he fell from sight, she exhaled and leaned against the fence, "Why can't I breathe when he is around?" Placing her hands high on her hips, she took a few fast and shallow breaths. "I want to tell him how I feel, but the best I can do is nod and smile when he kisses me. Are three little words so hard to say?"

Alit continued cleaning himself. "I could set him on fire? Worked for my parents. Although they did fight a lot." He stood up on his hind legs and put a paw on her shoulder. "Listen, it will come in time. Even if it takes years, as long as you love him, it won't matter. Your love will hold no matter how silly you are being about three words," he said.

"Do you really believe that?" she asked.

"Has to be true. I read it in one of those books Brena keeps in her bag. That woman reads some extremely strange things," he said.

She prepared all her things and readied to enter the watch commander's quarters. "I like him, but what do I say? When his friends hear, they will remind him that I'm an elf, and it always causes a fight."

Alit hurled a small rock at her arm, and the sting got her attention.

"He isn't worthless, and for the last time, he likes you and would follow you anywhere." He hopped down from his perch and entered the room ahead of Brianne. "Don't know why. Can tell you it isn't your charm."

She slammed the door and used the tip of her shoe to push him farther ahead.

"Are you ever serious?" she asked.

"Nope. The last time I got serious, we both know what happened," he said. He looked over the room and raised an eyebrow. "Why are we here again?"

Within the room, she found various ornate weapons and shields decorated with gold and silver trim. His armors were polished to a mirror shine, and his quarters were in immaculate condition. All his dirty linens were already in a bag, and he placed a basket next to them for fresh linens. "Were we just stopping to see how well he cleans after himself?"

"So, what, he is a little strange. I've only ever cleaned his room a few times. Brena always does it. I'm going to kill her," she said.

She put the supplies back outside and gathered his linens and laundry, leaving a sack of clean linens in the basket by the door. In frustration, she slammed the door and kicked the sack of dirty linens across the porch. Alit clawed her arm before she could kick it again. At the bottom of the hill, she saw the watch commander shouting angry obscenities directed at Shaw.

She ducked and grabbed everything and took the same route she used to reach his quarters. Racing down the secluded path to avoid facing him, she noticed the air of agitation around them both, and she would wait for Shaw to cool off before risking a conversation with him.

CHAPTER 8

 oodbye

MOST OF HER CHORES WERE DONE, AND BRIANNE eyed the guards on patrol and waited until they were out of sight. She tucked what few supplies she carried into an alcove behind the bushes and ducked into the partially open sewer grate. She did this a hundred times, and like most attempts, she slipped through unscathed.

She expertly dodged the randomly piled debris and stepped over the pools of questionable liquids. It became more difficult to manage. Every time they caught her, they either closed off her route or increased the number of guards wandering around the outskirts.

Using an old glowstone she slipped off the abbey alchemist, she navigated the winding paths below Sarntheris. As the years had passed, she had marked each path and knew the district given the symbol she scribbled. Most faded, and she forgot what each meant except for one. Passing the crude etching of coins meant she needed to reach the market. City guards and the lord's personal garrison avoided the main city, preferring to spend their time at the docks, but they often used informants to keep an eye on the crime bosses of the Consortium. The harbor remained off-limits being the most guarded portion of the city, but corruption spread enough for the Order to gain a foothold in illegal trade in the region.

She needed to reach Thealen. Her last effort to enter the city failed, and, in the year since, she avoided that method of breaking the rules. Her plan hinged on purchasing an item from him. He hadn't changed much over the years and still looked like any other withered old man lurking about the slums; frail skin and trembling hands guided his gentle touch, and his soft, strange words were refreshing for Brianne. But escaping the sewer required effort with it being the preferred means of travel for the less-than-savory members of the city. Most were delivering messages for the crime lords or carrying small items to and from their fences.

She made sure to cover her ears and face, as it would stand out for an elf to be in the city when so few lived in the Southlands, and being spotted would end her expedition rather quickly. She walked the streets with her head down and ducked into the cluttered alleyway among the broken wood and trash scattered about. Many of the tents were removed, and the people she helped to feed over the years were gone, their things in a smoldering pile in the middle of the street.

"Thealen, are you here?" she asked.

He was often nearby, but on this day, she saw no sign of him. Even his bags of assorted odds and ends were missing. She visited him for years in the same spot, and even a stain of a spilled potion from her last visit remained where his stall should be sitting. Two men entered the alley, and she froze. Without thinking, she quickly hunched over and snatched a piece of splintered wood. Holding the piece to her chest, she hobbled past them, mumbling about it, suddenly yelling in a strained voice, "Mine, not yours. stay away!"

The men gave her space and ignored her movement into an alcove opposite the alley. They carried on talking about random things until they reached the carved Catha wood doors, and after a series of knocks, the door swung open. They entered the tavern on the slum side of the alley.

She tossed the plank and meandered her way toward the tavern door. Standing outside, she could hear a few voices, from the very informal and often slurred speech of a Dwarf to the affluent tones of a human from the floating city of Fimorn. But there was no sign of Thealen's distinctive and often unnatural sounding voice. The guttersnipe who often slept by his stall predictably still slept in her makeshift tent. After finding nothing near the tavern, Brianne lurched toward her, acting like another slum dweller to not draw attention to herself.

"Ascoli. Ascoli, wake up." She shook the frail old woman's arm and roused her from her midday nap.

"What? I don't gots gold. They done took the old man and took Ascoli's gold, you no take sleeping spot," the woman said.

"Ascoli, its Brianne." She wrestled to get the

woman to open her eyes. Looking over Brianne, she moved her beloved keepsakes of mostly discarded bits of useless metal and scuffed beads.

"What do you want? They said I had to move in two days. Can't sleep here if that's what you want," Ascoli said.

"No. It's me! Brianne. Have you seen Thealen?"

"They said speak, and I will have to go too. This is my home. I don't want to find a new home," Ascoli said. She slipped back into her pile of trash and glared at a few people passing by to enter the tavern. Brianne kept her eyes forward until they passed, and she eyed both ways before asking again.

"Ascoli it's me." She pointed at herself. "Brianne, remember? I come and visit Thealen. where did he go?"

Ascoli shuffled back and made space between them. "Sands. They say the lady comes. Must clear the trash. Ascoli not join friends in the dunes." The disheveled woman cowered into her tent and hid, peeking only to see if Brianne remained nearby.

Brianne tossed a few gold coins into the tent with Ascoli and walked briskly to the guard post. She took some old rags and pulled them over her clean clothes, making it more difficult to be spotted. Once the guards left for their patrol, she slipped into their office and searched for any notice or sign mentioning the evictions.

She sifted through every piece of paper and folded notes and found nothing. She slipped out without notice and huddled into a corner and watched the priests greet people by the open doors of the cathedral. A boot hit her backside.

"Move along. Your kind belongs in the slums."

The guard made his rounds and ordered her to move on.

She kept her head down, bundled the awful-smelling rags around her chest and face, and scampered off to the alley. Once alone, she ducked into the sewer and tossed the rags. The smell clung to her clothes, and they would need a week's worth of cleaning before being rid of the smell. Alit, sitting on a pile of driftwood, was waiting for her when she climbed down, shaking his head and rolling his eyes.

"How many times do you try this? 'Oh, Alit, I need another this or that,' and boom, gone. I won't always be here, and what happens then?" he asked.

She patted him and pulled a piece of jerky from one of her pockets. He growled and accepted the bribe without question.

"Alit, if someone was taken to the dunes, do you know where they would go? Other than Sarntheris, of course."

He gnawed on the piece of meat and stared down the tunnel behind her, "Hermit's Den. Think that's what it's called. Just beyond the southern wall."

She kissed the top of his head and ran down the tunnel. Taking the turn, she heard his small feet racing up behind her. "Stop!"

She kept running and made it to the grate leading to the southern wall.

"Shaw was forced out of the abbey!"

She froze. Her mind raced, but his words didn't make sense. Shaw was forced out?

"What happened?" she asked.

"They approved your request to attempt the trials. I heard the others speaking, and from what I heard, he was against you doing the trials. and that caused the council in Oncier to relieve him of duty and send him away."

She grabbed on to the grate and used it to keep balance. "It doesn't make sense. He wanted me to take the trials, and now he doesn't? Do you know where he went?"

"Nope. He rode north, and I watched them lock the gates behind him. Lost sight of him when he turned onto the King's Road. Must be halfway to the farmland by now."

She slid down the crumbled stone wall and sat on a piece of flotsam left by the last hurricane to strike the coast. "If I go back, will it be the same?"

She looked to a concerned Alit, and he dropped the feline appearance and took his dragonling form, tiny in stature and resembling a lizard more than a fearsome dragon. "I'm worried, Brianne. Things aren't happening the way they should, and now without Shaw, I fear a dark tide is rising," Alit said.

She climbed through the grate. "I have to find Thealen. He deals in knowledge. Maybe he heard something from the guards, or maybe the Order knew about it." She looked around and noticed no messengers were traveling the tunnels and hadn't heard any voices echoing under the city. She ran through the rubble and stumbled out by the southern tower. She failed to look up and ran into Eandar standing in her path.

"Welcome, young paladin. We've been waiting for your arrival," Eandar said.

A group of paladins gathered around her and placed shackles on her wrists and ankles.

"I would hate for you to try another of your escapes. The day has come when you will go through the trials and become a true paladin. Once done, may you bring light to the world and allow our Order the glorious return."

They dragged her back to the cottage and threw her inside, only removing her shackles once they stationed a guard at the front and back of her cottage. She pulled open the hidden compartment on her nightstand and placed the pendant inside. A knock on her door came without warning and startled her. The door swung open and the seamstress Verna—a Dwarven woman—stepped inside. She had come to take measurements and decide Brianne's role in the Order, taking what was needed by the smith for her weapon and armor to be crafted.

"Remove yer clothes. Need to measure yer body, not some rags ya dug out of the trash." Her Dwarven accent had always warmed Brianne's heart, but this time, she found little enjoyment in hearing it. "Do ya want anythin' special?"

Brianne shook her head and did her best not to show she felt uncomfortable about being naked in front of another person. Alit even crawled out of the room until they finished their task. Verna opened an old sack and tossed a half-torn dingy robe on the bed.

"Ya wear that until the trial is over. Nothing else. Tradition is all, and from what I heard, y'all need it," Verna said.

Before Brianne could ask about the odd tradition or what to expect, the door slammed, and the pitter-patter of the old Dwarf's feet raced down the pathway from the cottage, followed by the groaning sigh of the guard out front. She pulled the robe over her body, and it lay uncomfortably against her skin. The bloodstains and splotches of dirt made her slightly nauseated, but she sat on the bed and looked to the ceiling to avoid thinking too much about the situation and her newly received attire.

She heard the shuffling of someone moving through the crawlspace and moved around behind to catch the only person who knew about it off-guard. Timul's head poked through, and he looked around, only to have her arms drape over his shoulders.

Brianne whispered, "Hi there. Trying to sneak another look at me changing?"

He turned beet red and avoided eye contact. "I wasn't trying to. Wait a minute, I never tried to watch!"

She smiled at his fumbled answer and kissed him. "Fun aside, what happened with Shaw?"

She helped him out of the narrow passage and sat beside him on the bed. They both avoided the window and spoke softly so as not to alert the guard snoozing out front.

"No one said. He just stormed off when they said you'd be starting the trials tonight."

Brianne sat on the floor and opened the nightstand. "I got you something. Tried to get a new chain, but this will have to do. If you don't like it, just say so, and I'll gladly get you something else."

She opened the box and placed the pendant in his open hand. At first, she tried to place it around his neck, but as she feared, the chain was too short to fit around his neck, so she wrapped it around his wrist.

He smiled and looked over the charm of Athys and Balessa intertwined. "Honesty and devotion." He smiled and put his hand on the back of her neck. "I love it. Not as much as I love you, but I love it all the same." They kissed, and his hands started to wander until a claw from Alit caught his elbow.

"Ouch!" He jumped out of reflex and heard the guard do the same. They scrambled, and Brianne shoved Timul into the crawlspace.

"I'm coming in and this isn't asking!" the guard said.

She swung the door to the crawlspace closed, smacking Timul's head before sitting on the door. The door to her chamber thrust open, slamming against the wall. She smiled at the guard when he entered, waving at him with a book at her feet.

He looked around and back at her. "If I hear so much as another peep from you, I'll kick the door down and drag you to the stockade. Eandar was clear in his orders." He stepped outside and yanked on the door, shaking the walls as it slammed. His grumbling could be heard through the walls as the creaking from the rocking chair returned.

She opened the crawlspace and lay on the floor. They kissed again, and she ran her fingers through his hair. "Tomorrow, I'll be a paladin. Do you believe it?" Her finger dragged down to his jaw and then to his chin before pulling him in for another kiss.

"Yes, and we can officially see each other. None of this running around and pretending we are just friends," he said. Upon hearing this, her hand moved away, and as she eased back, he grabbed her hand and softly pulled her back. "You don't have to say it until you're ready. I just wanted you to know how I felt, what I wanted. Don't feel pressured, okay?"

She grinned and kissed him again. "But I want to see the world, from Iskal to Mourningstar, and anywhere in between." Her head came to rest on his shoulder.

"And I'll be here. I'll always be here whenever the road feels too rough and you need a place to rest. This will always be home." He raised a hand to her cheek and wiped away a tear. "I love you, Brianne. I don't care who knows it, and I love all of you, from your pointed ears and especially your blue eyes."

She rubbed her face against his shirt. "Stop. You know I cry over stupid stuff like that."

He pulled back and raised her chin. "Stupid? What makes it stupid? Or are you hiding from how you feel?"

They rubbed their noses, but looking into his eyes, she felt a sinking feeling, the same feeling the day Kindri went missing. She wrapped her arms around his neck and squeezed. "I promise I'll always come home. No matter how far I travel, I'll find my way back to you."

He smiled from ear to ear—short-lived as it may have been. Footsteps fell hard against the porch step, and Eandar's voice called out. "It is time!"

She kissed Timul one last time, pushed him back into the crawlspace, and shut the door. Knocking the dust off her filthy robe, she stood at the door and took a deep breath. Alit hopped out the open window, and she watched him run along the wall toward the crypts. With a quick pull, she opened the door, and Eandar stood in his ceremonial armor. Paladins lined the path, holding their shields against their chests and staring straight ahead.

"It is time to join us. We can be one in the light," Eandar said, closing the door behind her.

CHAPTER 9

he Veil

BRIANNE SCRAMBLED TO HER FEET. SHE LAY IN water a few inches deep, but oddly enough, her clothes and skin remained dry. Beads of water rolled off her clothes and skin. Her body ached, and she found it difficult to remember what had happened when they had entered the crypts. She watched the beads of water roll off her hands, merging once more with the flowing water at her feet.

"Alit, what is this?"

She found no answer, only a soft breeze rustling her clothes and fading into the distance.

Her eyes rose to an endless lake, and at its edge, she saw a brim of light, the same in every direction. She started to run, but her feet were so heavy, she could hardly move. Out of breath and gasping for air, she looked up to the sky. A hollow blackened sun pulled away into an endless abyss above her. She felt a tug, as if she were being pulled into the chasm, but when she looked down again, the feeling stopped. Her eyes darted back and forth, and her heart raced,

Where am I?

She heard a voice from below, and within the water, she saw herself lying on the ground sleeping. Alit took human form and resembled her. He sealed the door with him outside.

I'm sorry, friend, but what is to come cannot claim you, he said.

She reached toward the reflection. "Alit, what happened? Why are you leaving me?"

But touching the water caused it to change again. Her reflection held the door shut. Hands were forcing their way through and were grasping at her, clawing at any flesh they could reach. Another rose behind her. One of the clerics fell in some sort of conflict and now lurched forward, reaching for her.

"Behind you!" she yelled, but it fell flat. The walking corpses overran her and forced her to the ground. She touched the water as her reflection met a grizzly end.

Timul's voice came through, echoing all around her.

Today is the happiest day of my life.

She looked at the reflection and saw Timul speaking to Alit as Shaw walked her down the aisle. She wore a white gown with a flower pattern and a veil with only her golden eyes shining through. Everyone she knew attended. At the end of her walk, she let go of Shaw's hand and locked arms with Timul. Tears rolled down her cheek, landing in the water below. They exchanged vows and kissed, and people came to congratulate them with kind words and gifts.

My little girl is all grown up. Guess I didn't hold on tight enough.

Shaw placed a hand on her back and greeted her with a smile. She hugged him, and the joyous moment carried on, and soon, they were to leave in a carriage. Brianne felt empty—hollow—and out of the corner of her eye, a wave dragged along with another breeze. With speed, it approached, and Brianne wished for it not to come, that she could have another moment. Hollow as it may be, she wanted to enjoy a bit of peace and joy.

I promise to love you for the rest of my life, Timul said.

The ripple washed over, taking away the beautiful moment. Afraid, she kept her eyes closed, but peeking through her fingers, she saw a broken shell of herself. Tattered robes and pieces of magical armor fused to her body. Shaw's shield lay on her back, and she carried a sleek sword with the same pommel as Thealen's cane. A scar ran from her forehead to her chin, and its depth left a frightening shadow across her face. Around her were bloodied and broken bodies, human and Dwarf, Elf and Ualeon, all races lay broken by her side, but she stood firm, facing the glowing vessel of the Divine. They clashed, each strike causing more death around them. Before they could meet a final blow, the reflection became clouded.

She touched the water again and saw herself standing before a broken pillar. The runes were darkened, and its magical hum faded. A Dwarf and human woman stood at her side, and Alit waited behind, holding the door.

All possibilities, some more likely than others, a voice said from all around her.

A ripple raced across the water again, changing the reflection. She stood outside of Oncier, watching herself stand in front of a headstone. She wanted to see the name, but her vision became blurred and out of focus, bleeding as tears rolled down her face into the still-open grave.

"Who am I burying?" she asked.

The voice didn't reply. Another ripple spread across and changed the reflection again. Alit lay bleeding on the ground. Spears riddled his body, and chunks of flesh were missing from his wings. The city of Iskal lay in ruin behind them to the north, and the bells lay broken and sunk into the earth. Alit reached up to the version of her beyond the water's surface, the real her.

Do not cry. Dragons do not experience death as mortals do. We pass to Aethera, and in time, we return. I just hate that will miss adventuring with you for a time, Alit said.

Thealen placed a hand on his snout. *She will not be alone. We will finish our task, and when you return, there will be plenty of time to regale you on what we accomplished.*

The human woman put an arm around her and pulled her close. *It's okay, Blue. I'm with ya.*

Alit looked to the real Brianne again, through the veiled water. *Be strong, little one. Dark times are ahead that will challenge even the strongest of us.* His eyes closed, and the life faded from his body, passing through the Veil and into Aethera. The reflection turned to a bed of black stones with a slight trickle of water rushing over them.

The voice called again, *I brought you here to give a warning.*

A sharp wind raced across the lake, passing her without disturbing her clothes or even pushing against her. It went through, and out of instinct she braced and turned away, drawing her attention to a room floating on the water.

Shelves and furniture were lit by the soft glow of candlelight. A human man sat with a book in his lap. He raised the edge of a page, and as it folded over, everything around her changed. She nearly lost her balance while standing still as the world ripped past. Above them stood the crumbled gates of Bruin. He turned the page again, and the sand sifted away and rain fell around her. They were on the northern coast by the city of Maknora. Violent waves crashed along the shore, and a battle raged in the hills just beyond the city gates.

"The world is so small that no matter which page one turns to, it is always the same. Mortals kill each other in the name of gods. Soon, you will join the fray and leave broken bodies in your wake. But I must ask: in whose name will you leave a trail of blood?" The man placed the book on the shelf and walked toward Brianne.

She eased back. "Who are you?" she asked.

"Answer my question. Whom do you serve, Child of the Veil?" the man asked.

"I don't serve a god. I serve the people, as all paladins do," she said.

He laughed and waved a hand. They returned to the endless lake. He changed forms to that of an old Dwarven woman, and using her cane, she tapped the water. A ripple raced past Brianne, and the reflection showed her at the gates of Bruin. Kindri stood beside her. She reached for the reflection, but the woman grabbed her wrist.

"Allow it to unfold." She smiled at Brianne. Her leathery skin was covered in wrinkles, and her sagging brow concealed her eyes, but there was a soft look about her.

"I don't want to watch. I've tried to forget that day, but it keeps coming back." Brianne tried to cover her face, but even in her mind, the events played out for her to see and feel again.

"You fear events that have already taken place?" She placed a trembling withered hand on Brianne's shoulder. "Watch. The pain has already been inflicted. It is safe to relive the past. It is the only way one can truly be prepared for the future."

Brianne opened her eyes, and Kindri reached for the woman's hand. Everything played out the way it did that night. She sank and put her hand through the water, ran a finger over Kindri's face, and let a few lonesome tears roll down her cheek. "Why do I need to watch this? Why do I need to suffer these feelings again?"

"Suffer? You do not suffer. You feel pain, but to suffer? Can you heal a wound with a blade still in it?" the Dwarven woman asked.

She tapped her cane again, and the reflection changed once more. Brianne sat on a bed with her children. They waited for Timul, as they did every day. Soon, he would round the corner and walk up the path toward their home.

"This could have been your life, but . . . but—" The woman knelt and changed to an elven boy, and even the being's voice changed with each form, but his manner of speaking did not. "But sadly, this future is out of reach. Would you really have wanted to marry and remain at the abbey for the rest of his life?"

Brianne smiled at the look of their children. "Why is it out of reach?" She looked at the boy, tears welling in her eyes once more as she tried to hold back the rush of emotion.

"Time is often not on our side. I sent Alitherus to watch over you until you were ready, but it would seem this is nothing like the many times I peered into the future. Things are always changing, and no matter how I view them, no future is ever certain. Only those that can no longer come to pass." The boy walked along, not disturbing the water, holding a hand to Brianne as he pressed forward.

"You're Emual. The Great Dragon," Brianne said.

The boy smiled. Still holding the cane in his other hand, he tapped the ground—not a reflection, but a living, breathing place—from beneath the lake hills, and structures rose. They were standing just outside a coastal town, home of a tribe of Wolvar. They were preparing a body for his final voyage.

The people tied ribbons to his clothes and braided his long gray beard, bonfires were built, and they cooked roasts and placed their musical instruments by the dock. They put his fishing rod in his arms and pulled his nets up like a blanket. After pushing him out into the bay, the singing and dancing began. People were laughing and telling stories and enjoying a wondrous celebration. Brianne and Emual were standing among the waves as the fisherman's body passed them to be carried out into the open sea.

Emual looked at the people and smiled. "This is

what they do for every member of their tribe, no matter how big or small. Tonight, they will tell stories of his many adventures and stuff themselves. Tomorrow, they will return to hunting and fishing, making clothes, and teaching the children. To them, a single life matters. No one is ever alone, and they come together to bid farewell to a life well lived. I often spend my days admiring their simple way, but there are two sides to a coin."

He tapped the ground again, and the water at their feet turned to hard cobblestone bricks. The waves became walls, and the streaks of lightning turned to glowstone lamp posts. They were standing next to an alley with an old man drawing ragged breaths while bundled up in old rags left out by the mission. His sickly cough weakened as his body turned cold and his life faded. Another of the destitute rifled through his pockets and took anything of value before leaving him under a pile of garbage.

"This man was once a great soldier, honorable and brave, choosing not to end lives but to save them, but the horrors of war left scars no one could see. They festered within, causing him to lash out and push others away. Knowing the path he walked, he used any means necessary to stop the horrors held behind his eyes, but it was only a matter of time before he ended up here. The feeling of hunger became greater than the memories, and his thirst drove him to not care for his fellow man."

They stood over his lifeless body and watched as rats started at his flesh.

"This is the Beggar's Ward in Oncier. His life meant nothing, and soon, he will be nothing more than another rotting corpse tossed into the Ossuary.

All of his deeds will be forgotten, and his loved ones will never have closure."

"Why not help them?" she asked.

Emual stopped and scratched his chin. "Because what could be done? They are fleeting, specks of dust floating in the night sky. It is not that we help, but that we don't abandon them. Though short-lived, they are just as important to this world as any other." They stepped out of the alley. People were moving about and getting on with their day, and no one noticed the man lying in the alley mere feet from where they walked.

"Then what should I do?" she asked.

"A question for the priests and clerics. There is one more thing I must show you before the trials will start."

"Do all paladins start the trials like this?" she asked.

"No. Sadly, you won't ever be a true paladin, but more on that in time. I have brought you here because you have a part to play in what is to come. Countless lives will hinge on what lessons you learn today."

He hunched over and became a young Wolvar woman and tapped the cane again. The streets peeled away, and above them swirled a sky filled with smoke. They stood over a battlefield. Bodies were strewn about, with Brianne standing in the middle of the endless rows of carnage, changing from a broken woman with shards of black glass fused with her skin to a stoic figure holding her staff high and channeling a torrent of arcana at the Divine, Kere'tora.

"Why am I constantly changing?" Brianne asked.

"Because this is a possibility. The choices you

will make could send you down any of countless paths. What you must see is that at this moment."

They clashed, weapons meeting, lightning arcing, and many other versions of herself overlapping with the Divine's. It became more clouded as the fight progressed until the fog blocked the scene from view.

"I have always been able to see what lies beyond, but now, I cannot see past this moment. Something has tampered with events, and if we do not understand how to undo the damage, this is the outcome of every possible future."

The clouds faded away and Kere'tora stood over her, hands around her throat, her face and body changing to match the different versions of herself, but all still in that position. With a thrust of her immense energy, the Divine boiled the blood in Brianne's veins. Her body fell to the ground, and her army routed.

Freezing the moment at that point, Emual knelt and watched as every version of Brianne lay in the same pose, blood trickling from her eyes and nose, the world poised to collapse under the Divine's unimpeded might.

Emual tapped the cane once more, and they were standing in the Veil. Water rolled over Brianne's feet, and she held a piece of folded parchment.

"These waters hold the key, but I cannot see before the Divine's creation or beyond your death. Something clouds my sight, and this troubles me. I leave you with a map that your mother left with me. She could not tell me of its importance, nor did either of us know what it meant."

She unfolded it to reveal seven locations. They were randomly scattered over a map not matching any she knew. "How will I take it from this place?" She tucked it into her pocket and followed behind him. He ignored her question and walked into his study. Taking the form of the human man, he sat by the fireplace and flipped through his book once more.

"Take care, young one. Alitherus is required elsewhere and will return to you in time. Another will take his place. Though not as resourceful, he is a noble soul. Farewell, last of the Anian."

Emual waved his hand, and a cresting wave rushed toward her. Bracing, she felt it roll across her skin like a soft breeze. The warmth caused her to drift off to sleep and land peacefully on the ground.

CHAPTER 10

$\mathcal{G}$athering Light, 1333

Brianne pushed herself off the dust-covered stone floor, finding it hard to move with her sore joints and aching muscles. It felt as though she slept too long. A thick layer of soot covered her skin. The candles had burned out and were nothing more than pools of wax that trickled down onto the floor and were covered in a thick layer of dust. All the glowstones offered no light, and she could only see from the few narrow shafts of sunlight coming through the several-foot-high ceiling above. Having her bearings, she tried the door she entered with Alit, but it wouldn't budge. It being barred from the other side meant she would need to delve deeper into the trial chambers.

The grumbling in her stomach caused immense pain, causing her to feel nauseous and weak. Brushing it off, she took a few of the glowstones down and focused a slight bit of energy into one—dim, but usable. After gathering the rest and stuffing the two pockets with as many as she could carry, she righted herself and held the dimly charged stone overhead while she inspected the entrance to the trials. The torches were spent on either side of the long chamber. Cobwebs and dust overtook the room. The door to the side entrance was collapsed, filled with roots and dirt and with shafts of light near the bend.

The pain in her stomach returned, causing her to sit on the steps leading into the first trial. A sense of dread washed over her as the draft from below sent chills up her spine. She had visited the crypts before and even stood in this chamber, but never felt so alone or felt so abandoned and hollow. No clerics or priests were traveling the halls, and the eerie sound of empty space made the cold bite a bit harder.

The cold, damp air rising from below felt unnatural, but she would need to move forward if she wished to be a paladin. With the pain gone for now, she slowly walked down the long stairs, hundreds of steps extending into the depths, vanishing into a pit of darkness. She walked slowly, but even squinting, she could not make out the walls nor the bottom of the cavern she entered.

A woman's soft and eerie voice rumbled in the deep.

"Do you wish to find solace in this place?"

When the silence returned, the ground quaked. Dust shook loose from the seams between bricks, and the steps under her feet moved slightly. The shaking subsided, and she raised the glowstone.

"Hello?" She waited for a response, and another

draft rose from below and cut through the thin robe. Fighting the urge to shiver, she forged onward.

Her one source of light faded, forcing her to channel a bit more energy to maintain it for a while longer. This time, it held a bit longer, and with a brighter glow. She could see farther, and on either side of the stairs, she noted the drop into the abyss. In low light, she couldn't see the ground, but she could see a patch of fog resting over what she believed to be a platform a few hundred feet down.

The voice returned.

"So long has it been. Has the Order forgotten tradition?"

The ground quaked again, causing Brianne to lose her footing and slide down several steps. The pain ended, but the air became stale and smelled of the earth. Seeing a faint light on the far end of the shrouded platform, she held the glowstone out. "Hello, are you Balessa?"

The light moved about franticly but did not give her a response. It moved from one side of the room to the other, stopping briefly and taking off again. She slipped again and slid down more than a dozen steps and found herself looking at the floor just below the fog. Gathering herself, she took a deep breath and made her way quickly to the ground below, her legs wobbling the whole way down the slick steps.

The momentum caused her to stumble at the bottom and crash into a pile of books.

After regaining her balance, with a chance to look around, Brianne took the change in pace in stride. She was surrounded by rows upon rows of bookshelves, each standing a few stories high and packed with faded tomes and empty scrolls. She opened one of the books and found it to be nothing more than a dingy journal without a single word written. Each was blank or the words were smudged, and a few were so badly degraded, they fell apart in her hands when she lifted them.

Having found nothing of value, she made her way to the glowing light moving from shelf to shelf. At first, she thought it to be a torch or lantern, but as she came closer, it became clear that it was like a living glowstone moving about—but brighter than her poorly charged light—allowing her to see her surroundings better. Like the rooms above, there was a crypt with tombs and another large door at the opposite end from where she entered. The engraving on each tomb had worn down so much that it was impossible to make out how long ago or which of the fabled clerics were entombed within.

She drew near the orb and heard it speaking.

"No, no, no, not that one. Ugh. Gods, why send me to retrieve a book if you don't know the title?"

Cautiously, Brianne walked closer to the floating orb and stood behind it. "Hello," she said.

It turned and floated to her. "Another trainee? The door is that way. Have a good day." It moved a bit and stopped. "Ugh, forgot." It bobbed toward the far end of the platform. "See the door with the runes? That is the one. Forget I don't have hands sometimes." It floated off and returned to bobbing up and down each row of shelves.

"What are you looking for?" she asked.

It moved up and down another set of shelves and would stop for a moment, grow brighter, and then dim again before moving on. This pattern repeated until it searched an entire section, came back to the starting point, and prepared to enter another.

"Hey. Why are you going up and down the same rows?"

It stopped and moved back and forth in the middle of a row. It looked to be contemplating her words, but as before, it returned to moving along each section.

At her feet lay an old, tattered binding. The pages had worn away centuries before, but the ridges on the cover were still visible. A journal from the god Nyasom. Its value now lost to the ages, she placed it on a shelf and took a step, staring down row after row of ruined tomes and scrolls.

The orb raced to her, asking, "What is that? What could it be? I have searched for a thousand— Or was it a hundred? Wait, how long have I been searching?" It bobbed about, its light becoming brighter and then dimming again before it stopped and moved back to the shelf. "What is this?" It looked closer and grew increasingly bright, forcing Brianne to close her eyes. "Ugh, it's not the one. You'd think with so many books, I would find more than one copy of what Balessa wanted."

"Wait, you serve Balessa?" Brianne asked.

The orb paused and moved close. "I didn't see it before. You aren't a paladin, thank heavens. The ancients return, and I can retrieve my physical form." It became as bright as before, and Brianne looked away and blocked what she could with her hand.

"Sorry. I get a bit excited. Been down here . . . How long was it again? Umm, no matter. So, as you may know, I am Flicker. Some people called me Ke'vin, but since I don't have a body anymore, it kind of doesn't fit." He circled her and bobbed up and down over the uneven floor.

"So, why would Balessa send you to find a book here? Didn't they live here? Both Athys and Balessa?" Brianne asked.

"Gods no, they lived. Umm, so how long do you got?" Flicker asked.

She looked around and back at him. "Not sure. They said I was to complete the trials, but I can't imagine this is what everyone goes through." She sat on a crumbled bench that was little more than a few pieces of smoothed stone elevated from the rest of the floor.

He came to rest beside her. "Been there. Wasn't always a floating orb of light without eyes or a nose. You know, people don't often think about it, but a nose is pretty important."

She didn't understand how, but she felt that he looked at her. The unnerving feeling made it difficult to speak with the floating ball.

"Noses aside, you never answered my question," she said.

"Oh, well, umm, so, I don't remember what you asked," he said. She went to speak, but he cut her off. "Oh yeah, where they lived? Right? Athys and Balessa? So, they lived in cities like everyone else. This was a library and sometimes a vacation spot. Well, I called it that. Not sure if anyone else would, but, hey, like my brother Tyrn always said— Wait. How do you convey creaking noises into meaning? He became a suit of armor and couldn't talk, so I just had to think the sounds of his armor moaning and creaking were his way of . . . What were we talking about again?"

A smile crept across her face, and she let out a quiet giggle at his way of speaking. "Do you get many visitors?" She smiled at him, and his light changed color to a dull red. "Are you blushing?"

He moved away. "Maybe. Don't get many pretty ladies down here, and I get a bit nervous is all. And no, I don't get many visitors. Let me think." He returned to his normal golden glow and moved around her in a circle. "Best I remember, it's been years since anyone has come down those stairs. Not sure how long, because most don't stop to say hi or ask how I'm doing. Quite rude, if you ask me, but, hey, I get it. Who wants to speak with an undecided-number-of-years-old floating orb of light, and, like you said, time to do the trials and leave me here alone for another eternity."

"I'm supposed to go through those doors? Know any tricks, or am I on my own?" she asked.

"Nope, never been near it. Came down here to find a book, and I will keep looking."

He floated back to the first row and started to search again. "Have a good one. Nice to see people still have noses. How weird would it be to not have a nose? Right, I don't have a nose. Keep forgetting."

She smiled at him and walked to the door. It was smooth like a river rock, without a blemish or marking, and above it bore the runes of an unknown origin. She had never seen any like these in all her journals and scrolls. Even the mass of books Shaw brought her during her youth offered no insight into the languages written above the door and on the walls surrounding it. It was even without a handle or keyhole—only a rim of light around its frame.

"What halts your progress, little thing?" the voice from before rumbled in the deep.

"How do I pass? I cannot read the words," she said.

The ground shook, and the door opened. On the other side, darkness blanketed the room, and she could see the light of her glowstone shining off sleek black limbs that were moving. She took another stone from her bag and imbued it with enough arcana to glow for a few moments and rolled it into the room. Large spiders scattered into the corners of the sealed-off room. Bones littered the floor within, and she could see torn pieces of cloth matching her current attire.

"Wouldn't go that way." Flicker made his way over to investigate the commotion. "Those stairs. Oh yeah . . ." He bobbed over to the side of the room and waited over a winding staircase that cut back and forth into the depths below. "People always stood at the door. Some went in, and the others went down there. People that went down here screamed a lot less than those that went into the room."

She looked him over with a look of horror. "Why would Balessa make a room of death?"

"They were a lot smaller when I first arrived, but they get hungry after a while. Anyway, figured I'd see what was happening. Back to the books."

Before he could float off, the voice from the deep called again.

"Flicker, the book is no longer needed. Follow her, and once her task is complete, find your brother. We will be waiting."

Flicker moved over the chasm. "Yes, my lady." He turned back to Brianne. "Guess we go down?

Maybe we should rest, because you look awful now that I have gotten a closer look at you."

"That's rude. I think I look fine. And you try to make this crappy robe look good," she said.

"You are pale. Paler than the usual visitors I get. And you look like you haven't eaten in years. Sure you're up to this?" he asked.

She took a swipe at him and stood over the first step down into the chasm. "I'm fine. If we get this over with, there will be a party and all the food we can eat."

She turned to him and noticed his light dim as he moved toward the first step and paused. He moved back slowly and looked at her. "I've been here so long, you'd think it would be great to leave, but I feel more comfortable here."

She took a step closer to him and investigated what she believed to be his eyes. "It's fine to be afraid, but we must always look ahead."

He turned to the stairs, moved down a few, and looked at her. "Are you coming or not?"

Smiling, she watched the screeching door to the spider-infested room slide shut, and the hissing from within fading behind the thick stone. She paused and put away the one glowstone she charged because Flicker radiated enough light to illuminate their path. She followed him down into another veil of fog hovering within the depths.

CHAPTER 11

Etched In Stone

BRIANNE AND FLICKER MADE THEIR WAY THROUGH the dense fog and found themselves at the entrance to another large chamber bound with runes and sealed. The door opened as her hand neared the stone pedestal at the base of the steps. She could feel the thrum of magic at her fingertips as she held her hands against the stone walls around them. Flicker moved up high, revealing a great dining hall.

Rows of tables and chairs filled the room in every direction, and plates and platters were set out, missing only the food and drink to make it a feast. The candles and braziers were cold and unlit. Witnessing it in such a way made it feel dead, like life had vanished in an instant. Without music and shouting from table to table—as was common—it felt hollow. All along the ground were pieces of parchment—nothing more than tattered pieces of books and scrolls, likely fallen from the library above.

She wandered about the empty halls and admired how the crafters carved each from stone and held the markings of Kasridak, God of the Mountain and Forge. She ran her finger over the dust-covered table, and under the thick layers of residue, she saw gold trim set into the heavy marble slabs, as well as silver dinnerware that had tarnished centuries before but was still elegant in its design.

At the room's center, she found a raised platform where a band would play music for the host of revelers. The instruments were still leaning against the seats. The wood rotted away, and nothing remained aside from the metal trim, but she could make out each by their shape. She could almost hear the music and laughter, but as Flicker came down to join her, the moment faded, and the cold running up her spine took precedence over idle daydreams. She listened as a short-lived vibrant sound gave way to the silence of the great hall.

"What do you think?" Flicker asked.

Brianne flicked a silver bowl over, sending a plume of dust into the air. "So, Kasridak threw parties here?"

Flicker floated behind her. "Yeah, they were the best. Didn't get to attend though." He bobbed into her field of view again. "Can't really drink and sing without a mouth, and people always found it strange that I was always just hovering around."

She giggled and moved on to the sealed door. A brazier sat at the center of the path, and above were the names of all the paladins that had come through before. There was Timul, the last to be etched in the plaque that stood hundreds of feet tall, and the first was Kere'aton—and next to that, squire to Kasridak, Galen Mias.

She inspected the multitude of names and found no sign of Shaw. Curious, she ran her finger along the names and raised a glowstone to read it. Flicker wandered off and left her in the low light of her glowstone. She found the names of Eandar and Falun, but not Shaw. She even found Verna. While searching each row, she remained lost in the names of adventurers and scholars alike, many she had read about over the years. From behind, she heard a grunt and looked at the brazier.

Beside it stood a Dwarven figure. It was translucent and faded to a thin outline before regaining its appearance and returning to the pale gray figure. She knew him from her lessons: the visage of Kasridak. He spoke in smooth and calming tones.

"Using their will, a paladin must carve their name in the wall of remembrance. Here we keep records of all that came before, and all that will come after." Kasridak vanished, leaving her alone to watch Flicker travel around the edges of the room.

She took a knife from the table and started chipping away at the wall. Each piece she broke loose filled back in before she could remove another. After failing to leave a mark, she tossed the knife and sat on the cold cobblestone step. She felt the rush of a magical current below the great hall. It ran deep, far enough that she couldn't tell what type of magic it was, and only the raw power rubbed against her mind.

Closing her eyes, she reached out to the current

but felt a strange sensation—not the connection to a thing or tear in the Veil, but a voice, bound, silenced. The feeling passed, and she found herself sitting on the cold ground. Her fingers and toes started turning purple, and she could no longer stop the shivering.

Each brazier had a few planks of wood and a striking stone attached. She gathered what she could and broke loose one of the striking stones. Stacking the wood and filling the pile with pieces of parchment close by the brazier, she hit the striking stone against the bricks and ignited the small campfire she prepared.

The warmth brought comfort, allowing her to fall asleep for a brief nap. Flicker hovered over her as she woke.

"Good," he said. "Scared me for a moment. Thought you were a goner, and I would have to go up all those stairs by myself. You do look a bit better now, still rough but better."

He moved to the other side of the fire and floated a safe distance from the flames.

"How long did I sleep?" she asked.

"Not long. Guess the fire has magical sleep powers or something. You went out the moment you sat down. Oh, you don't look so blue. I mean your eyes but— I'll shut up now," he said.

She fought against her waning strength and stood. Her stomach turned and cramped, and it became a dull pain that wouldn't go away. She looked at Flicker and pointed to the door. "Any idea how we get a name carved into that door?"

He turned and glared at it for a bit, not making a sound and with his light focused on the stones. She felt another rush of pain and gripped a nearby chair.

Keeping herself upright, she waited for the feeling to pass and returned to Flicker staring at her.

"The door, no idea, but you don't look so good again. I hear Nyasom has a garden somewhere down here, and maybe there is some fruit. Or some leaves. Can you eat leaves? I haven't eaten anything in a very long time. Where was I? Oh, you look awful again."

"Gee, thanks for the help and making me feel so much better about things. How do you write—" Pain gripped her again. "Uhh. I'm going to sit down for a bit." She sat down by the fire again.

The crackling flames eased the cramps, and she felt a bit of comfort while resting. Looking over her hands, it became obvious that something weakened her body, from the trembling to the cracked, colorless skin around her fingernails.

"How can anyone complete these trials if it drains you so much?" she asked.

"Hmm, don't think this is a normal part of the trials. Everyone that came through the library seemed happy and full of energy—well, those that didn't go into the spider hole. You look like you skipped a hundred too many meals," he said.

She felt along her side and could feel her ribs. The sensation made her uneasy. Her muscles were gone, and she couldn't sit for long, or her bottom would become sore. Turning from side to side, she watched the flames turn to embers and then coals.

All warmth faded, and a quaint shiver rolled up her body. It caused the droning pain to worsen, and she could hardly keep still for the aching in her bones. Every so often, she would jerk violently only to be followed by her wincing in pain. She didn't have enough energy to make another fire and needed to save her strength to make it through the remaining trials.

Two more gods remained, and she could feel her strength bleeding out with the last bit of warmth from the dormant campfire. Flicker hovered over her, trying to use his light to warm her, but it garnered the same reaction as placing a glowstone on someone's skin, pulling away the warmth rather than adding to it.

She noticed a mural of the Dwarven god Kasridak. He held up the mountain, and veins of gold sprouted from its peak. "Kasridak was the first shaper?" she asked, fighting the pain and cold to stand.

"No, he was a smith and scholar. When Idra came and taught the first shapers, he cataloged their successes. This was one of the few built by Idra herself. Magnificent, isn't it?"

She looked at him and threw a light rock in his direction. It passed through his form and struck a bowl behind him, knocking it from the table and causing it to clang against the floor.

He looked at the bowl and then turned back to her and asked, "What did the bowl do to you?"

"Idra taught the shapers to use written words to etch things in stone," she said.

She scrambled to gather a piece of parchment, and gathering a piece of charred wood from the brazier, she scribbled the letters as best she could and laid them in the bowl.

Unable to stand for more than a short period, she crawled to the striking stone and back. Using what strength she could muster, she pulled herself up onto the side of the brazier and rammed the striking stone into the stones around its edges.

The paper went up in smoke, and her name formed on the wall, etched beside Timul's and the last to be written. Kasridak appeared by the open door and greeted her.

"Welcome, young one. I offer a boon to any that should require it." His hands were outstretched, but his form faded before she could reach it.

"My essence. Essence. Rejoin. Broken. Depths." His visage faded completely, and even his voice merged with the slow hum of the hall.

She leaned against the wall and slid down a long, narrow corridor, nothing like the rooms before. Everything was covered in damp webs that stuck to her skin, pulling against her and making it hard to move forward. At her feet were a few scattered bones and a layer of an unknown substance, making it hard to keep balance. It stretched to a source of natural light. She felt the warmth of the midday sun on her skin and caught the aroma of spring flowers rolling through the hall, accompanied by the sound of trickling water. Her feet stumbled over each other, and she fought to remain standing.

Flicker moved ahead and vanished into the light. Her strength gave way, and she slipped down to the floor. Crawling along, she felt the hum of magic more clearly than before. The door to the grand hall closed, leaving her in the dark. The only source of light lay ahead, and she could feel the cold from the floor sapping her will to keep pushing.

She shimmied herself along the floor, stopping only to regain what little energy she had left before starting again. The scratching sound of arachnid legs came from high above. She couldn't see them, but the sound moved closer with every inch she moved forward. Adrenaline started to pump, and she gained a second wind. Climbing to her feet, she fumbled about, hardly able to control her legs and feet but still pressing forward. The light narrowed and the path started to shut. Above her, the skittering drew near, and she could hear the hissing as they closed in.

She could see their shiny black limbs coming into the light and reaching to collect their next meal. Her off-balance walk turned to a run as she squeezed through the door. Soon after, it slammed shut, crushing the few spiders that tried to claw their way through the opening.

The warmth of sunlight and the mattress of soft grass under her greeted her. She stood in the garden of Nyasom, Protector of the Ancient Grove and Keeper of Lore.

She crawled along a soft patch of ground, struggling to reach the clear stream running through the verdant grove.

Flicker hovered overhead and bobbed next to a ripe piece of fruit. "Hey, this should help." He couldn't touch it, nor could he help her other than to point out things of interest.

She felt the last bit of her energy fading, and her eyes could no longer remain open. Her sight faded, but she could hear Flicker saying, "Come on, just a bit longer. Please, I don't want to go back to that dingy old library. I mean, books and scrolls, some of them aren't even written and were transcribed with arcana so only the person who wrote them could read it. I just need you to hang on a little longer."

"Fine, just be quiet for a moment," she said.

Her hand dragged the water's surface. She cupped her hand and drank what little water clung to her fingertips. She did the same a few more times and pulled herself up the thin tree and plucked the piece of fruit before falling back into the soft grass. The sweet taste of the peach overwhelmed her. The pain in her stomach receded, and she felt full after only a few bites.

Unable to stand, she closed her eyes. "I just need a nap. Just a bit of sleep before I go any farther."

She fell into a deep sleep. Hearing Flicker's words would only pull her back so far before she collapsed again, slumbering in a deep and restful sleep.

erdant Grove

SHE WOKE TO SINGING. THE WORDS WERE BEYOND her understanding, but they were a sweet melody. Mixed with the sounds of birds chirping and with the rustle of wind through the trees, it made her feel safe and at peace. Her eyes weren't open, and she wanted to drift back to sleep and enjoy the calm of the grove a bit longer. The soft kiss of spring rain landed on her cheeks. Rolling over, she felt a bit of her strength return—not fully, but she would be able to press forward.

She could finally admire the grove: miles of forest covered in lush grass and thick moss, streams packed with fish, and all kinds of beasts roaming the wild. Her eyes widened at the trees wider than her arms could stretch around and vibrant flowers of so many colors, she could not name them all. Her eyes were drawn to the sky and the countless birds fluttering about the canopy. She froze at the sight of

The Seer, Nyasom, one of the Hanuwei. Her books told of their origin, legends of how the elders shaped them to resemble the heart of the forest. They looked to be a cross between an elk and human. Their horns stayed year-round, and they were known to only dwell in hidden groves far from the prying eyes of the mortal races.

Before her stood the real Nyasom, not an illusion or a dream. Catching sight of Brianne, the Seer fled into the forest, his tracks glowing bright green, and led her toward the trunk of a great tree. She stumbled forward and over the natural bridges formed from vines and roots. Flicker came down and joined her along the moss-covered stone path.

"Do you know anything of the Seer?" she asked.

"Never met 'em. Balessa and Nyasom argued over the nature of man. Was always so boring that I never listened but never wanted to come around after their falling out," he said.

"Could you tell me what they fought about? It is a long walk after all," she said.

"Sure, going to be boring though. Balessa believed that humans could be pure and learn to cherish the groves and deep places. She felt that, given the chance to grow, they would learn to appreciate the world and its many wonders. I miss her. The voice in the deep is just a memory, something left behind to help others with their quest for purity and valor. At least that's what she called it. I often told myself it was because she knew I'd get lonely without someone to talk to, so she left a piece of herself."

"What did Nyasom think?" Brianne asked.

"That is complicated. He believed ever since the

elders"—he bobbed a bit closer to her—"your people, left the world that none would care for the groves. Even the elves were careless in his eyes, and so one day, he closed off his groves and made sure that neither humans nor elves could find his shrines, but more importantly, he hid the Baeothen. Was always weary when it came to humans. Didn't like elves, and only cared for a few Dwarves. Your kind, he loved. Thought they were the most important beings in existence."

She stopped walking and stared at him. "I'm an elf, and I have the same glowing eyes and pointed ears that every elf is born with. Even have the pale skin."

"Nope. You might not see through magic yet, but I can see you. Same *golden* eyes. The thing that gives it away the most, the hair. Never knew a single elf with silver hair and golden eyes. Also, you have blue skin. Don't know if it is blocked by something too, but that tells me that you're an Anian. Balessa and Athys called them the Aldar. Also, the only elves with blue eyes vanished when Bruin fell. Sadly, it is a magic spell. Always liked the blue eyes."

"Wait, a magic spell? How come I can't see it? I can see spells and feel magic auras," she said.

"Because it was cast on you. My guess is a powerful being placed the spell. But— Wait . . ." He moved closer and circled her a few times. "You aren't just Anian. Not sure what else, but someone really wanted to keep you a secret. These interwoven spells are something else."

"What else am I? And why didn't anyone tell me this before?" she asked.

"Hmmm, would say it is likely they didn't see it.

Balessa granted me sight, among other things, because most of her scrolls and books were written with arcana and cannot be seen by most. Hence, I can see spells, and you are wrapped in a whole bunch of them."

"Wait does that mean I'm—"

"A mystery?" Nyasom stood on the path ahead of them. "Come, Child of the Veil. Much has happened, and we must speak where their ears cannot hear. Servant of my sister, remain here. I will return her unharmed."

Flicker dimmed and floated off toward the great tree. "Okay, guess I'll just talk to Myusa until you return. Didn't want to go anyway. Always boring to join in on things."

Brianne didn't speak and followed the god of nature. They reached a portcullis, and with a breath of his magic, it came to life. The swirl of color blurred the image of another grove beyond. He stepped through and beckoned her to follow, but she paused and looked at Flicker talking to the trees. He was laughing and joking with creatures yet unseen to her eyes. Taking a deep breath, she followed Nyasom through.

She stood in a grove like the one they left, but she felt the scars and corruption. The plants were broken and wilted, the bones of animals and withered trees littered the forest, and the stream ran dry and without life.

"What happened here?" she asked.

"Forgotten. I could not tend to the groves, and in my absence, they have withered. Only a few remain, and fewer still have a chance at surviving what is to come. I blamed mortals for a time and searched alongside Emual for a chance at subverting their course, but I found the truth."

The moan of dead trees and the cracking of rotted branches rolled through with a sharp, cold wind. A few starved deer wandered through, picking at any foliage they could find. With hollow eyes and splotched fur, they wandered deeper and vanished into the fog surrounding the once majestic grove.

"From all sides, life fades. The light and darkness are not enemies nor allies, but pieces to a puzzle. Without all forms, the world will fall to decay, but even then, it will not consume this world. Balance is needed." He walked over the brown grass and dead leaves with the great tree at the center lying broken on its side, dying a silent death.

"I must ask a favor. You must find the stones of binding and destroy them. Without this, all efforts to stem the tide will be in vain. They prevent magic, and they are reducing the Great Dragon's sight."

"Are you the real Nyasom? Or a vessel? Visage? Or a reflection of arcana?" she asked.

"I am the only true version of myself. I do not know what became of my brethren. Without my groves, I am without strength, and with many such as this, I will soon be powerless. Your path will lead you to Tania. There you will find the first stone. I do not know where the rest are, nor do I know how to shatter their influence."

Crows flew among the trees, and their calls tore at Brianne's ears. Around them, rabid beasts crept closer, their fangs dripping in a foul substance. Their glowing eyes filled Brianne with dread. "How will I know where to find the first?" she covered her ears and closed her eyes.

Nyasom touched the great tree, and it mended. Leaves sprouted from its once-dead branches, and the grass turned a shade of green. This return of life forced the crows and rabid beasts from the forest and called back the deer and a few colorful birds perched in the branches above.

"Find the Baeothen Idra. She is the eldest and will know of the first. From there, I do not know, nor do I see the current that pulls you. Another is on the same path, yet his course is set against yours and pushed on the winds of forces that would wish you harm." He walked with her to a hollow log, and inside lay a dead animal, its flesh decayed and a feast for flies and maggots. "Others will join your cause. Understand that even decay has its place among the cycle. Once you leave my grove, your soul will be in peril. I can send you from the depths and back to the surface."

Her eyes opened to the sight of life returning. "No, I must complete the trials and prove that I am a paladin." She puffed out her chest. "Then I will travel to the forests of Tania and do as you ask, as a paladin."

Nyasom patted her head and held out a hand, waving her back to the portcullis.

"I will offer you something, guidance and a gift." They stopped before entering, and he looked at her intently. "Pain awaits you, and in time, you will feel suffering most will never know. Take the lessons of your mentors and heed my warning: even the most corrupted can be redeemed."

He then placed a charm made from the bark of one of the great trees and carved into the rune of birth into her hand. "And a gift. Carry it with you. Dark places can still hold life, and should you require its protective magic, it will not fail you."

She stared at it for a moment before tucking it into her pocket. "Could I ask you something?" The swirl of magic within the portcullis shifted and swirled in the opposite direction.

"Of course. What question troubles you?" he asked.

"Am I that important? Am I destined to be a hero?" she asked.

"No. You are a piece to a puzzle. Countless lives will alter the flow. Should one be out of place, the whole of our efforts will fall apart, and our world could crumble. I waited for you, not because you are fated to be a hero, and not because you were of the first, but because the others have chosen paths that will take them far from my reach. I believe in you Brianne, daughter of Melisande. We must return now. I fear our time grows short, and the hour grows late."

With a nod, she followed him through. They were back within the verdant grove. Flicker remained near the portcullis chatting with the trees, and the animals were moving about peacefully. Nyasom placed his hand on the portcullis, and in the swirl of its gate, she saw another grove, one made of stars and filled with impossible shapes.

He turned and pointed at a small log resting by the stream. "I will be watching, and in time, I will call on you again." He stepped through the gate and vanished. Its power faded, and the portcullis became dormant once more.

She inspected the log, and within, a full set of paladin armor lay wrapped in a silk towel. It bore the symbols of the first paladins and was made of silver armor and white clothes—no blue—and on the chest, it bore the symbol of a tied scroll: the marking of Balessa and not the torch of Athys. Bound within the bundle, she found a sharp sword and a staff made of Catha wood and black glass. Last, there were a few pieces of dried meat folded in paper and tucked into a satchel alongside a waterskin.

"Whoa, that is some neat stuff. Guess he really does like the Anian more than most. Guess we're ready for the last trial?" Flicker asked.

"I guess. Did you ever meet a Melisande?" she asked.

Flicker moved away and his light dimmed. "No. Why would you ask? Did someone say I did? Can't prove it either way. So, nope, never met her. I mean, don't even know who you are talking about."

Her eyes narrowed on him, and she held the tip of the staff toward him. The black glass pulled against his form and drew his light to it.

He moved away quickly and stared at her. "Fine, yeah. She was a person with stuff. She led the people in Ciro until . . . Ha, I don't remember. I should remember, but I don't. It's like someone plucked the memories from my head like a bad dream. I mean, what goes for a head when you are, well, you know." He moved close to her again. "If you wouldn't mind not pointing that staff at me, that would be great. Black glass can suck the arcana out of stuff, and I'm about all arcana. I'm afraid it could end badly. Just a suggestion."

She reached out and placed her hand on him. Cold to the touch, his shell-like form pulled at the arcana flowing through her, and when she moved her hand away, the skin turned a light shade of red. No worse for wear, she slapped one knee and grinned.

The path through the grove wound along rows of spring flowers and trees covered in thick green moss. It felt like walking on a fragrant pillow. They walked alongside a pond with fish snapping at bugs flying just above the water and herons waiting for the right time to snag a fish that swam within their path. The sun sat high among a partly cloudy sky, and the faint mist of a spring shower moved through.

At the end of the path, she came across a darkened cave. Stalactites and an eerie light welcomed them back to the depths below the abbey —a drastic departure from the grove and its beauty, but the only path forward. She took one last look around before ducking in. She turned to see the sun and greenery, to feel the mist land on her cheeks, but bleak gray stone walled her in and returned to a darkened tunnel.

She took the time to change out of the dingy robe and into the paladin armor, placing one of the glowstones in the inner pocket. It warmer than the cloth, and it offered a bit more protection from the damp tunnels and rocky paths than being barefoot wearing a paper-thin garment.

As she finished tightening and tying the weapon straps, she looked at Flicker. "Were you talking to the trees?"

He bobbed ahead and confidently floated over to her. "Yep. They tell the worst jokes, but they do have the best laugh." He stopped and grew bright. "Wait, are you telling me you can't hear them? Must be a shame. Could explain the stares I get. Even Nyasom thought I was touched, but those trees, let me tell you."

She sat up and waited for him to continue, but he just remained silent. She looked around and back at him, but nothing. "Yes?"

He looked at her and dimmed. "What? Is there something behind me?" He turned around and then back. "What are you on about?"

"You said 'Let me tell you,' and I'm waiting."

He bobbed and moved away toward the path ahead. "Already told you in tree speak. Guess you still didn't make anything of it. Anywho, this way. Might as well get going. If that party is as good as you say, we should get moving."

He zipped out of sight and vanished into the tunnels ahead. With her armor ready and weapons in tow, she followed him down the long, narrow path toward the sound of what she could only think to be heavy breathing. She drew the sword and walked deeper in. At the door, she found the runes of order, meaning one thing. Ahead, she stumbled into the domain of Athys. She stepped through the doors, and the sound stopped. Flicker moved behind her and remained silent as they walked toward the next opening.

CHAPTER 13

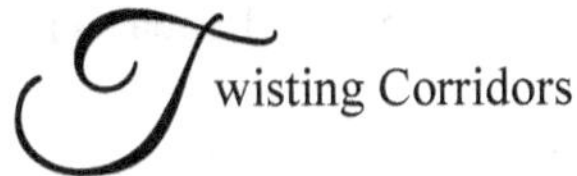

wisting Corridors

A DEEP RUMBLE CAUSED THE GROUND TO QUAKE again, and when the final tremor receded, the slow breathing returned. The floor heaved with each breath, making it difficult to walk over the smooth, damp stones. Flicker, having no issues, hovered down yet another narrow passage. After a few seconds, he floated back and followed the path down another.

Brianne took a moment to catch her breath and watched as he moved about, his light dimming and brightening to match his movement up and down the crossroads. His color changed depending on how frustrated he became. Brianne felt another pain shoot down her body as her muscles contracted and the cramps returned.

They walked aimlessly down the myriad of tunnels for the past few hours and seemed to always return to this spot. She knew it from the markings above the entrance that she passed many times. The words had likely faded centuries before, leaving little more than a few crudely drawn letters and figures marking each path. After resting a bit, she took a notepad from the satchel, marked the different symbols, and started scribbling lines.

Flicker returned and hovered over her shoulder. "What are you doing?" His light dimmed before he noticed he had moved too close to the staff.

"When I learned about the sewers below Sarntheris, I used an old pick to carve symbols. I used those to get around the city, because if I was caught, they would drag me back to Eandar and Shaw."

"So? What does that have to do with what you're doing now?" he asked.

She dropped her hands, slapped the notepad on her leg, and stared at him. He proceeded to stare back with his light becoming brighter with each second. She said without blinking, "I'm making a map. See?"

She held it up to him and pointed to what she drew. His light dimmed as he turned toward her then back at the map.

"I get it. Wait. Why do we need a map? Only two ways we can go," he said.

She patted him, leaving him floating at the first crossroads as she took the path to the left and followed it to the next intersection. Using one of the glowstones along the wall, she found more worn writing and symbols. She marked the ones that were visible and carried on. At the second crossroads, she took the path to her right. The winding tunnel led to a pool of water in a small circular room with no markings on the walls, not like the other corridors. She found the movement of the water to be unsettling each time she came near. It hummed with arcana and gave off an eerie light. Not the first time she entered this room in her futile effort to find a path through.

She backtracked and went to the left. The winding path cut back and forth, leading her to a chasm on either side of the entrance where there were empty sconces. She noticed the symbols of light and dark but could not make out any more of the broken tablets under each. Knocking a pebble over the edge, she felt the ground sway, and the unstable floor forced her to cling to the cracks in the wall to keep from falling in behind it.

"Go back. These halls are not for your kind," the bellowing voice said from below, each word snapped and carrying a cruel harshness.

"How do I get through?" she asked.

Her voice echoed into the depths, but the words changed, and what repeated back did so in a strange language. She tried again, but this time, her voice barely reached her lips before fading.

"I will not suffer your kind, nor any other. Leave me to my slumber." Two large eyes glared up at her and rose from the depths. Light did not reflect from their pits but instead devoured it.

The creature reached the top of the chasm, but before it entered the light, Brianne found herself standing next to where she started, still holding the notepad. Flicker stared at her, dimming at his center but remaining just as bright as before.

"So, a map, huh? When will you see if it works?" he asked.

"I just did. I went down." She held up the paper, and only the first set of symbols were scribbled, no markings noting the different rooms she came to, nor any lines allowing her to have bearings.

"No, I went to the left here." She followed it again and reached a dead end. The walls were solid and blocked off. "No. No! *No!* There should be an intersection here."

Flicker bumped against her side. "I get it, maybe you need a nap. You stood there pointing a finger for a bit and didn't say a word. Thought you spaced out for a moment."

She crouched and ran a finger along the seam where the wall and floor met, but she found no sign of things shifting around the room. She let out a long, exacerbated sigh, and she returned to the first crossroads. They looked over her notes and back at the symbols, but they were shifted. The same ones, but in different places. She ran down the path to the right and found the crossroads from before, but each path now sat reversed.

Noting which marking sat above each door, she followed the one that led back to the chasm. Entering the room, she could hear the breathing again.

"I know how to play your game!" she yelled. The eyes opened in the deep but did not rise.

"There is no game, no trial, only the truth. You still do not see. Fear holds you from reaching the next trial." Its haunting eyes locked on to her, and she felt it stare through, into the depths of her regrets and doubts. Pulling away, she found herself standing in the main hall, holding the notepad with Flicker patiently waiting for her to speak.

"Okay, so you have a map. And?" he asked.

"Ugh, he did it again. I go down the path and

reach him, just to end up back here. What am I supposed to do?" she asked.

Flicker moved back from her. "You went where? You said you were drawing a map and then stood there like a statue for a moment. Didn't see you go anywhere."

She looked over the notes and the symbols, and, again, they were in different positions. She tossed it against the wall, and from below, she heard a low rumbling laugh.

Frustrated, Brianne yelled, "If you want to play a game, I can play games!" She gathered the notes and wandered the halls until she reached the chasm and yelled, "Ha!"

Flicker moved away, putting space between them. "What kind of game are we talking about? I really like chess. Oh! What about hide and seek? I suck at it because I'm made of light and all. You get the idea. But I love searching for people."

She kicked the pebbles across the floor and screamed an unintelligible sound as she pulled the staff from her back and ran back through the tunnels, making sure to follow the marks. She looked back down and held the notepad, with Flicker staring at her with concern.

"Fine, I'll find another path!" she yelled at the floor and stomped as she came back to the intersection.

"Umm, could I ask you something?" Flicker asked.

She shrugged and went over the other markings. "What is it now?"

"Are we playing a game now, or were you

waiting for me to pick? I'm not complaining, I would just like to know what the objective is."

She rolled her eyes and walked down the third path, which led to another crossroads. One marked with the chasm. She knew it from the symbol of a cave. The other two weren't as familiar, but she knew one from her many travels through the various tunnels. Ahead, the door was marked with the rose. She knew this led to the strangely smooth room humming with magical light. To her right, she eyed the marking of the carriage.

She looked around and noticed that Flicker had vanished from her side. Scribbling down on the notepad, she went to the right. Another room with a pool at its center. The walls and floors weren't smooth but were instead covered with an all-too-familiar substance.

The glinting stars floating in the pools around the room caused a sinking feeling in her stomach. The hunger pains were replaced with an overwhelming sense of dread. Behind her, the door closed, and no matter how much she pushed, it didn't budge.

"You came back."

Her breathing became fast and shallow, and her heart raced, all caused by his voice. She slowly turned to see Kindri, the same as the day he was taken.

"We can be together now. You can have the same joy that we have." His hand reached for her, and she knelt, covering her head with her arms as she wept.

Her eyes opened, and she found herself looking at the ground beneath Flicker.

Flicker sighed and said, "Fine, I didn't really

want to play a game either. Didn't think you would get so upset."

She wiped the tears away and looked down each path and returned to Flicker. "Have I even walked down any of these paths before?"

"Nope. You look around and then stop. Only thing is, when you start moving again, you act all weird. Screaming and crying. One time, you drew your staff and just stared at me like you were going to hit me, but then you put it away and started over."

"Not a game, not a trial, but the truth. His words must have a meaning." She sat on the rock again and looked over the markings. They were chipped and worn from time.

The symbol of the chasm repeated, but without the other symbols or words, she could not make out what she needed to do next.

"I guess I have no choice. I will ask him again. Worst that could happen is I'll be sent back here."

She climbed to her feet and walked past Flicker again, making her way down the hall. She passed the rose and the carriage, then the well, finally making her way to the chasm. The low rumble of the creature's slow breathing rattled pebbles loose, sending them down into the depths.

"What do you mean the truth? I have tried so many paths, and none lead to the next trial." Her words echoed like before, changing into a different language with each bounce and waking the creature below.

"I do not wish for company!" it bellowed.

"Please, show me this truth, and I will leave you to your slumber."

"You have yet to learn. Your deepest regrets and

fears are holding you from seeing the truth." Its eyes stared through her again, and she woke standing with Flicker.

"Did you speak to him? Or am I losing my mind too?" he asked.

She smiled at him and sat on the rock again, tapping the side of her forehead and watching a bug crawl across the floor. "My fear and regret."

Flicker lowered himself to the floor and looked up at her. "Maybe it's a riddle, like a thing meaning another thing but then turning into another thing. Nyasom once trapped Kasridak in the Veil. He came out of it at the wrong time and missed nearly two hundred years. All because he made fun of his riddles. They shared a laugh and drank until they both forgot the reason for any of it."

She looked past him, and with her eyes widened and mouth agape, she sighed. "I guess I have no choice."

She brushed the dust from the seat of her pants and walked to the intersection and followed the winding corridors until she reached the room with a rose. The smooth door opened, and beyond the threshold, she watched the water ripple across the pool at its center. Another rumble in the depths caused the ground to quake, and when she looked up, the room faded away. The room blended into dunes, and smoke billowed into the corridor. She stepped through the door and stood in the desert outside of the abbey.

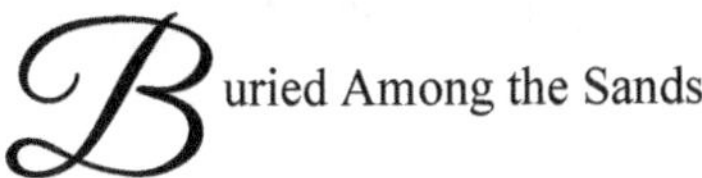

uried Among the Sands

THROUGH A SWIRL OF SAND AND DEBRIS, BRIANNE saw Shaw walking. His shoulders were slumped, and he dragged his sword behind him.

Using a hand to block the sand from her eyes, she called to him, "Shaw. Wait! Where are you going?"

Receiving no answer, she followed. His shield fell to the ground, and soon, his grip on his weapon gave way. He unclasped his shoulder guards and removed the straps from his chest piece. Each piece of armor landed in a trail across the dunes. Brianne grabbed his shield and saw it was split down the center. Chunks were missing, and blood stained its face.

The sandstorm raged and caused her to lose sight of him. She fumbled about until her foot landed on a piece of cobblestone. She stood at the entrance to the abbey. Her heart warmed, and a sense of calm fell upon her. She expected the familiar sounds and smells, the hammering of the forge, and the aroma of freshly baked bread. A smile eased across her face as she ran past the gate, but no sound radiated from the forge, only the harsh silence broken by the howl of wind against the walls and the flapping of banners that tore loose from their braces.

The stale air put a bitter taste on her tongue, and she felt the looming dread crawl up her spine. Her eyes caught a glimpse of a figure walking the streets, but when she followed it around the corner, she found an empty path. Beside her, a bloodied spear stuck out of the stone wall. Pieces of meat still clung to the splintered wood handle, and trails of blood led to the alleyway.

The figure again moved in the corner of her eye, and she raced to catch it, knowing it could only be Shaw, but like before, it vanished into sand, swirling through the passages without a trace. An eerie sound of sobbing echoed through the abbey, but with no source to be found. Whispers and prayers bled from the hollow buildings. Only the sand rolling across the ground joined her in the search.

She wandered every path and alley until she arrived at her cottage. Shattered glass sat up on her porch, and smoke rose from the smoldering remains of her home. She found more blood splattered on the ground blocking her porch, and the aroma of fetid flesh and some other putrid stench crawled up her nose.

Out of the corner of her eye, she saw a shadow moving in the courtyard below. It traveled in the direction of the washhouse, so Brianne took a shortcut through the shrubs and brush, slipping past the burned carts and arrow-filled crates. She arrived at the washhouse first. She did not find a person, but the mutilated corpses of the mules and horses. Even Topper did not escape the harsh fate. Such noble animals were left rotting in the hot sun. Her arrival spooked the vultures, sending them scattering into the sky. Their blackened wings left shadows swirling around her.

Doubt crawled in, and a few tears rolled down her cheek. The whispers returned, but a single voice rose above the rest.

"Another promise I couldn't keep."

Shaw's voice rang through the streets and cut through her, and she raced toward its origin.

"I should have listened, but no. I knew better than them," his voice called out again.

She came to a blocked passage and could see him kneeling over a body. He wore the attire of a commoner, and a satchel was thrown over his shoulder.

"Shaw, I'm here. Why can't you hear me?" The sound of her words vanished before they could reach her lips. She grabbed the crates and shook them, causing Shaw to turn and inspect the odd noise, but he shrugged and returned his focus to the body of a woman. Her armor looked familiar, with its color fading and the sand covering the breastplate, but at that distance, she struggled to make out who Shaw knelt over.

She crossed the street and ran through an alley, passing the watch commander's home. His body lay hunched over the banister, and countless others were lining the street. Many were piled up, and some were left hanging with their feet dragging the sand. She dared not look up and ran toward Shaw.

"What will become of us? A few . . . Only a few

remain, and we are scattered to the wind." Shaw's voice broke, and Brianne felt a sharp pain in her chest as she raced toward him.

"I should've let you go. This is all my doing, and I alone bear this shame," he said.

She ran down every path but found them closed off. She could only see him sobbing while picking up the corpse.

"So much . . . So much death. For what? if I had been here—"

Another voice cut through, "You, too, would be among those rotting in the sun."

She could not place the voice, but its familiar tone disturbed her for not remembering. A man for sure, but aged and soft.

"Where were you?" Shaw asked.

"Watching, waiting for a moment to retrieve her. But like all the rest, she fell," the man said.

Through a barricade, she could see a hooded figure standing behind Shaw. The green eyes were haunting, and his face uncovered, baring the look of a young man, but his gray, cracked skin mirrored that of a person nearing a hundred. Seeing his hands gave Brianne pause. He wrapped them the same as Thealen did, but she never saw his face, and he muffled his voice when speaking around others.

"To say we failed would be more apt, old friend," Thealen said.

"We are not friends. We served a purpose, and now, what are we? What could we hope to be without our charge?" Shaw asked.

"We must give this one a burial and then we can discuss what will come next," Thealen said.

She watched them carry the body, and dangling

from its neck the same pendant that she gave Alit when she entered the crypts. She followed them through the streets and made her way back around to the main gate. Outside, Shaw and Thealen were preparing the body. They wrapped it in a blanket and left the face uncovered for the final rite.

Brianne reached a full sprint and leaped at Shaw, passing through him and landing firmly in the sand.

He remained unmoved and started digging while Thealen placed bloodstained flowers in the arms of the woman and removed the pendant from around her neck.

Brianne stepped around them and saw her own face staring back. She wore her training armor. It was sun-bleached and covered in blood, and the armor was torn at her chest. A gaping wound cut through her body just below her collarbone.

Shaw finished digging and crawled out of the hole. Covered in dirt and sweating, he lay beside her body and stared at the sky. The sun neared the horizon, and a cool breeze rolled through. After a short rest, he rolled over and finished preparing the body. Using a rag and a bit of water, he wiped the bloodstains from her cheeks, but each stroke caused his hands to tremble and tears to pour. Her eyes were open; the blue glow faded, but her irises were bright green and staring back at him.

"It should've been one of us! This shouldn't be her grave!" Shaw said.

"When we are done here, we must travel west. A young man will require our aid in finding a path—"

Shaw stood and slapped Thealen. "Done here? Was she nothing to you? Did you see this as another pointless mission? Her life is over, and you speak of the others. What kind of man are you?"

Shaw returned to his task and covered her head, making sure to wrap the blank snugly around her body. Thealen turned to the real Brianne standing beside them and smiled before placing a hand on Shaw's shoulder. "It is time. We must let go and fulfill our oaths."

"Our oath was to her!" Shaw shouted. "I promised to protect her, just as you did, and to what end? She was my daughter, and I should have— I should have been here!" He rocked the body while holding it to his chest.

"I know your pain, old friend, but it is up to us. We must finish what was started."

Shaw put a rope under her legs and neck to ease the task of lowering her into the hole. Once at the bottom, he tossed the ropes in and started shoveling dirt. His violent thrusts came faster, and with each, his rage bubbled to the surface.

He swung the shovel at Thealen, blindly striking at him and missing his mark. Thealen did little more than dodge and deflect his blows until his arms wore out. Knelt in the sand and winded, Shaw tossed the shovel at him and sat against the abbey wall.

Thealen picked it up and proceeded to fill the grave. After patting down the surface, he put two pieces of wood together and planted a cross at the front of her grave, which cracked and burned but would mark her resting place for a time. Shaw strode past him and stabbed her staff into the sand beside it and stepped back. After a moment of silence, Thealen held out her pendant, dropping it into Shaw's hand and pushing him forward.

"We lay you to rest now. We send you to the lands of your ancestors." Tears rolled down Shaw's face, leaving streaks in the dirt on his face. "May you walk with them in the beyond, and . . . And—" His voice failed to come, and his pained moans sent chills down Brianne's spine. She reached for him but could not touch.

"I'm right here! I'm right here! Shaw, I'm right here!"

Thealen stepped between them and finished the words. "And may you find peace that in life you were not granted. Rest now, Child of the Veil." He squeezed Shaw's shoulder. "I go west. I hope to see you there, old friend."

Shaw replied with a nod and draped the pendant on the cross and let his hand come to rest on the mound of dirt. The air grew cold, and the sun faded behind ominous clouds, leaving the land dark and without warmth. Taken aback by the sudden shift, Brianne failed to notice Shaw and Thealen leave, walking into the swirling sands. Alone, she turned around. The howling wind pushed the wall of sand toward her, and the pained cries became louder.

She ran into the abbey, and the swirling wall of sand followed, swallowing everything around her until she reached the watch commander's house. The bodies of everyone she knew were hanging, and above her, the body Timul dangled in a cage, gutted and feasted on by the birds. He hung from the archway leading to Shaw's office. His hand reached for her, but his eyes and lower jaw were missing. A low moaning came from his throat while insects crawled from his mouth.

She stumbled back and bumped into the body of

Verna. Her eyes opened, and the hollow pits were fixed on Brianne. She turned to find everyone standing around her. All their eyes were blackened and hollow. Their corpses lumbered closer with hands outstretched. Timul, no longer hanging in the cage, reached out to her. Blood dripped from his mouth, and his insides were dragging the sand. While they closed in, Brianne knelt and covered her face and reached toward him, trying to keep him at arm's length. Her eyes closed, and she felt the sand engulf her.

"Are you okay?" Flicker asked.

Her eyes opened, and she stood in the main hall at the crossroads. In one hand, she held the crudely drawn map, and in the other, a glowing crystal.

"I'm fine," she said, wiping the tears from her cheek. She stood and knocked sand from her clothes. A few deep breaths was all it took to compose herself. With a broken smile, she left him floating in the main hall. Around the first, turn she collapsed to her knees, and she held a hand over her mouth as she sobbed.

The rumble in the deep returned. "What you have seen is not the future, yet the past. In time, the pain will change, be molded into something you truly fear. But for now, mourn what your mind perceived and prepare for the next wound to be deep and gushing." A bellowing laugh followed and faded.

She wiped away the tears and found her way to the chasm. Placing the crystal caused an ethereal bridge to form, but it only reached halfway across the chasm.

"Can you overcome regret? He awaits. Will his words tear you asunder, or will you make peace with the truth? I shall enjoy it either way," the bellowing voice said.

Brianne turned to face it, only to be returned to a spot outside the room where she faced the visage of Kindri.

A voice from beyond called to her.

"Welcome back. Shall you join us on an adventure?"

ast Regrets

THROUGH THE NARROW OPENING, SHE COULD SEE Kindri standing in the vacant room. His hollow eyes were fixed on her as she stood in the darkened corridor. A tremor rolled across her body. With it, the feeling of terror set in. Her knees became weak, and tears welled in her eyes. The ground quaked, and she felt the creature in the depths move. A bellowing laugh echoed through the halls.

"Your fear was strong, but what do I sense? Yes, even with all your strength, it is regret what binds you to this place. Does it tear at your thoughts? How interesting. A paladin cannot pass with such feelings."

"He shouldn't have taken her hand! Why wouldn't he listen?" she asked.

"Oh, now, isn't this wonderful? You blame him for your decision. Was it not your efforts that led him to that place? Or do you recall it differently to spare your own emotions?"

"We both wanted to go! We had planned that night for weeks, and it shouldn't have happened that way," she said.

"The lies we tell ourselves to feel better, but even now, you don't believe it. If you did, the way would be open. No, you forced his hand. You mocked and belittled him. It was your ego that pushed him toward this end."

"No! We both wanted to go. If he had refused her hand . . . Why didn't you walk away?" she asked.

"I have said what I must. It is your choice now. Face it, or join the hallowed spirits that walk the depths with me. Many must find their way to the afterlife, but few can give up the regrets that bind them."

The rumbling in the caverns below faded, and she felt alone once more. Kindri still waited in the chamber beyond, staring, following her every move. Her feet dragged over the uneven stone tiles. Her stomach rose to fill her throat, and the tremors caused her whole body to shake. Sweat formed on her brow as she stepped through the door. Her eyes were fixed on the ceiling, but nothing could keep her from seeing him. His movements were rigid and haunting, with his eyes never closing and staring through her.

"Have you come to join us?" he asked.

She closed her eyes, and her lips quivered as his warm breath pressed against her cheek. The lump in her throat made it hard to breathe, but she dared not move a muscle nor make a sound.

"We can offer you peace and happiness. A release from this torment that claws within."

She remained silent, clutching the sides of her tunic tightly in her clenched fists. He stepped back, and the voices of Dhral faded while only Kindri's remained, the same voice she had listened to for hours each day.

"Why can't you look at me?"

She felt a harsh wind pass through, and soon, the sounds of the abbey were all around her. The warmth of the summer sun kissed her skin, and she felt a cool breeze at her back. Shaw's voice carried over the sound of the smith's hammering and Eandar shouting at fresh-faced recruits. "You two better get your chores done by the time I get back, or Falun will have my head!"

Her eyes opened to her and Kindri playing with toys on the cottage porch. They pretended to delve into a deep ruin and were fighting off skeletons and spirits on their way to treasure and glory.

"Someday, I will be the greatest adventurer the world has ever known," a young Brianne said.

"Ha, and you think I would let you have all the glory?" Kindri said.

Tears rolled down her cheek and pooled at her chin, dripping into the sand at their feet. "Why do you show me this? Is it not enough that you're gone."

The visage of Kindri walked behind her. "Because this is your regret. You buried it deep, but nothing can be hidden in this place."

Walls rose around them, and they were in the chapel, sitting together in the back and giggling as they pored over every page of another of Reduwar's journals. The sermon continued, and the people paid no attention to their bursts of hushed laughter and shouts with each turn of the page.

"We were so close, yet you shame my memory and have lied to yourself," he said.

"I never forgot you. How have I shamed your memory? I spent so many nights haunted by what happened that night," she said.

People started to leave the chapel, but they remained planted under the back row of pews, their feet dangling out and kicking the air. She leaned in, and with a peck on his cheek, she giggled and returned to reading. He stared at her with a smile, his cheeks turning red. Everything froze, and the visage of Kindri knelt by their hiding spot.

"There, the moment I chose to follow you anywhere. In the years to come, we would chase each other around. I thought it was love. But did you feel the same, or was it a game to be played and my emotions were the prize?" he asked.

"I did, but we were young. It was a childish thing," she said.

"Wasn't it you that decided to go that night? Toyed with me and teased me until I said yes?" he asked.

"No! We had snuck out many times. You wanted to see the awakening without your mother hovering over you, so we went into the sands," she said.

"Oh, the lies we tell. Do you not remember?" His fist slammed against the pew.

The chapel faded, the board tore away, and the ground slipped from under her feet. They were together, their arms were wrapped around each other, and each time he leaned in for a kiss, she turned away.

Brianne turned from her youthful self and refused to look. She could hardly breathe through her sobbing. "Why must I see this again? Can't I have peace? Or should I relive this again and again? At night, when I sleep, I see you. I remember what happened, and it doesn't go away."

"Why do you think it happens this way? Because you hide from the blame. You tell the lies and pretend that the dragon forced your hand, that it would be better to keep it a secret," he said.

The ooze-covered walls returned. "Why didn't you tell her the truth? My mother? She spent years blaming herself. When her son ran away, her guilt caused her to become cold and distant. She could have mourned my passing." His voice became angered, and the ground trembled under their weight. "Even Shaw could no longer stand the sight of you, the monster you became. He saw through it and offered a chance."

The walls rose around them once more. She sat outside the cottage, staring at the ground and drawing lines in the sand with a stick.

Shaw sat against the banister. "Can you just tell me the truth? Blue, I know when you're lying, and damn it, it's written on your face. Is he hurt? Or did he just run away? We can find him. Just let me help."

She threw the stick and grabbed the door. His hand caught her wrist and held tight. He stepped closer, but she remained turned away, hiding the tears in her eyes and the agony she felt.

"Don't do this. Just tell me the truth. No one will blame you," Shaw said.

Tears streamed down her face, and she pulled away and slammed the door, burrowing under the covers and refusing to listen to any more of his words.

The visage of Kindri stepped to the window. "This was the day he left. After that, he could no longer stand the sight of you, what you had become. He no longer saw his daughter. You wondered how he knew, but that night, he checked the northern tower, and your lie sealed it."

The memory froze again. Brianne's hand shook as she touched Shaw's cheek. "I should have told you. I never should have kept it from you. I never knew you'd become cold, that you wouldn't speak to me without anger again."

"But you did hide it! You left me in the desert. How was it fair? Think of the pain a single lie has wrought." He tapped on the window, and everything fell away. They were both standing in the hollow room. Her hand was still held out, reaching for him, but she stood alone.

"Brianne, did I hear your voice?"

Behind her, an old, withered Shaw was sitting in the corner of a tavern, his hair turned to mostly gray and his skin wrinkled. He returned to his drink, no longer wearing his armor, nor did he carry a shield upon his back. He huddled over a warm lager, and as he took a drink, a smile rose on his face.

"This is him now, an old man withered by an unforgiving world. You are nothing more than a fragment of a dream, a terrible nightmare, faded with time and forgotten by the world," Kindri said.

"No! I wasn't forgotten. They are waiting for me. When I walk through those doors, I'll be a paladin, and this will be just a dream. Nothing more!" she screamed.

"Why do you fight so hard to cling to a false memory? Was it not enough to lose me? Would you rather blame me for what you had done? There will be time for agony after," he said.

The walls fell away, and, again, they were standing at the gates of Bruin. "There we were, children playing pretend. If only you had let me go home. If only it had been different. I'd still be with you, a companion until the end, as I said in those days."

The agony returned, and she felt the same rush of terror and sadness that she did that night.

"I know. I shouldn't have made you, but I . . . I wanted us to have an adventure together. I wanted to spend time with you." She walked up to the visage of Kindri. "I did love you."

She put a hand on his chin. More tears fell, and his eyes narrowed on her, but her words continued, "And I never should have lied. None of us deserved that. And I will do my best to make it right. I promise." She closed her eyes and pushed their foreheads together. "I'm sorry, Kindri."

A draft rolled up, and the chilling breeze caused her eyes to open. In her hand, the second crystal formed. Kindri faded into nothing, and she returned to Flicker.

He looked over the crystal just like before. "What ya got there?"

She walked past him. "Our way forward." She wiped the tears from her eyes and walked down the winding corridor. She stood over the chasm, but the memories were still clawing at the edges of her mind without a sense of closure.

She placed the crystal, and she stood with Flicker again. The maze merged, and before them, a single path formed. On either side, the chasm stretched beyond light's reach, and below she could see the creature stirring.

"Knowing what perils you face, I do not envy your path, but should you prevail, the world will be better for it," it said.

She knelt on the bridge and peered into the depths. There was nothing below, but beside her stood a Dwarven girl with black stains stretched from her eyes down her cheeks. Her mouth did not move, and her feet did not touch the ground. The girl smiled and greeted Flicker with a nod.

"Time runs short, Champion of Ruin. Should you stay too long, the way will shut, and you will become trapped in this place."

"I will go, but could I ask you a question?" Brianne asked.

"Hmm, you remind me of the only being that ever stopped me from collecting a soul," she said.

"What are you? A spirit? Or are you like the gods?" she asked.

The small girl moved closer and held out her hand. The bloodied tips were devoid of fingernails, and her wrists were cut with many deep gashes along her arms.

"I am a dragon. The Ecephen is what they called me, brother to Emual, the Keeper of Possibilities. It is my task to grant absolution and ferry the forgotten souls to the beyond. For the paladins, I was asked to aid them in their cleansing rite," she said.

Without effort, she moved, hovering toward the stairs leading down, and pointed. "Best for you to be going. The Deep isn't a place to waste time."

She smiled at the Ecephen and gave a bow as she walked past. Her footsteps felt lighter, and even with the heavy weight not being lifted, it felt lighter somehow.

"Goodbye, kind dragon, may your time be well spent," she said with a smile.

After stepping through the passage, she turned to find a flat slab of stone behind her, with no sign of where she entered, leaving them to move forward, down farther into the depths.

CHAPTER 16

Lake of Stars

THE PATH OPENED BEFORE HER, AND SHE STOOD AT the edge of a lake, its water undisturbed. On the other side, a modest chapel sat at the top of a hill. It was hard to make out, but she saw candlelight flickering in the windows, and the doors were open. Her hand whisked back and forth in the cool water. There was no way around, and the only way across was a small boat resting against an old half-sunken dock. Its planks were missing, and the posts were leaned over or rotted; more of it sank underwater than not.

Her weight was too much for the few planks that remained, so she hopped into the waist-deep water and inspected the boat. Fish swam at her feet but moved away as she moved about in the crystal-clear water. A single paddle sat on the seat. The hull remained in solid condition, and it looked comfortable.

She pulled it to the shore and climbed in, and Flicker hovered over the seat as she used the paddle to push off the smoothed stones in the shallows. Above them floated a starlit sky, thousands of twinkling lights reflecting off the pristine water. Like winter nights in the abbey, it brought a sense of calm after the hardships of the trials. A cool breeze at her back eased the boat across the vast expanse of the lake. She paddled softly, and though her stomach growled and her muscles ached, she ignored it to enjoy the first moment of awe since she started the trials.

"How long have you been here?" she asked, turning to Flicker.

Flicker hovered over the water at this point, avoiding the few fish that snapped at him like they did to the glowbugs floating over the water. His light shined brighter than before, and he hummed a tune that she did not know. "Don't know. They were in Aud Nua and needed a tome—or was it a scroll? Anyway, Balessa sent me to retrieve it, and I have been down here ever since, floating about. The difficult thing is, I could only read the books on top. Don't have hands, you see."

He soared into the sky but came back down, resting over the seat beside her. "Are the meadows around the abbey still beautiful? I used to glide over the spring flowers and enjoy the kiss of humid air after a spring rain."

She stopped paddling and allowed the boat to glide peacefully across the water. "The abbey is in a desert, and the meadows and springs are to the north. I have only ever smelled the aroma of flowers and spring rains on the wind."

His light dimmed. Looking up at her like a child facing punishment, he brightened at his core. "Do you think the Lady was mad at me?"

"No. Why would you think the Lady of Devotion would be mad at you?" she asked.

"I've never failed a task before. Maybe if I had succeeded, things would be different?"

A soothing chorus rolled across the water from the chapel. Inviting and warm, the sweet melody caused the fish to glow with a dull blue light and swim alongside the boat. They fluttered about below the tiny waves lapping against the sides of the boat.

Brianne placed a hand on the top of Flicker's glowing shell. "I don't think you failed. One thing, if you hadn't been there, I wouldn't have made it this far."

His light brightened around the edges, and the dim center moved to look over the water. "Will you do me a favor?"

She smiled at him. "What do you need? If I can help, just say the word."

His light changed to a pinkish hue, and he turned to stare at the floor of the boat. "I don't know where Tyrn went. He was sent to a Dwarven ruin, and I don't know how to find it." He turned back to her. "Will you help me find him?"

She leaned back and kicked her feet up on the side of the boat. "Well, after the ceremony and feast, I will gladly help in your quest. I'll be a full paladin, and every paladin can choose their first assignment. Mine will be to help find Tyrn, wherever he may be."

His light shined bright, causing her to squint and turn to the sky. Due to his joyous expression, she laughed and watched the stars sparkle with a pale blue moon set against the dark sky. Its shape changed, and it grew larger. Wings sprouted from its back, its body elongated, and it descended from the sky. Wind rolled across the lake, and the gust followed the serpentine creature and pulled a wave across the water that rocked the boat as it flew overhead.

The chorus rose, and the dull blue light spread across the creature, illuminating its scales as it grazed the water and flew over their boat again. The flying serpent came down and dragged a claw on the surface, and with a snap of its enormous wrist, it pulled a fish from the water, returned to the sky, and hung on its perch once more, as a moon in the starlit sky.

Brianne eased back and pulled one of the pieces of dried meat from her pocket. The aroma so sweet, it caused her stomach to rumble and turn. She took a bite, and the mouthwatering morsel was tender to the tooth.

She relaxed and enjoyed the gentle sway of the boat. The warm breeze rolled over her like a blanket, and Flicker nudged against her side and hummed along to the chorus. Even without using the paddle again, they were gliding across the water peacefully.

"Do you think this is what being an adventurer is like?" she asked.

"Wouldn't know. I've only known what it's like to be a squire. Or a glowing ball of light."

She turned to him and rested her chin on her hands. "What was it like to serve a god?"

"Not much to say. The only thing that is different now is I cannot hear her voice the way I once did. When I first joined the Order, we weren't paladins, nor were we templars, just knights. Tyrn and I took the oath because our village was burned to the ground, the first casualty of a war that nearly devoured the world. The undead had washed over Narrisia, and we joined to bring an end to the war." He, too, looked at the stars.

She rolled over to enjoy the sight, and his light shimmered with the same wave of light as the stars. "Did you ever regret saying the oath?"

"Nope. I would have missed the parades in Cadris Apol and the great march to Iskal. The Dwarves rang the bells, and Balessa sent us to aid her brother Kasridak." He turned back to Brianne. "Do you regret joining the Order?"

"I didn't join. My mother left me with Shaw. I never knew why. Can I ask you something personal?" she asked.

"Fire away. I'm an open book. Well, not really a book; you can see that." He turned and shifted. "So, what do you want to know?" he asked.

She smiled at him and put her hand back onto his shell. "How have you kept from becoming cold and bitter after all these years trapped in this place? It surprises me that you aren't weighed down."

"I'm not trapped. I was busy. Big difference." His light slowly became a soft blue. "Also, how many thousand-year-old floating balls of light do you know?"

"Not sure I've met any other than you, but doesn't it get lonely?"

His golden glow returned. "No, sometimes rats would come in, and the devoted used to come and read from the library. They haven't come in a long time though. Wonder if they're alright?"

"So, people did come to see you?" she asked.

"No, they often ignored me, but a few would say hello and leave me to search. Once, a saddened lady used to come, and she told me I reminded her of someone. Not sure how long ago it was that she last came to visit. Used to tell me wonderful stories of what it was like in the world above. Said her son would be an adventurer someday. Wonder where she is now?"

Water splashing against the rocks caused her to spring from the comfortable position. They were nearing the shore. On the hill, the soft candlelight shone out the door and illuminated the meadow. Along the stone slab path, fireflies fluttered about, and a heartwarming hymn played within. She could hear the sweet tones of the chorus joining the instruments. It felt welcoming.

They arrived at the dock, and it was in immaculate condition—very well-kept. Not a board was out of place or a nail missing, the wood was beautifully stained with a chestnut finish, and other boats were tied off. Each boat had a creative flare, from gold trim to a glass bottom. They were a sight to behold, but Brianne cared more for the chapel than admiring the boats at the dock.

Brianne tied off her boat and climbed up. The glowstone lamps guided their path, and at the top of the hill, the shadows moved along the walls. The sermon began, and she could hear a priest speaking to his congregation.

She could hear people shouting in agreement, but she heard none of the words being spoken. It sounded muffled, and she could see the lights wavering with each shout. Flicker remained on the dock. Brianne walked a short distance up the path before noticing him waiting behind. He moved side to side but would not cross the final plank onto shore.

"What is the matter?" she asked.

His light brightened as he looked at the chapel. "You shouldn't go. Something doesn't feel right. Like, umm, like my light is being drained. Don't you feel it?" he asked.

"No, I feel fine. Maybe you should hang out here until I tell you it's okay," she said.

"Alright, but if you get in trouble, just, umm, yell, and I'll come. Not sure what I'll do, but if I remember anything about evil, it's that light is terrifying. I'll be here waiting, I promise," he said.

She smiled and patted him, and his light returned to the soft golden glow from before. She walked the path, and as she neared the steps, she noticed people standing in the meadow. Their backs were turned, and they swayed with the wind. She looked back at the chapel, and the lights were out—no candles and no glowstones. Flicker was the only source of light in the distance, and his frantic movement gave her cause for concern.

The neatly placed stones were cracked and uneven, and the chapel sagged, becoming broken down. The windows were shattered, with a few pieces of glass still hanging in their frame, and the roof was caved in, with water dripping from the ceiling. Even the singing faded, replaced by the shutters knocking in the breeze.

Inside, she could see a single candle wavering against the draft through the aisle, and in the front row, a figure sat praying. She stepped up, and the boards creaked and moaned. She felt a rare sense of disgust while inspecting the interior. The walls were covered in mold, and the carpet bore holes and missing sections.

"I can do this." She climbed the next step and watched the person inside.

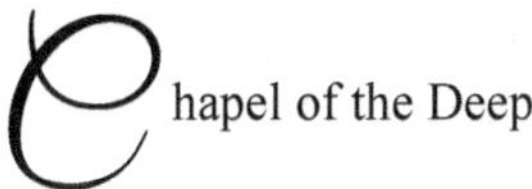

hapel of the Deep

BRIANNE'S HAND SLID ACROSS THE OPEN DOOR. Splintered wood and paint chips snagged her fingertips, and the light touch pulled against the rusted hinges. The carpeted aisle was shredded and damp. Several of the pews were missing, and the rest were in pieces—except for the one with a person seated in the front row. She felt a sense of unease by the holes in the ceiling and the water dripping around her. The smell of mold hung in the air.

Stopping just out of sight of the person in the front pew, she looked over the hundreds of candles that had burned out. Only one remained lit, and its flame dwindled. Along the walls were coffins and bodies that were haphazardly stuffed inside, with arms and legs hanging from the open lids.

She removed the staff from her back and stepped away from the person. The doors shut, and the air sucked from the room. The person, a withered old woman, turned to face her. Many of her teeth were broken or missing, and the rest were blackened with bleeding gums. Her eyes were empty sockets with blood trickling down her face. She grabbed hold of Brianne's arm with an unnatural strength.

"They said you'd come. Oh, we have waited. The taste of you will be so sweet." Her tongue rolled across her lips, peeling the skin and causing black blood to ooze from the torn bits of flesh. "Put that away. You'll need no such thing here."

Brianne's weapon vanished and appeared against the wall. "You bring these things to my chapel, but you must submit." Brianne's armor vanished, and she wore a dingy old robe, the same one she wore at the start of the trial, stains and all.

"Better. Now, sit with ol' Kala." She returned to the pew and watched the candle flicker. Her raspy voice started singing the same hymn Brianne had heard from across the water. Her screech was joined by the screaming and wailing from the bodies scattered around the edge of the room.

Brianne stepped away, her feet sliding back against the floor, making as little sound as possible. She turned to run, but Kala stood in her path. "Fear? A paladin should have no fear."

Brianne's eyes ran past the feeble woman and were fixed on her weapon. Kala laughed and moved closer, sending Brianne back into the pulpit. With nowhere to go, Brianne grabbed a blackened metal candlestick holder. The thick layer of soot made it slick, but she held tight and swung it like a weapon.

"Stay back! I do not wish to hurt you, but I must collect my things," Brianne said.

The woman grasped the base, and it vanished.

Her hands then clasped around Brianne's neck and forced her to the ground. They struggled, but Kala overpowered her and squeezed. Blood dripped from her hollow eyes, landing on Brianne's face. She fought to breathe, but her airway closed completely. She started to see bright colors, and her hands started to go limp.

"Yes, sleep, and you shall join our congregation. A lovely group," Kala said.

Brianne reached for anything as her vision went dark. She felt something at her fingertips and latched on to it. The force of Brianne slamming it into Kala's head released her grip enough for Brianne to slip her grasp.

She gasped for air, coughing and writhing on the floor. She crawled toward her weapon, but her hands came to the gnarled toes of Kala. Her toenails were missing, and bones protruded from her legs. Her hand grabbed a clump of Brianne's hair and dragged her back to the front pew.

"You could have joined our family, could have become one of our nurtured flock, but instead, you wish for damnation. Wearing armor and carrying weapons, even the first paladins weren't so clever." The voice changed and was joined by others. Each word echoed with thousands of voices calling out and fading as it spoke the next word.

"Enough of these games. You are within our realm. We shall feast, and with you, we shall be sated for a time," they said.

"Dhral? But this is a holy place! The paladins—"

Dhral's laughter interrupted Brianne.

"Your precious paladins. All of them served us in one way or another. We offered them many things, and they bent the knee before the end, just as you will." The woman tossed her into a closet. "How long will you take to break? Your betters lasted days. The chorus will sing when you accept our price."

The door slammed shut, and Brianne stood in complete darkness, with no sound and no light. She felt the walls closing in but did not struggle. Soon, the air became hot, and touching any surface burned her skin. She endured the blistering heat, searing the skin from her feet. Her screams stopped, and the tears no longer ran down her face as her numbness took hold and the pain faded. Soon, her body collapsed. Engulfed in flames, she felt darkness creep into her mind and the fire reaching into her lungs. As her body melted away, everything turned black, and she woke in the closet screaming.

She felt a click under her feet, and another. Panic washed over her as she heard Dhral dragging its nails on the outside of the door. "What will it take? How far must we go to bring you to our arms?"

The floor gave way, and she fell with the rushing air deafening her. With nothing to slow her descent, her heart started pounding in her chest. With the ground rapidly approaching, she whispered a prayer with a thud. Her body slammed against the rocks, bones cracked, and blood filled her lungs. Her eyes darted about as she gasped for air, but blood poured from her mouth and nose. Only her eyes moved, and she didn't even feel the bubbles rolling up her throat.

Everything went black again, and she stood in the darkened closet. The injuries were healed, but she felt the agonizing pain rippling through her body. Cold air fell from the ceiling, and the walls froze. Her bones ached, and the numbing pain swept through her body. She wanted to curl into a ball but couldn't. The walls tightened, and water rose. It brought relief from the cold but soon reached her chin. It crept higher until it complete submerged her. Holding her breath, she fought against the urge to gasp for air, but with her heart still racing, she soon faltered, and water filled her lungs.

She clawed at the walls, but her actions were slowed, and in moments, she felt everything fall away. Her mind went blank, and she stopped struggling. The darkness crept back in. Her sight narrowed, and she could no longer feel her own body.

She blinked, and once again, she stood in the empty closet. She gasped for air and coughed, water spilled from her lungs, and she grasped her knees.

"How long can you hold out? Will you falter like the rest, or will you die to your own pride?" Dhral asked.

Brianne closed her eyes, and, controlling her breathing, she eased the panic within. The wall moved, and each piece of wood came to life and turned into a grasping hand. They grabbed at her, tearing the robe and pinching the skin. Becoming more aggressive, they tore chunks of cloth loose, and the hands pulled at her body, digging their fingernails into her flesh and tearing away pieces of meat.

With a loud pop, her arms were wrenched from their sockets. Next were her legs, and soon, she could not move. The hands pulled harder, and the flesh pulled apart. She felt them severing her veins and arteries. Blood spilled from her fractured body, and she felt hands wrapping around her neck. They tore her head from her torso. She tried to scream, but being only a head, she old made a gargling sound. The pressure rose, and her eyes felt as though they were going to pop from her head, causing her to pass out from the pain.

Waking in the closest again, she leaned on the wall, her body whole. Tears rolled down her cheek in anticipation of what horror came next.

"An eternity can be a long time. None have outlasted our torment. It is just a matter of time before you give us what we desire." The door opened, and a hollow figure stood before her. Without shape, it undulated like water holding the shape of its container after it broke. After a moment of silence, the creature took Brianne's form. Her hollow doppelgänger pulled her from the closet and slammed her into the broken pews. "It is imperfect, but once you are a part of us, it can be fixed."

Brianne struggled against the physically stronger creature, being tossed about and beaten. The staff leaning against the door became her only goal. Each time the monster thrashed, she positioned herself to be sent closer to her staff. Blood dripped from her chin, and a few of her teeth were scattered in pools of blood. She felt the pain of several broken ribs and struggled to breathe while putting up a pathetic defense. With what strength that remained, she snatched the staff and landed a single blow on her attacker.

She struck the wall of the closet and found herself still locked inside. Her knuckles were bruised, and her body ached, but she never left. Another hallucination starting to wear on her mind.

"Pride is such a wonderful sin to claim, don't you think? We thought your guilt or fear would slow you, but no, pride! Can you believe anything in this place? Or will you go mad?"

The door to the chapel opened again, and it was filled with faces she recognized. From Eandar to Verna, they welcomed her with a smile.

She refused to exit. "No paladin would give in. A paladin bargains for nothing, for they have all which is required." Brianne closed her eyes, and the chorus of voices grew louder. They called to her.

Her eyes snapped open when a set of hands latched on to her. They took her and laid her on the altar. Timul stood over her with a knife. His eyes were hollow and black, but a smile crept across his face. Everyone surrounded them, and the singing stopped. She stared at him as he held the weapon high and waited for Dhral to give the order.

"It was nice to have them serve. Now, it is only you. But you will carry us into the world. Soon, you will join the chorus, and your voice will bring about the ruined dawn."

Brianne reached out to Timul, but she could not speak. Her mouth became stitched shut, and trying to speak pulled them apart, tearing at her flesh and filling her mouth with blood. She wanted to cry, but no tears came. With a sharp turn of his head, Timul looked at her, and the smile wiped away from his face. Without emotion or hesitation, he brought the knife down into her chest.

She felt the blade plunge deep into her body, but when she looked down, her head banged the door of the closet. Everything she could endure was laid out before her, endless torment and pain.

"We do relish in your failure, above the rest. How long had he tried to keep you from us, his greatest failure, and he never knew we were here? By now, he is wandering back to his old ways. Maybe even at her side once more."

She felt the glowstone in her pocket, the only weapon at her disposal.

"Is that hope we smell? No. No. No. You aren't allowed to hope. Have you forgotten the price?" Dhral asked.

The door cracked, and parts of the wall tore away with it. The creature cast Brianne into the empty pews. Blood-covered tendrils wrapped around her wrists and ankles and tied her down, with another snaking its way around her neck, constricting but not cutting off her airway completely.

"What gives you hope? Do you not fear that your world is gone? Do you not wish to join those you loved? If you leave this place, if you deny us, then you will lose everything you've ever cared for. Not by our hand, but by the hand of our brother. Emual has taken everything from you, and you have yet to see it."

Brianne stared at Dhral, refusing to falter. Her eyes closed, and she focused on the stone in her pocket.

"You don't know? Oh, the taste of your despair would be so sweet, yet we mustn't allow you to leave this place. Not without our prize."

Brianne struggled against the tendril around her neck. "What are you really? A demon? A spirit perhaps?"

It ran a finger along her cheek, and the torn bits of flesh smeared blood on her skin. Another voice came from its maw, a loud voice, one familiar to her. "We are the Dhral, but once," the singular voice called through the chorus, "I was, and am, the hunger in the deep. Many parts of me exist." It faded and was replaced with the deafening chorus. "We gave it purpose, and in time, we will do the same for you. Join us! Join us, and be free of all that pains you."

Brianne's chest shined, a radiant light that drew the being in. It plucked it from her pocket. The glowstone rested in its palm, and Brianne opened her eyes and stared at it.

"Do you really think a tool for sight could stop us? You truly are lost," Dhral said.

Brianne's stare intensified, and the stone grew brighter, forcing Dhral to turn from it. With a final push, Brianne caused it to shatter, and radiant shards were sent in every direction. What remained of the windows shattered, and pieces of stone were embedded in the walls. The tendrils around her neck released, and the doors opened. She raced to the door, grabbed her weapon, and turned to face the creature.

It had vanished. The chapel was empty, and the air became still. She gathered her things and stepped out the door and started down the path, but Flicker did not float by the shore, and the boat drifted across the water to meet the dock on the far side. She stopped partway down the path, and laughter rang out from within the chapel.

"Did you think it would be easy to stop us? A physical form is meaningless. Do you not feel it in your heart? Do you not know the truth? You haven't won; you are merely giving up."

Her body ached, and she felt a pain in her chest. Everything returned to black, and she stood in the closet. Shards of the glowstone were embedded in her body and the walls. Blood trickled down her skin, and she ran her hand up her body, gently running a finger over a chunk protruding from the gaping wound in her side. It broke a few ribs but harmed nothing vital.

"Do you see? It is meaningless," Dhral said.

"Whoa, you are an ugly one!" Flicker said.

"Fool! Have you come to join your friend in misery?" Dhral asked.

"Not exactly. Brianne, open your eyes," Flicker said.

"It is no use. She cannot escape. Her mind was so easy to break," Dhral said.

A shimmer rolled across the closet, and she felt as though her eyes were closed. She felt pressure, as if she were laying on her back. With the throbbing in her chest, the shimmers came faster and faster, tearing her from the nightmare.

Her eyes opened, and she lay on the floor of the chapel, still in her armor, but she caused the glowstone to explode under her breastplate. A warm trickle of blood ran down her waist, and she felt it pooling at her back. Her body was bruised, with a black eye and bloodied lips.

"No! We cannot be overcome!" Dhral's voice faded, and only Kala remained.

Brianne climbed one of the pews and braced herself with the staff as Flicker hovered near her. "What made you come?" she asked him.

"I heard you scream. I was afraid I would let you down too, so I ran. Hovered? No, *flew* through the window and found you. Told you they don't like light." He moved close to her chest. "Might I ask why is there a glowstone blasted into pieces under your armor?"

She gave his glowing shell a pat. "It was a trick I learned. Never thought it would come in handy."

"You will not be free of us!" Kala's voice wavered, and she ran into the chapel's basement and sealed the door behind her.

The walls started crumbling around them, and the ground quaked. Brianne hobbled along the broken pews until she made it outside the chapel. The wall crashed in, and the chorus fluttered away. Behind the pile of rubble, a row of stairs became visible, and the light radiating from above called her toward it.

assage of Time

HER HANDS TREMBLED AS SHE CLIMBED THE FIRST few steps. Flicker hovered over and changed to a blue tint. With the chapel crumbling and the last trial done, they could leave the depths behind and be certain she became a true paladin. Battered and bruised, Brianne climbed slowly on her hands and knees up the thousands of stairs leading to the end of her journey, putting one hand in front of the other.

"Do you really think people are waiting up there?" Flicker tried to help nudge her forward, but he lacked the strength to move anything more than a blade of grass. "Maybe I should go ahead and check, what if they forgot and the door is locked or something?"

Brianne rolled over, resting her head against the stone slabs. She looked at him. Her black eye and other wounds were aching, but she pushed past her pain. "Stay with me. I-I don't think I can do this alone."

He nudged against her again. "Then let's get going. Can't have a party without a paladin! Hmm, not sure that goes together . . . Let's get moving."

Her eyes were heavy, and her body was exhausted, but she pressed on, climbing another few steps before putting her forehead on the cold stone again and enjoying a moment's rest.

She sat up and opened the front of her armor, tore a piece of her tunic, and made a few strips of cloth. She placed the chest piece beside her and started removing the chunks of glowstone from her side.

"Do you think it's sunny? Maybe we will burst through those doors and people will be waiting to celebrate!" Flicker hovered back and forth over the stair above Brianne. "Wait you've seen people come out before, right? Is it a big deal? Maybe I should be a nice shade of purple and— Wait, what color am I now? Am I colorblind?"

Brianne smiled through the pain and reached up, patted him, and returned to packing the wound. "You are a warm golden color, like an evening sun over the dunes. I've never seen a person exit. Even Timul's trials were held at night. They celebrate after the joining ceremony. Not sure what else happens."

Her hand reached a larger piece protruding from between two ribs. The smaller shards were placed on the step beside her, and their glow made it easier for her to work. She grabbed it and pulled it. When it moved, she felt pain shoot down her body. It pressed against one of her ribs. It barely moved, so she tried again. Slowly, it eased out of the hole in her side, and she packed it with what cloth she could spare and laid back to collect herself before pressing onward up the stairs.

Beside her head was Timul's name, etched into one of the crumbled stones. She looked over the steps and walls and saw there were a great many names, from Eandar to Morris—each had carved their names during their climb to the top. She picked up a splintered shard and scratched her name next to Timul's.

She ran her finger over his name. "You know, when we get back, I'm going to do what I should have done."

Flicker moved closer and then back away. "Take a bath? If I had a nose, it would be running away. Even the flies in the place are avoiding you."

She swatted at him. "That too. I was thinking about him." She tapped his name. "Maybe he will be waiting for me alone." Biting her lip, she let a smile pull at her cheek.

Flicker lowered to read the name. His light turned pink, and he turned slowly to her. "Someone's in love. I was in love once . . . More than once. Ha! We were married, had two kids, and I even had legs then. Was a strange time for me, to be honest. Also, it is strange to think I have been without legs longer than I lived with them." His light returned to a soft blue, and he bobbed up the stairs and back down.

"Do you miss them?" she asked.

"I don't know. It was so long ago. I can still remember her smile. She was proud of me. She always was. The kids were cheering, and when I signed the charter to join Balessa's mission, we celebrated." His light dimmed, and he came to rest against the stone above Brianne.

"I remember how I'd run my fingers through her long dark hair. I could never keep a secret, and she was never surprised by anything I did, no matter how foolish. And the kids were monsters, always getting into things. But no matter how I tried, I could never tell them no." His color deepened but quickly returned to his bright golden hue. "That is all over now. Time to get moving.

"Flicker, are you alright?" she asked.

"Yep. Never better! In fact, I might go to the top step and back. Could really use the air." The edges of his sphere were returning to a blue color, and he could hardly keep above the ground.

"Flicker?!" she yelled.

He looked away. The blue light filled him, and nothing of his golden visage remained. He came to rest again next to her.

"What is there to say? After a few years of war, I returned home without a body. Just a suit of armor, like Tyrn after me. I stood outside our farm. She and the children were in the yard, and I watched. The man I was died on the battlefield, and all that remained was a shell. I wanted to join them, but I knew. I knew she needed to move on. I had Tyrn go see her, and that night, with me standing there, she answered the door, and he gave her the news." Almost all the light drained from his shell. "That her loving husband—that I—was dead. As she cried into his shoulder, I wanted to comfort her, to tell her it would be alright, but I couldn't. I knew that she was better off not knowing the truth."

She put a hand on him, and where she touched, he brimmed with a light again. "I'm sorry." She sat up and pulled him closer.

"It's alright. It was better that they moved on. I would patrol the road past our house. In time, she remarried, and the kids grew up and moved away. One day, I walked past our house, and they wore black. She succumbed to age, and in time, so did our children and grandchildren. Then, I was alone. Balessa called to me once more, and I answered, for there was nothing left of the life I lived." He looked Brianne over and turned a bright gold all over. "But it's ancient history. No need to dwell on it. Let's get to that party. You said there's wine."

He moved up the stairs. "I can't drink stuff. The problem of not having a mouth. Come to think of it, I don't have eyes or a nose or even ears, but I swear I can hear, see, and smell things."

She smiled and crawled up the next few steps, with her strength returning, but she needed to climb slowly until she fully recovered. Hours rolled by, and she put one hand in front of the other. There were twice as many steps below her as above, and she could hear drums and whistling above.

"Hear that? Sounds like they are celebrating," she said.

Flicker traveled to the top and back down. "Not sure what type of celebration that is, but clearly, they need lessons."

She shoved him and climbed to her feet, falling back to her knees with nothing to hold on to. She climbed faster and faster. The seam in the doors was just ahead, and she reached for it, a bright light offering comfort and warmth. They were slightly ajar, so she wedged it open with her staff and slipped through.

As she landed in the inner crypt, she heard the

banging, but the whistling stopped. She stood and leaned on a broken coffin. The door behind her caved in, and she would need to navigate the hallway filled with rubble to find her way out. The glowstones had burned out, and the candles were gone. Roots grew through the ceiling, and rats traveled the holes between passages.

"Wow, this place really needs some cleaning up," Flicker said. He shifted colors when looking at her. "Thought you said the devoted still lived here?"

"It wasn't like this when I started the trial. The lamps were lit, and candles were placed along the path. What happened?" she asked.

"You sure they didn't just forget about you and leave during the night?"

She waved him off and pressed forward. "They were here, I promise."

Brianne ducked through the cluttered tunnel and pushed her way past the matted roots. Ahead of the ceremony chamber, a raised altar and pews circled a single seat at the center of the room. Cutting through the roots, she managed to slide into the chamber, and on the seat, she found her armor. A set of paladin armor, crafted just for her, her name engraved on the breastplate. It was covered in dust and tarnished, the cloth was tattered from animals gnawing at it, and the leather had hardened and crumbled away, leaving it a pile of scrap.

"They made this. It was my armor. Is this part of the trial? Or am I missing something?" she asked.

Flicker bobbed around the room and floated back. "I think you've been gone longer than a day."

Again, she moved past him and left the ruined garments on the pedestal. She climbed through the crumbled stone into the narrowed passage. The ground looked as though it had remained undisturbed for years, and she used the bloodied fragment of her glowstone to guide her path. Flicker remained behind. His color turned to a dark blue. "Brianne, I don't think anyone is here to celebrate."

She shrugged him off and pressed on until she arrived at the entrance. A dull evening light came through the clouds and illuminated the room, but by the door were the remains of a person. She couldn't make out who they belonged to, with nothing but rags and bone remaining.

"I know what this is. Some of the recruits are toying with me. Right?" Her voice cracked, and her lips quivered. She looked around, and the few crypts that weren't claimed by the earth or crushed by cave-ins were covered in thick layers of dust and were sealed shut.

"I don't think anyone is here, Brianne. Maybe time travels differently in the trials?" he asked.

She shook her head and grabbed the door. She pushed and pushed, but it didn't move. The door was bound by the walls pressing in, some of the hinges were broken, and she couldn't get it to budge. She kicked it and started beating it with her staff, but nothing helped. She wanted to call out, but she feared no one would respond.

Flicker moved between her and the door. "We aren't getting out that way, Brianne. Something isn't right. Don't you feel it?"

She clutched the staff and ran to the corner of the room and launched it, knocking loose one of the windows with no glass in the frame. It broke into pieces of rusted metal and splintered wood. She climbed up and peeked through the opening. Through the bushes, she could see the banners were still hanging over the streets, and she could see someone slowly hobbling along the path to her cottage. She dropped down and shoved her bag and staff through.

"When we get through, I'm going to introduce you to Alit. I think the two of you will get along. Well, I don't know, he is a bit strange about new people. But I bet he knows about Dwarven ruins."

Climbing through the opening, she noticed the body by the door held a weapon and had arrows in its ribcage. Flicker remained in the crypt and watched until she made it through alright.

he Withered

SHE STOOD UP AND KNOCKED THE DUST FROM HER clothes and motioned for Flicker to follow. His dim blue light hovered through the opening, and, wary, he floated a few inches above the ground. Brianne looked around the courtyard. A poorly put together old tent and remnants of a campfire were all that stood out. She wandered between the buildings, and though she tried to force them open, none of the doors would budge. Sand claimed much of the abbey, and she wandered aimlessly from door to door.

One set of footprints was the only sign of life she found, and they trailed in every direction as though the person wandered a ghost town and remained the only soul within the abbey for a long time. Overhead, the banners were tattered and barely clinging to the walls, though most had fallen or were used to make the tent she passed in the courtyard. The doors were swallowed by sun-dried twigs and ribbon hanging on them—the wreaths that were placed for the return of the soldiers. The main gate was missing, and the abbey walls had toppled over while she attempted her trials.

"Brianne, what happened here?" Flicker asked.

She remained silent as she walked the path to her cottage. Tears did not come, but she wore a face of despair. Her eyes were heavy, and her shoulders were slumped. She sat on a stone slab that had broken from the northern wall and stared at what remained of her cottage: a sunken, charred pile of debris. Sand covered the floors, and her belongings were lost.

Flicker moved about and came back to her. "How long were you gone?" Not returning to his normal color, he floated around the broken remains of what used to be her home.

The sun sank low on the horizon, and she looked at a single pillar of smoke rising along the edge of the city. She jumped up and ran to what remained of the northern tower. She climbed over the broken planks and pawed her way up the sand-covered steps until she reached the top.

Sarntheris felt abandoned. Even the trash vanished from the city streets. Many of the buildings had collapsed, and the dock sank into the sea. Not a soul moved, and she turned to Flicker floating at the bottom of the stairs.

"Am I still in Dhral's nightmare?" she asked.

He moved to her, his light still a dim blue, and he nudged against her side, "No. I don't know what this place should be, but this is real." His color lightened for a moment as she slid down and came to rest against the wall.

"Where is everyone? Alit was with me when

Emual pulled me into . . . someplace. And when I woke, it was like I had been away for so long." She wiped the tears from her chin. "Did the trials take that long?"

Flicker did not respond, only burrowing against her. In the courtyard, she could see a figure moving with hobbled steps between the shadows. It moved slowly, vanishing from sight near the ruined campsite.

She remained in the tower until the sun fell, and a single source of light other than Flicker filled the landing before the barracks with light. The moon and the stars were blocked by a patch of clouds rolling in off the sea as a winter storm formed on the horizon. Brianne climbed to her feet and made her way down the winding stairs and back to her old cottage. The few sounds within the abbey were the howling wind and shutters smacking the buildings.

"Do you think we should go?" Flicker asked.

"Where would we go?" She walked past the rubble. Her feet dragged the sand, and she stared into the distance, making her way to the gate and barely having the will to look up.

Flicker nudged her, and when her eyes left the trails in the sand, she could see an elderly man sitting at a campfire, roasting what looked to be a giant rat the size of a dog, but the smell made it alluring.

She slowly approached the campsite and stepped into the light.

"Hello, could I rest by your fire for a moment?" she asked.

The man jumped up and pulled a broken, rusty hilt from his waist. His frail body could hardly hold it steady as he aimed it slightly toward her left.

She stepped closer. "I am tired. Could I sit by the fire? Just for a moment?"

Hearing her voice again caused his hand to tremble. She could see that his eyes were clouded from cataracts, and his skin was dried and cracked, with thin white hair on the top of his head. The wrinkles on his face relaxed, and he dropped the hilt and covered his ears.

"Be gone!" he yelled. "You aren't real!"

His voice stung her. Morris! Through his frail form, she could see the man that once followed her through the abbey. He was only a shadow of the man he once was, but even that would have more than what shivered in her presence.

"Morris? Morris, it's me. It's Brianne. What happened?" she said.

"Brianne? No, no, no. It can't be. She is gone! Like the rest of them! Why must you haunt me, young one? Are you another of my demons come to claim me, or has my mind truly given to madness?" he asked. "No! You died! I watched as Bashok, the foul, blood-soaked, horned demon, cleaved your chest. No, you are a ghost, a memory of my failure." He pulled away and tried to free himself of the ghost that had appeared before him.

"Morris, I used to leave an extra pillowcase in the drawer by your bed. It's truly me. Please tell me what happened," she said.

"What is it you do not know? Mad as I have become, arguing with memories. I did it!" He looked to the sky, his arms open and falling to his knees. "I did it! I watched from the shadows. A coward! I watched as they killed my friends and as they killed you and did nothing! Is that what you want?"

She put a hand on his shoulder and pulled him closer. "I'm not a memory. It's me." Tears ran down her cheek. "Morris, when I was little, you used to follow me around the abbey, making sure I stayed out of trouble. Don't you remember?"

"Always sneaking into things. I'd follow you about and play pretend until Shaw was done with his daily routine. No, you can't be real. So many years since that day, and you are still as beautiful as . . . as—"

He reached for his left arm, and Brianne held on to him as he dropped to the ground.

"Oh, let it be over," he moaned. "Brianne, be you ghost or memory, we all died that day. My body has just taken time to catch up." His breathing slowed and soon stopped. She knelt, holding his body and crying over him.

"No, you can't go! I don't want to be alone! Please, Morris. *Please!*" Her words echoed through the empty spaces and were only answered by a deathly silence.

Flicker nudged her shoulder. "Brianne. He's gone. Please, let's go. You have a waterskin and that big rat over there. This place is nothing more than shadows and nightmares."

She stood and walked to the washhouse. In the dark, she still managed to find a shovel lying on the top rack, just where the stable hand often left it. Her tears did not stop, and returning with the shovel, she started digging. Weakened, she stopped and took a rest by the fire, eating a bit of rat meat. The thought was repulsive, but the gnawing hunger within didn't care.

Flicker returned to his normal color and floated by her. "Are you going to bury them all?"

"He should be buried. He shouldn't be left here to be eaten by animals," she said.

The night dragged on, and in the early morning hours, she woke and started digging again. When finished, she prepared his body and lowered him into the hole.

"Sleep well, Morris, son of Arden. May the beyond welcome you." She gathered a few wilted flowers and placed them on his chest with the broken hilt. She filled the hole and took a rest under an old, gnarled tree. The day dragged on, and she just sat, watching shadows dance across the ground.

Wind from the north brought the chill of the snow falling on the farmlands. The sun reached its apex, and with her waterskin empty and her throat dry, she made her way to the washhouse. The well still held water, and the pumps worked. She slowly ventured into the city with a full waterskin. The gates were missing, and nothing barred her entry to the remnants of the market.

She had become accustomed to entering through the sewers and forgot the beauty of the fine stonework. Taking a deep breath, she searched the shops and alley stalls for anything worth using. She even entered the palace and found piles of ash, where campfires had been made in the main hall. From the gaudy estate, looters had taken all the gold, and the precious artifacts were also missing. She found the bedroom and slipped into the walk-in closets. Rows of dry rotted clothes and shoes lined the walls from floor to ceiling.

After searching the estate, she found needle and

thread and a few healing poultices. She carried on to the slums, where the buildings were mostly burned, and, in the alleyways, she could see skeletal remains half covered by the sand. Her spirit was slowly breaking, but she refused to give up. Finding an old clothing shop between the slums and market, she snooped around.

"Don't you think we should leave?" Flicker asked.

"Yes, but I need a few things first. Can't go wandering the desert like this. And those clouds mean we will get rain soon. Don't want to be in the dunes if that happens." She raised her left arm and showed the wound, which was still open and being picked at by insects.

"Going to get these supplies back so I can avoid worse injury." She snatched a few tunics that were stashed away in a drawer and a few towels from a sealed box. They were dingy and off-colored, but still usable. "I can clean it up, and after a bit of rest, we can be gone. I did promise to help you find Tyrn after all."

"Maybe we should take it a bit slow. It's been a thousand years since he went missing. Not sure a few days of rest would hurt too much," he said.

She ducked under the fallen awning and started down the path to the armory. Flicker followed close behind.

"What do you think happened?" Brianne asked.

He moved over to the holes in the walls and studied the scorch marks. "Looks like a battle. Did the city have enemies?"

Near the main gate were gibbets filled with

skeletons, and bodies were piled by the enormous iron gates.

Flicker's light dimmed a bit. "Yep, a battle. Wonder how long you were in the Veil? Like the stories say, you can enter and leave, but never will two people step out together."

She turned to him. "What do you mean? Step out together?"

"Oh, the way Nyasom explained it, the Veil is outside of time. Could be gone an hour or a hundred years. Would explain the look of things around here," Flicker said.

"Then how long has it been? How many years have I missed?" Brianne asked.

"My guess, a lot. Maybe someone we meet will know," he said.

She stepped through a broken section of wall and sifted through racks and shelves. All the armor and weapons were useless, withered by time or devoured by rodents. She made her way around the supply room to a few sealed crates that were hidden against the back wall and were full of random gear from a merchant in Oncier.

She cracked open the first and found weapons— steel swords and shields—crafted by the Dwarven smiths in the Oncier forge works and smuggled out, the insignia of the Empryss Legion emblazed on the face of each shield. She took a sword and scabbard and tied it to her waist. The second crate was filled from top to bottom with heavy plate armor of blackened steel, weighing too much for her to carry, let alone wear. She closed it back and opened the last. Inside were neatly stacked mail and leather armor pieces. She collected one of each and tossed them into a sack.

"Guess that is all we are going to find. Was hoping to find a bit more, but this will do."

Flicker looked over the sack and turned a shade of purple. "Why do you need new armor? Those look fine to me."

She tapped the insignia of Balessa engraved on the shoulder. "Even without what happened here—whatever that was—the pantheon could never be openly worshipped. If I want to make my own way, I'll have to give up being a paladin while we travel."

Walking back, she took a detour to the harbor. The docks sank into the sea, and the boardwalk had burned to ash. The hulls of ships and masts sprouted from the water in the bay, and some were crashed into the rocks, with the lighthouse destroyed and only a mound of bricks standing in its place.

She followed the shore and looked upon the wreckage of a dozen or more ships. Most were decayed from age, but some were newer, with corpses still rotting in the salty sea air and scattered along the coast. Out to sea, the raging winter storms from Tania were approaching the coast and would soon bring heavy rains.

She returned to the washhouse and took the time to wash the dingy clothes she gathered and dried them in the afternoon sun. After folding them, neatly she filled a basin and removed the pieces of armor and clothing, tossing aside the blood-soaked pieces and wincing from the air touching the seeping wounds. Using some soap and a wash rag, she cleaned around the wound and used a bit of ointment she carried to keep it from getting infected.

After covering the freshly packed and treated injuries, she washed her hair and removed the dirt and other substances from her skin. She laid down under the tree again as the sun sank low on the horizon, and her strength gave way to exhaustion.

Flicker came down from his perch overlooking the dunes. "I'd say you need another day to recover. Those wounds looked awful."

"We will need to find a place to shelter us until the storms pass. And I'll need to find some food before we travel," she said.

"Hey, those rats looked tasty. Maybe find another one of those, and you're all set," Flicker said.

Her stomach turned, and she rolled her eyes at him. "I will find something less rat-like to eat. I hope."

She made a fire and leaned against the barracks door. Hours passed, and they shared a few jokes and enjoyed a meal of yet another roasted giant rat before preparing for sleep.

"You know, I used to spend every day hoping to go off on an adventure, and now I just want to go back. Part of me wishes this was all a nightmare and I could wake up in my bed with a terrible headache and Alit right there beside me. Where is he? Makes it hard to believe that it's really been so long."

"I'm here. Is that part of the nightmare?" Flicker turned blue and bobbed away.

She reached over and rested her hand on his shell. "You're the one thing that keeps me going. Without you, I'd be lost."

He turned pink and aimed at the ground beneath him. "You mean it?"

She pulled him close and hugged the shell of

light. "Yep, without you, I'd be alone, and I hate being alone. You also saved me from the chapel, and that is more than I could ask for in a friend." She let go and curled up in a blanket. Bundled up, she stared at the stars and felt the weight of her eyelids dragging her off to sleep. "Night, Flicker."

He hovered over by the wall and grew brighter than the moon cresting the walls. Brianne watched him and smiled before dozing off.

CHAPTER 20

Hunting Supplies

AFTER A ROUGH NIGHT OF TOSSING AND TURNING, they got an early start, and Brianne wandered the city again. Digging through the stables, she inspected and tossed random odds and ends into a sack. She gathered all her things and piled them by the barracks, and she spent the better part of the morning preparing what she needed to carry on their trip, from extra water to clothes and weapons.

She would need to gather food along the way, and anything would be better than eating more rats, so she more than wanted to leave.

"What are you looking for?" Flicker asked.

He hovered around the exterior, peeking in and dodging the random things she sent flying at him as she discarded them. Although he couldn't be physically hurt by anything, it was a reflex for him to move, so he remained at a distance. She burst through the doors and kicked an old wooden bucket through a shop window.

"It's useless. We need a cart or sled to carry all our supplies, and if those storms get closer, we'll need to prepare. Everything has either been left out in the elements to be ruined or broken from the fighting however long ago."

"We could make one. Use some boards and ropes and maybe use the metal bits off that old one," he said.

She grabbed what pieces she would need and carried them back to their camp. Among her collection was nails, rope, twine, and a collection of boards. She looked at Flicker hovering over the chapel spire. "We need a few more things."

"Can we go shopping?" he asked.

She rolled her eyes and took a crumpled piece of paper from her pocket, cringing and taking a sharp breath. The sting on her side had improved but still caused intense pain when she moved the wrong way. She grit her teeth and started writing. "So, we need a hammer and some extra cloth to cover everything and keep the sand out. Oh, and we will need to get some glowstones."

She tapped the quill against her temple and watched Flicker talk to himself while he hovered over their goods.

"Can you think of anything else that we might need?" she asked.

"Hmm, good question. Guess we could use some extra water," he said.

"Already have enough."

"Do we have any gold?" he asked.

She looked past him and fixed her gaze on the

roof of Shaw's office. "I'll get that when we are closer to leaving."

She hopped up and walked back into the city. She started at the armory and searched the supply room again, finding more crates in the storeroom filled with random odds and ends, but she managed to find several uncharged glowstones. Finding nothing else of value, she sauntered off to Crafter's Alley.

She crawled through the forge and found a hammer. It was rough around the edges and a bit rusty, but when she swung the heavy forge hammer and slammed it against the anvil, it rang out, spooking the birds nesting in the attic. However, it was larger than she could manage, so she kept searching, finding a smaller one they used for shoeing horses, light in weight and sturdy.

After a time, she gave up searching for gold while rummaging through the shops. The sun would soon be setting, and navigating the streets in the dark wasn't on her list of things to do that day.

Her search for extra linens started at the washhouse supply building, where she found several sheets and blankets. She sifted through the tattered and molded pieces of cloth and kept only what she could use and needed. Climbing through the barracks window, she searched the desks and drawers for anything of value.

Under one of the mattresses, she found a well-kept knife. Tucking it into her pocket, she found a letter. On the outside, the name faded, but the impression was from Timul's handwriting.

She opened it and revealed it to be a letter he never sent to his sister. Brianne thumbed through the few pages and hung over the last few lines.

I know you told me not to keep after Brianne, but I love her. Not sure it will last, but for now, she is all I can think about. Also, she will complete the trials soon, and we might come to visit you in the fall.

She folded the letter neatly and placed it in her shirt pocket and searched the remaining rooms, finding nothing but a few blunted knives and random odds and ends. She returned to camp and started piling wood for their fire.

Flicker floated over everything she had gathered. "So, what are we missing? I see the hammer. Good. Nice plenty of linens. And with your deft hands, with glowstones, we can use them as weapons. Okay, so what else?"

She caught his glance while she lit the campfire.

Waiting for the fire to burn down a bit, she prepared a small ardoc, a six-legged reptilian creature native to the dunes. She had run across it when she'd climbed out of the barracks window. Her mouth watered at the thought of eating anything other than another rat; full grown ardoc were about the same size as a house cat and were a delicacy in the north.

She used the few spices she'd found during her exploration the day before to season the meat before placing it over the fire to listen to it sizzle. Seeing Flicker approach, she kicked her feet up and blocked his view while drawing in her notepad.

"Hmm?" Flicker bobbed, watching her.

She moved her feet apart and saw him glowing red and staring at her. After a moment, she asked, "Did we find any gold? We have plenty of stuff to get us out of the desert, but this stuff won't last forever. Have you seen the prices on stuff lately? I mean, I haven't, but I can only guess things are much more expensive since I last stopped at the general store."

"Didn't you say you knew a place where we could find some gold?" Flicker floated about, turning purple as he lectured her.

She rolled her eyes and stood up. "If I go get some gold, will you stop worrying?"

"No, but I won't bother you about gold. Maybe. Look, we just really need to buy you some food. I don't eat or anything, so all good on my end, but you really chewed for a while on that rat meat. Wait, what is that thing? How many legs does it have?"

"Just watch it and try to scare off anything that comes by to steal it. Okay?"

She froze by the hill leading to Shaw's office. The flash of her trials returned to her mind, and a rush of emotions washed over her. "Maybe we can sell some things in the first town, make some gold that way?"

"What are you afraid of? Been up there a few times. Just a few skeletons and sand, but nothing we haven't seen elsewhere in this boiling paradise. Also, what can we sell? I'm no merchant. Honestly, I think we have established that I am a handsome floating ball of multicolored light—possibly the most handsome—but if I were a merchant, I wouldn't buy what we have. In fact, I would throw us from my shop and lock the door. Though you do smell better today."

"Are you done?" she asked.

"Just saying. I'll go back to the spider rat you have cooking," he said.

He turned a shade of blue and returned to the camp, bobbing about and muttering to himself about random things and changing colors with each turn around the fire.

Brianne walked the path to the watch commander's house. The door was sealed shut, with sand rising halfway up the door, and the windows were all broken. Sand drifted inside the once immaculately cleaned space.

Everything remained in place, and she slipped through without issue. Even Brena's chair and book were still sitting in the corner. Time had ravaged the pages, and sand filled most of the rooms, but seeing it brought a smile to her face before she started the search. Looters had pilfered everything, and Shaw's office received no special treatment; nothing of value remained aside from a few gold pieces tucked in a pillowcase.

On the wall above the fireplace, she saw the portrait of the watch commander and Shaw in their youth. She enjoyed the sight until the squawking of ravens roosting on the gibbets snapped her out of the moment. Placing the ten gold pieces into her pocket, she climbed out and knocked the sand from her clothes.

Keeping her eyes down, she maneuvered under the cages and steered clear of any that sat in her path. One from the archway had landed in her path and was buried after years in the elements. The cages being partially buried offered a reprieve from her fears; the bodies inside were submerged. She managed to reach the door to Shaw's office without seeing any of the paladins' remains.

It was a challenge to move with the roof sinking and the walls folding in from the pressure. Being forced to enter through a window, she slid over the mounds of sand that filled the first floor of his office.

After searching through what wasn't covered by sand and pocketing the few gold pieces and silver jewelry she came across, she pilfered everything and made her way out. The second floor was inaccessible, with the stairway broken and no other way up from the inside.

She would need to find another method of reaching the second floor. The only route caused her to have a sinking feeling, but she pushed it away. She tucked away what she could, and she peered out at the shadows getting longer on the sandbank.

The ardoc would be fully cooked soon, and she ducked out of Shaw's office and reached camp.

She found Flicker glowing green and hovering back and forth by the campfire.

"About time. Find anything? Oh food's done? Can't tell, just realized I don't really smell things, and it is really getting to me," he said.

"At best, fifteen gold pieces, and I'm not sure about some of this jewelry. It's rather tarnished, but there is one room left that I could search," she said.

The aroma of herb-roasted ardoc made her mouth water, and the steam rising as she cut the meat made it difficult for her to wait for it to cool down before eating. She gathered some desert pears and peeled them, cutting them into neat slices and placing them on the side of her meat. They weren't ripe, but she couldn't be picky, given the circumstances.

"It is a gamble, but there is a hidden safe in Shaw's office. Used to watch him stash things inside when I was little. Might have some gold." She chewed and hastily chugged down some water before waiting to take another bite.

"Maybe we should leave first thing. Could be better to just risk it and do some odd jobs to get some copper. I hear people pay money for item retrieval." Flicker turned a dingy brown and eyed what remained of the ardoc still sitting on a spit over the fire. "Why did you stab this thing? For fun?"

She set the plate on a bench and carried the inedible bits and tied the rope off the far side of the main gate before she sat down and refilled a glass of water, taking a cautious bite. "With the storm looming overhead, we need to prepare."

"Prepare for what?" Flicker asked.

She started making spikes to narrow the path leading to their camp.

"When the winter storms come, the Prowlers come out of their dens and hunt from the southern dunes to the farmlands south of Oncier. The last hunting party from Sarntheris was torn to shreds, and the matriarch left the bones piled by the King's Road, licked clean and sun-bleached. It was spring before anyone found the remains."

She took one of the old spears and popped off the broken metal tip and sharpened the wood, stacking it into a pile of others. "Shaw once told me that Prowlers were likely to sneak into places on nights like tonight."

The moons were blocked by clouds coming from the west, and the rumble of thunder caused Flicker to move a bit closer to Brianne under the barracks awning. "We need to place all of these to make sure it cannot sneak around behind us. also why are you hiding? You are a floating ball of intangible light!"

"Because I remember stories about the desert cats. Also, I can be afraid of things too. Don't need a body to experience fear," he said.

She rolled her eyes and placed another spear on the stack. At her side, one of the tarnished steel swords and the black glass staff leaned against the sealed doors. Prompted by the cold air rolling in, she would need to gather as much firewood and stash it in a dry place, and place as many of the spears as she could to ward off anything that would wander too close. She placed glowstones in sconces on either side of the path and made sure the posts were sturdy.

The first raindrops landed with heavy thuds, and they stung a bit against her skin. She raced to finish the task of setting out everything she needed before being drenched and forced to take cover by the fire once more.

"How does someone kill a Prowler?" Flicker asked.

Brianne scratched her head and looked him over. "Shaw said they have thinner armor on their bellies, but I wouldn't want to be in a position where I could see their belly."

"I agree. Maybe they have a weakness to fire?" he asked.

Shaking her head, she curled near the fire. She needed to get a bit of sleep before the long watch through the night started. Lightning sprawled across the sky like spiderwebs, and thunder shook the ground beneath them. She pulled the blanket up to cover everything but her eyes as she watched the single path into their camp.

he Prowler

THE RATTLE OF RAIN ON THE ROOF OF THE BARRACKS made it difficult for Brianne to sleep. So, she watched the narrow path between the spears. She had set a few iron bear traps out as well. They were not made for Prowlers but would serve her purpose well. Flicker hid, tucked away under the blanket, avoiding the sight of lightning and trembling each time thunder tore through the air around them.

She held tight to the sword's grip and ignored a fly crawling across her cheek. The spray of rain stung her skin and rolled off her chin and jaw, but she remained fixed on the path. Low growls moved through the darkness just beyond the walls, and she followed the sound.

"Think you could go see what is out there?" she asked.

Flicker turned a shade of yellow before turning blue. "I don't often say this, but I'm scared."

She caught a glimpse of something moving near the meat she hung by the gate. The flash of lightning had been too brief for her to make out any detail.

"Why are you scared of them? Feel like they wouldn't get far since you're a ball of light." Her frustrated tone snapped at him while her eyes scanned the edges of light from the campfire.

"Lightning . . . It feels weird and causes me to black out for a bit. Really hate getting hit by the stuff. How aren't you scared?" Flicker poked out to see but slipped back under with another loud crash of thunder.

Her hands were trembling but held tight to the sword, and in the other hand, she held an unlit torch. "What do you mean? A paladin is never scared."

In the corner of her eye, she saw one of the banners falling. She jumped and dropped the torch, gathering a spear and hurling it at the banner. With precision, she pinned it to the door of the dining hall.

She sat back down, breathing heavily and shaking as she watched for more movement before curling up and hugging her knees, leaving the sword close enough to grab should something arise. She took a deep breath and tried to calm her frayed nerves.

"Did I tell you about the time I met this old Dwarven adventurer? Nishal was his name. An odd character. Kept asking about the ruins of Ciro and wondered if I had been there. Why would anyone want to go under a mountain? Anyway, was a stormy night like this, and we had bandits all around and some Inquisitor lady hunting our trail. Ah, those were good times." Flicker sighed.

Brianne leaned toward him without moving her

eyes or blinking. "Nope, you never told me that story. What happened?"

"Oh, what happened? Well, we were traveling with this cranky old magister, and they were searching for the Pillar of Starlight—like anyone could find one of the seven pillars without a map. Came to me and promised to help me find the book if I led them to Ciro." He turned red. "They never came back to help me find the book, but . . . What was I—? Oh, so we came across this valley just south of the Borethen Mountains, and they discovered that we were being followed," he said.

Out in the darkness, she could see the eyes of something moving—fixated on her—and her eyes followed it. Each strike of lightning did nothing to reveal whatever lurked just outside the gate. She leaned over and tossed another piece of wood onto the fire. "I'm listening. So, what happened next?"

"Well, old Nishal placed his hammer under his blanket, and the magister prepared spells and used an illusion to convince them we were in one place, but we were in fact in another. They were a wonderful team. Not sure how they met. Think the magister had blond hair, but maybe it was brown, the elf sort. But he had this attitude like he was above everything. Who cares if he's that tall? Where was I? Oh, right."

The eyes vanished, and the winds picked up. Rain drenched Brianne and dimmed the fire.

Her hand slid to the sword with a finger tipping the edge and flicking it closer with each attempt. Another loud growl made her shiver, and the ear-piercing squeal of a giant rat being torn to pieces reached her ears before the tapping of rain picked up and deafened the sound of gnashing and snapping sounds being carried on the wind.

"When they made their move, we were going to be ready. Nishal slept with an eye open. Strange how he always did that. Not sure why, but he said it was comforting or something. The magister said, 'Stupid ball, try to dim your light so we aren't given away when they approach.' He was always a fun person. I floated up onto the ridge and watched the bandits sneaking through the pass."

Another crack of lightning rippled across the sky, and she saw the outline of a catlike creature moving just beyond the gate. The flash faded, and its eyes were once again locked on her. Another flash, and it was gone, but the eyes remained.

"There had to be nearly thirty of them, and it was just me and my two intrepid companions. A storm rolled in, and the illusion faded—something about interference and the nature of magic or something. Bathor—the magister, that was his name. He was always funny. Said we would have to fight and stared at me, so I turned red and gave him my best battle cry and charged into the night."

He fidgeted with another crackle of lightning and slid a bit farther under the blanket. Wind forced more rain in and dimmed the fire further. With the wood damp, the fire dwindled, and only a few flames danced among the cold coals.

The eyes moved closer. Brianne could feel the ravenous gaze fixated on her. She poked the fire and brought back some of the flames, enough to cover the edge of their camp.

"I was flying through the trees and thought, 'What am I doing?' Not like they could hurt me, or I them. So, I returned and waited with them. Nishal and Bathor were roused by the bandits making their charge. When they came over the rise, Bathor struck them with a powerful meteor and set several of them ablaze. Will say it wasn't as cool since they were screaming, but it was interesting spell—not like the elves of old, but it was nice to see real magic being used."

The eyes vanished, and with another flash of lightning, it no longer paced just beyond the gate. She gripped the sword and uncovered the unlit torch. Another swirl of wind pushed the flames, but they managed to remain lit.

"How did they get out? Did they fight their way, or did they have to flee?"

"Nope, Nishal used this strange artifact and said, 'Aye, pointy ears, keep 'em at bay so I can get this workin'.' Bandits were rushing us from the pass. Bathor looked back, and for some reason, he called him some name in his native tongue and returned to raining fire down upon them. I was flying about just startling people, and, in hindsight, it was awful, because so many of them were set on fire and didn't get back up."

Another gust of wind tore through the camp. The flames dimmed but held. The eyes moved closer, and with the light pulling away, it moved with haste.

"Nishal got that thing going, and boom! Just like that. Nishal said, 'Farewell Flicker, I'll find another way.' And with a loud bang, they were gone. I really wonder what happened to them. Maybe they're alright."

The last few flames died, and the eyes raced toward them. Brianne leaned forward and focused on the path leading into camp. As the footsteps reached the steps, she pushed magic into the glowstones she hid. With a flash, they exploded and blinded the beast. It thrashed about, catching Brianne with a single claw and gashing her abdomen. She drove the torch into the coals, and the heat caused it to ignite. The beast's hardened scales were wet and shining, but even a strong swing of her sword bounced off, leaving no marks and sending a tingling shock down her arm.

She rolled away, and the warm trickle of blood down her stomach and legs garnered her attention. With another swipe, she deflected with her sword, only to have it flung from her hand, sending it sliding across the sand.

The force threw her into the spears lining the path but, luckily, they were aimed in the opposite direction, so she wasn't impaled; hitting them still knocked the air from her lungs. Her torch lay on the steps, and her sword was somewhere in the darkness. She grabbed a spear and searched the inky black for the creature and only caught the silhouette following another lightning strike.

Its eyes appeared and raced at her again. She managed to turn in time to splinter the spear against one of its scales, which knocked her back into another row of spikes.

The beast became dazed but recovered and charged again. She rolled and jumped out of the way of its lunge and pawed her way to the burning torch. Its light wasn't enough to spread across the camp, but it would deter the creature and buy a bit of time.

Flicker shined with a white light, while still hiding under the awning so he remained out of the weather. She waved the torch around, but the creature vanished into the night. A low rumbling growl came from the shadows beyond her sight.

Collecting one of the spears and backing up the stairs to the fire, her vision blurred, and she could hardly hold the spear steady. She wiped away the water on her forehead, and it mixed with blood, running into her eyes. Through her blurred vision, she could see the beast preparing for another attack.

She tucked herself into a corner and laid the spear beside her, aiming down the path away from the camp. Another heavy gust of driving rain stung Brianne's skin as she watched the beast charge, gaining speed as it leaped, clearing the steps and reaching forward with its claws.

She raised the spear and wedged it into the corner for leverage. She caught the beast between its scales, landing the tip of her spear in the soft spot, puncturing its chest and impaling it. The beast started thrashing but slowly wore down until it hunched over lifeless on the spear.

Letting out a moan and a final ragged breath, the Prowler's body went limp and hung on the spear, sliding down as the shaft worked through the creature. The cold lifeless look in its eyes gave Brianne relief, and the adrenaline bled from her system. She felt the pain of a new injury; its paw pressed on the side of her chest and had shattered some of her ribs. Jolts of pain rippled across her body in waves as she crawled from under it before it reached the ground.

She grabbed some linens and the needle and thread, placing them at her side and breathing new life into the fire. Once the flames were rising and the warm glow permeated the area around the camp, she started her work. Using a bottle of whiskey, she cleaned the lacerations to her stomach and scalp.

She held the needle over the flame and cooled it with whiskey and started closing the fold of meat on her stomach. Her cries of agony echoed through the abbey, and Flicker came close only to give a bit more light.

The process took more time than she would have liked, as she blacked out a few times during the suture, but she managed to completely seal the wound and dress it before working on her scalp. Using a broken mirror piece she found in the barracks, she guided her hand along her hairline, closing the fold of skin and using a bit of alcohol to clean it before placing a bandage over it.

Her breathing became increasingly more painful with each passing moment, and she felt the ribs shift each time she turned or reached for the injury. Her body trembled and ached, but she continued, fighting against the torrents of burning pain radiating from her side.

The wound from the glowstone reopened, and she stitched it again. Each time her hands reached to complete the task, she could no longer breathe and would black out and see stars for a moment before bouncing back and restarting. She took a deep breath and held it while finishing the stitching before she blacked out again.

Her body went limp, and she could hear Flicker speaking, but his words were garbled, and she could not make any sense of it. Her eyes opened again, and she rubbed a healing poultice on the new wounds and old. Her head rocked back and landed on the soft pile of cloth and wood that hours earlier she called her tent. "Next time, I'm locking us in one of the towers and lining the stairs with spikes."

"Sorry I wasn't much help." Flicker came down and nestled against the side that wasn't hurting. "Maybe next time we can just not be in an abandoned city surrounded by hungry beasts?"

"Hahaha, deal. Tell me something," Brianne said.

"Sure?"

"How did you get back to the library? Wasn't it sealed off?" she asked.

"How did I get back? How *did* I get back? Oh, I remember! I traveled through the mountains and passed some strange floating lights rising from the meadow, and when I reached the chapel, all that was here was a small chapel and a few monks. Strange people. And did they smell! Or I think they did. Anyway, I told them I had returned, and I went below to hear the Lady's words again. Being near her voice used to bring me peace . . . Maybe I'll hear it again someday."

Brianne's eyes closed with the last bits of rain passing over the area, she drifted off to sleep listening to the remainder of his story. The pain of her injuries subsided, but black striated lines spread from the gash on her stomach, and she fell into a deep sleep.

CHAPTER 22

*N*ever Too Late

MORNING CAME, AND BRIANNE USED A FEW SLATS OF wood and cloth to bind her chest so she could move without doubling over in pain. With their camp in ruin and the spears she set out broken and scattered across the courtyard, she gathered up what hadn't been destroyed and sighed. She chugged down a healing tonic, more for the pain than any healing it offered.

Her gear remained in usable condition and tucked away inside the dining hall. She pulled the Prowler's teeth and removed its outer scales before dragging it to the main gate. The plates were harder than steal but light as a handful of straw, and the teeth were a rare and valuable item in most places around the kingdom and beyond. She looked at the arch beside Shaw's office, and her eyes narrowed. She grabbed a curved piece of metal and one of the bundles of rope.

"Where are you going?" Flicker asked.

215

"We need more than a few pieces of gold and barter goods to travel across the mountains to Oncier," she said.

Flicker moved into her path. "You need rest!" He moved to her side and turned red. "Look at you, still bleeding! If I were bleeding, I wouldn't— Can I bleed? Hmm, never mind. And have you looked at those lines coming from the wound on your stomach?"

She walked off, leaving him to catch up.

"Brianne, stop. If you don't rest now, we'll never make it to—"

She stopped, dropping what she held in her hands. Her feet became too heavy to lift. Flicker came around her to see that one of the cages had fallen. The skeleton inside remained huddled, with a spear through its ribcage.

"What's the matter? Brianne? Brianne? It's just another skeleton," he said.

She ran back to camp, pulled the forge hammer from her pack, and raced back. Raising it high, she brought it down with force, breaking the lock. The high-pitched whine accompanied the door opening hurt her ears, and the body slipped out. Nothing remained but a bit of tarnished armor and tattered cloth. Around its wrist swung a pendant with the symbols of Athys and Balessa intertwined.

Her hand trembled as she lifted it from the sand. The weather had taken a toll, but she knew it to be the one she gifted to him.

"I'd hoped. I hoped—" She sat it back down gently and collected a blanket and the shovel. Next to Morris's grave, she started digging. With the sun beating down, she pressed on. Sweat caused her wounds to sting, but she became singularly focused on the task.

Taking no breaks for water or food, she prepared a hole. Once done, she climbed out and carried the blanket back. The remains were still resting in the sand, and she rolled them into the blanket. With a soft hand, she wrapped them and folded the ends over, taking the pendant from the wrist and placing it in her pocket.

She carried the bundle and sat it beside the hole and walked to what remained of the gardens. Before, flowers had remained in bloom for most of the year, and her favorite were white lilies. Luckily, it seemed the flowers had no issues growing in this new world. She gathered a bouquet of them and a bit of thistle. plucking them one by one and placing them on a piece of fine silk before tying them with a neat bow.

"Who was he?" Flicker asked.

She remained silent and carried the bouquet, giving him a pained glance before making her way back to the hole. She returned to them still sitting there. The wind had pushed open one end of the blanket, but she folded it back over and climbed into the grave with the body, setting it down and climbing out.

"Beyond . . . Take . . . Take—" Her voice broke, and tears poured down her face. She could not form the words through the pain.

"Beyond, take him. Carry him to peace, and may his days never end," Flicker said. He glowed a deep blue and moved to her side.

"I know, Brianne, I know." He returned to his golden glow and moved back, giving her space.

She shoveled in the first bit of dirt and then

tossed the single rose she had found blooming at the edge of the garden. Taking the shovel, she dumped more dirt. Hours rolled by, and her body grew tired, but she would not stop. Through the pain, she pressed on until the hole was filled. She took a stone slab and mounted it as a headstone. She returned to her cottage and climbed through the rubble to find her small box of odds and ends before returning to the graves.

She took out a pick and stabbed it into the side of the stone, hanging the pendant from it and watching it swing while the sun set behind her. Tools in hand, she carved the name and dates, leaving a few kind words from her favorite book. She stepped back to where Flicker hovered and stared for a long while. Her stomach rumbled, and her mind wavered, but she laid the bouquet and knelt over the grave.

"I love you. What is it you said? Better late than never? Guess I was later than either of us planned." She kissed the pendant and fluffed the flowers before leaving for the northern tower.

She climbed the steps and sat at the top, looking at the sand blowing across the northern end of the desert. The King's Road stretched out unto the horizon. A narrow path cut from the edge of the green to a village a day's walk north of the abbey, and lights twinkled from the small buildings. The ringing of an evening bell carried across the valley.

"Do you think anyone got away?" Brianne asked.

"If I tell you what I think, it might not be what you want to hear," Flicker said.

"Part of me hoped that I would walk into a tavern someday and see an old man and know, but I guess hope is an awful thing," she said.

"Why would you say that? I hoped, and then I found you. Some things we hope for come true. Others, we just weren't lucky enough. I know I can be a bit different at times, but never give up hope. It's the reason I joined the Order; I hoped for a better place for my family."

"How have you kept hope with everything you've lost?" Brianne asked.

"Lost? What did I lose? My children lived full lives, and I served my god. Even my wife died holding the hand of the man she loved, just wasn't mine in the end," he said.

She laid back and closed her eyes, letting the world drift away, going back to the place she wished to be. The purple hue of late evening blanketed the land in a cool breeze, and white smoke rose from the chimneys against the darkened sky. The smell of charred wood and the sound of faint echoes of life brought a tear to her eye.

It passed, pulled back by the bell ringing in the distance. Giving Flicker a pat, she walked back down and started a fire. Its warmth did little to comfort her, and she wrapped herself in a blanket and watched the flames dance.

Embers floating into the sky danced their way back to the ground around her. "Flicker, I'm leaving tomorrow. I don't care to find more gold, and I would rather leave this place behind than see any more of what was lost."

"You sure? Might be better to know how much is lost than to wonder what is left," he said. "But if you leave, I'll be right beside you."

She pulled the blanket up over her shoulder and tried to fall asleep, but each time her eyes closed, she saw flashes of arrows raining from the sky and people shouting.

Please help me, Brianne! Please!

She heard Shaw's voice calling through the chaos, and she woke to the moons shining bright and Flicker moving past the outer walls, his light bobbing along. His mumbling could be heard for miles around, and his light was easy to follow.

She struggled to stand. The pain of her wounds increased, and an unnatural infection took hold. Using the staff, she walked along the streets of Sarntheris. It felt eerie in the moonlight—hollow, devoid of all life, and forgotten by the world. So many years since anyone traveled these streets and spent time within these walls, and it looked much as it did the last day she left.

She wandered along the cracked cobblestone. Clumps of grass started growing through and were being covered in sand. Standing next to the bakery, she could almost hear the soft tones of the owner shouting that pastries were done and were cooling on the windowsill. The wooden counter broke loose, and the ovens remained cold and without a single ember burning. The sinking feeling she carried since her return only worsened, and she found no respite from the agony of knowing she would never know what truly happened, nor could she find where everyone that time scattered about the world.

She walked along the alleys and narrow passages she had once traveled to avoid the guards, and now, only a few rats and snakes moved among the debris. With the tide rolling in, she could hear the gulls nesting along the rocks. Flashes of light drew her to the shore. Just behind the horizon were bright flashes, and she could see them spreading across the mountains, reaching the towns to the north.

She raced to the nearest tower. Her body ached, and she found it difficult to raise her feet, but she climbed to the top and watched a rider carrying a torch racing into the town. Shouting broke out only to be followed by cheering. Over the next few hours, fires were lit, and singing carried on the wind, reaching Brianne.

Flicker moved up the stairs behind her. "Had me worried." He stopped beside her. Matching her gaze, he turned purple. "Wonder what the fuss is about?"

"Whatever it is, they seem to be having fun." She walked past him. "I'm going to prepare what I can; I'm not staying here another day."

"Brianne?" Flicker asked.

"Yes?" She stopped a few steps down and looked at the floor, her hand bracing against the wall. Her body swayed a bit, and her knee started to buckle.

"You need rest. Think you could do that in the morning?" he asked.

"No, I'll be fine," she said.

Back at camp, she stuffed everything she could into the sacks and tossed them on top of her makeshift sled, binding everything together with ropes she found. Having prepared all she needed or could get her hands on, she took a breath. It neared time to rest, but she felt something wet running down her leg. She looked and saw the stitches had burst, but she wasn't pouring blood. The skin became red and tender and felt hot to the touch. Pus came from the open wound, and she became lightheaded.

The world started to spin, and she stumbled to the ground, grasping at the box of healing supplies. She managed to get a bit of cloth and pressed it against the wound.

"Flicker! Flick—" She started to fade in and out. Her vision was blurred, and she could hardly concentrate. "*Flicker!* Help! Help me!"

She crawled closer to the fire and reached into her pocket and drew the knife, placing it into the fire and holding it there. Darkness covered her vision, and she only woke when the handle became too hot to hold. She rolled onto her side and tried to bring it to her skin, but everything went black again.

Flicker's panicked voice called out to her, "What's wrong? Brianne, what's wrong?"

She fought to raise the scalding blade to the wound.

"Oh god, that looks awful. Wait here, I can go get help," he said.

"Flicker, wait. Wait! I, just—" Her body went limp again, and she blacked out.

She could hear howling and the low hum of the beast growling again, but she could not move nor open her eyes. Voices approached, and she struggled to open her eyes. She could barely see a shrouded figure but couldn't make out a face between slipping in and out of consciousness, but she heard his words.

"This will hurt, young one, but it is needed to keep the infection from spreading."

Before she could force the words from her lips, another sensation came. Warm at first but soon burning, hotter than the scorching sands, and she screamed and writhed until she blacked out again.

Her eyes opened, and she stared Thealen in the eye. She clasped tightly to his robe as a red-hot piece of metal pressed to the skin on her stomach and her flesh, only to sear the flesh away.

"You won't be lucid for long. A Prowler has infected claws, and without proper medicine, a victim will succumb within a few days. Luckily, your glowing friend found me by the dunes," he said.

The pain caused her to stop breathing, and she tensed up. Her eyes rolled back, and she went limp. The sky started to swirl, and she could no longer feel the pain nor hear anything as she lay on the linens.

"Sleep well. Tomorrow will come soon enough."

he Last Dragon

BRIANNE'S EYES PEELED OPEN, AND SHE COULD hardly move. Her body ached, with every muscle sore and every joint stiff. Her throat was dry, and she could hardly form words, but she crawled toward the waterskin leaning on the banister. With her stiff joints, she could hardly make any progress and proceeded to land face-first in the sand piled beside the campfire.

A hand landed on her shoulder and pulled her back into the makeshift bed, forcing her back down and offering her a sip of cold water. Her eyes gained focus. Seeing Thealen's gray skin and tattered black robes was a shock, and she spat the water into the sand.

"You aren't real! You were gone, and . . . . And! you would be—"

He smiled and raised the cup to her lips once more. His green eyes were just as she remembered, and around his right wrist a strange form of stitching. "Old? Oh, child, I have lived many a lifetime, and being old isn't a description. Ancient would fit more adequately. You've been out for a few days, the product of a Prowler. I have waited for many years for you to return."

When ready, he sat her up and placed a bowl of stew on a small table he brought to her. At the gate stomped a mule, bound to a cart and ready for travel.

"What do you mean many lifetimes?" She pushed herself up but managed to slide a bit lower in the process. "Like an elf or a . . . an—" She caught her breath. Just speaking became a chore, and she could hardly accomplish thinking of the words fast enough to say them.

"Rest, rest. Let me do the talking. I owe you that much." He wiped a spoon clean with a flap of his robe, stirring the bowl before raising it to her lips.

"Where to begin . . . The day of your trials, I was told an Inquisitor was coming to inspect the grounds. My being an undead, let's say, would have complicated things."

He raised another spoonful and waited for her to be ready. "From the dunes, I watched the city burn. Was a horrible thing. From my guess, they were searching for you."

She froze. Her hand managed to push away the next spoonful. "What do you mean? Why would anyone look for me?"

He swatted her hand and shoved the spoon in her mouth. "Not while I am speaking. The time for questions will come, but for now, eat."

Through his shawl, she could see an evil grin. "I guess Shaw waited too long. You were to be one of a few: born to lead. But through failures and poor choices, the others fell away." He wiped a bit of stew that ran down her chin. "Then came you. Daughter of our greatest, destined to lead, but the people of the abbey were hiding a darker secret than Shaw realized, and when he tried to step in, they forced your trials."

He held another spoonful, but she refused to open her mouth. "What secr—"

He jabbed it in her mouth the moment she spoke and grinned. "Act like a child, and I shall feed you like one."

She sneered at him. "Fine."

He raised another spoonful and held a cloth to her chin to catch any that might dribble out. "Shaw came to me after his expulsion. We were going to race in and break you free. Always the soldier, that one. When we arrived, the city was in ruin, and ships were bombarding the walls from the sea."

She finished the stew, and Thealen helped her ease back into a more comfortable position.

"When the dust cleared, we entered the city and found his worst fear, but I knew what really lay in your place. Mimicry was always one of their best talents. I had no choice but to send him north. And so, I waited. For twenty years, I waited for you to emerge, and in a way, I'd given up. Figured I would spend the last of my days watching sand move from one pile to another."

She lifted the bandages to reveal the blistered flesh covered in a poultice, but she couldn't feel any pain.

He moved the bandages back and patted them. "An herb to numb the pain. You would rather not dry it out before it is time. The food might not sit well with such pain."

She put a hand overtop the mass of bandages and leaned her head back. "So, it was twenty years? Am I still destined for anything?"

"Yes, and no. You are the daughter of Melisande, but the time of heroes has gone. The Divine has found herself a champion, and the hearth gods claw at the edges of our world. Nothing any of us can do but hope; it is all we have, and it is better than lying down." He placed a wet washcloth on her forehead and let it cool her feverish body.

The infection wasn't fully gone. Blackened lines still webbed across her body, and an accomplished healer would be required to guarantee her full recovery.

"When the infection is dealt with, I shall see if you are capable of what is needed to stand against the tide. Honestly, I would rather not fight anymore. I've become weary of bloodshed and would rather watch the world fade into nothing than to spill more blood in an endless cycle of death," he said.

Flicker returned. A golden glow revealed his joy before he said, "You're awake! Found this thing roaming the sands, and with how bad you were looking, it was better to get him, even if he looks worse than the skeletons around this place."

Thealen smiled at him. "This one was once a proud knight. Faced him in the arena when he was little more than a suit of armor. A formidable opponent, but now he is a fool, lost to his own form of madness I suppose."

"Hey, I'm not a fool! Alright, maybe a little, but I'm better looking, and I smell way better despite being a thousand years— Wait, did you say we fought in the arena? Aphelion or Destrana?"

Thealen grinned. "Something we can discuss another time. For now, we must prepare our friend for travel. An alchemist in the mountains will know what to do about the infection, and the longer we wait, the less likely anything can be done. Until she is healed, we will not speak on our next move."

He started sifting through what she had gathered, tossing anything without any real value. He looked through the collection of silverware and a satchel full of inert glowstones. Setting them aside, he looked at Brianne and raised an eyebrow.

Finding her bag of armor, he tossed it aside along with her staff. She tried to move, but straining caused her to nearly black out, so she just grabbed a rock and hurled it past Thealen's head. "Thealen!"

He turned and glared at her. "For someone without much you make it difficult to tolerate your behavior."

"Why are you tossing all of my things?" she asked.

He held out a finger; the gnarled appendage was missing some skin and was nothing but bone at its tip, having no fingernail. Taking a moment to bring some water to his mule, he sat beside her and gave his undivided attention.

"They offer a challenging problem. Black glass is approved for only the nobles, and your armor would cause issues in the places we must go. Carry a sword if you like, but things that common folk aren't afforded will bring more trouble than we might care to receive."

"What about the rest?" she asked.

"We can only carry so much. Anything worth keeping will be taken, but things we can live without will remain here. Unless you would prefer I leave *you* to such an awful fate. Now, if you don't mind, I would like to return to the task of getting us far from this place."

He sat a cup on the table and filled it with water. "And if you would like, I will get you something more tangible to eat for supper. Enjoy the water for now."

He spun around and tossed a sack of linens onto the cart and started making a space in the back, placing a seat and making sure it was comfortable. Flicker floated along the walls, grumbling about random things as always and keeping an eye on the dunes to the north. Brianne took the letter from her pocket and opened it, she read it over a few times before returning it to her pocket. When she put it back, she noticed the map Emual had given her remained tucked in beside it.

When ready, Thealen returned and lifted her, helping her into the back of the cart. The seat was a perfect fit, and she could lay back and nap while they traveled.

He put a journal in her hand. "I found another of his works. Enjoy it. We have a long road—many weeks—before we reach the mountains, and if we're lucky, it won't be too difficult to pass through the valley."

Flicker joined her at the back of the cart, and Thealen climbed into the seat and urged the sturdy animal forward. They reached the gates, and Brianne kept watch over the walls as they passed into the dunes. The exterior walls were peppered with charred marks and holes. Along the northern wall, she saw a stick protruding from the ground and something glinting in the sun.

She grabbed the floor of the cart and pulled herself out and landed with a thud on the hot sand, crawling toward the stick, dragging herself along and grabbing handfuls of sand as she pulled herself closer.

"Hey, smelly, she jumped," Flicker said.

Thealen hopped down and ordered his mule to wait and walked up to her. She crawled a few feet but fought the whole way and made little progress in her attempt at reaching the object.

"Brianne, we need to get you back in the cart. There is nothing left here. Must you do such things? He gave his life to convince the world you were dead. Do not diminish his sacrifice," he said.

"No! He was going to wait for me! He said he'd wait!" Tears didn't form; rage was the only emotion she had left within her heart.

Thealen helped her to the staff that marked his grave. She saw the necklace Shaw gave her when she arrived at the abbey—the pendant of Athys—dangling in the breeze on a plank of wood.

She started digging with her hands, pawing away to uncover the body beneath.

Thealen grabbed her and pulled her against his chest. "I know your pain, young one. The dragon knew the cost. As did we all. Let him rest, and in time, the pain of this chapter of your life will lessen, and you will be stronger for it. Let us go and tend to what is left."

"T-the dragon? You mean this is . . ." Brianne choked up. "Alit? Not Shaw?"

"I'm afraid so, young one." Thealen nodded. "Shaw left the necklace for him."

Brianne turned back to the grave. "Where were you? I searched for you, and after all of this— He was my friend. My best friend! The only one that never left me." She gripped the staff and pulled herself to it. "We were going to travel to Iskal. He told me about the Dwarves and how dragons circled the mountaintop. Together. We were going to do it all together."

Thealen pulled the staff from the ground and draped the necklace around her neck. "I wish it were different, but we are here. Shed tears if you must, but we must press on. Oaths were taken, and we will finish what was started, Brianne. Too many have perished to give up now. The world doesn't care about what was lost, it will only care about what we gain."

He wrapped his arms around her. She fought against him, trying to break free of his grasp, but she remained too weak.

"Hate me if you must, but I will complete my task. I made a promise," Thealen said.

He placed her in the seat and put the staff in her hands. The mule pulled again, and the cart started moving away slowly. With distance, the empty feeling in her stomach became a bottomless pit, a chasm of nothing, but she could not cry another tear. It wasn't apathy, and it wasn't anger. She felt hollow, and her focus burned for the one person she wished harm above all others. Gripping the staff, she found a new purpose: to find the Ualeon Bashok.

Flicker pressed against her side, turning blue and

looking at her. "I think I would have liked him after all."

She put her arm around him and squeezed as the abbey slipped below the dunes. "Goodbye Alitherus, spread your wings and maybe someday we'll see each other again."

PART II
AHKARAD

CHAPTER 24

Setting Sun, Year 1286

From his room, Ahkarad could hear the royal guard shuffling about the winding halls of the keep. In recent days, tensions were high, and everyone remained on edge with the tribes naming Netoma as host to the next council meeting. Like most mornings, he tried to keep out of sight and stayed under his covers, pretending to be asleep. If he weren't the prince, he would have been pulled into service and trained as a soldier long before his current age, a fate he didn't care for and avoided. He enjoyed the lavish parties and gifts from the nobles wanting future favors from the king in waiting. Being twelve offered many challenges, and he found himself preparing for the pact and wanted little to do with tradition. His thoughts almost worked against him as he nearly missed his mother's footsteps as she entered the room.

"Ahkarad, a young man should always be on

time. Tak, make sure my layabout son makes it to his lesson." She leaned over the bed and pulled the blanket back, taking a moment before tickling his underarms and forcing a bit of laughter.

He looked up at her smile. With its warmth, it offered a feeling of safety. She carried herself like any other noble, with grace and dignity. Her long black hair framed her face and a clouded left eye. With an accompanying scar down her face, one would think her gruff exterior would be difficult to get along with, but most considered her gentle until she became angered. Few were unlucky enough to see her fits of rage, but most feared her prowess in combat almost as much as the sharpness of her tongue. Both were equally fearsome to an opponent, the blade more so if she wasn't in the mood to talk. He sat up on the bed while Tak carried his clothes to his bedside and laid them out neatly for him.

"Will the council be bringing gifts for this session?" Ahkarad asked.

"Now, now, have you no subtlety? We aren't hosting nobles and lords. We greet the tribes tomorrow, and seeing our people is gift enough," she said.

He slumped at the edge of the bed and pulled a tunic over his long, spiraled gold-capped horns. They were a sign of pride to him, having gone through the same process all heirs receive; his horns were dipped in gold shortly after birth. The distinctive black and red color of his skin gave a distinctive sign of his age, but the blue line between the colors on his skin gave away his lineage as much as his horns. Now fully dressed, he gathered the satchel of weapons and armor and prepared for his journey to the barracks.

"One day, you will be a brave soldier. I fear it will be a long time from now, but it will happen," his mother said.

He stepped toward the door, and she called to him, "I forgot, Elissar will be returning soon. She needed to resolve an issue in Morningstar and will be here much sooner than planned. Her daughter will not be coming this time."

"She always brings gifts and candies. Do you think she will bring more of those Iskalan chocolates? The Dwarves know how to make the most delectable sweets," he said.

She leaned over the bed and kissed his forehead, giving a smile to Tak and beckoning him to the door. "No, but she will be staying with us for a while. If you are good, I can see if Nishal can bring some during his next visit."

"That's fine, I guess. What abo—"

She cut him off and gave him a hug in front of the crowd of royal guards and nobles then knelt and gave him a pat on the cheek.

"Son, there will be time for this after the day's business is done. For now, Usuara is waiting, and he never likes waiting for long. I will see you after the delegation has arrived."

He frowned and glanced at the snickering guards. His face became redder than normal before ducking his head out of sight. "Okay. Not in front of them." He gave her a shoulder hug before darting out after Tak.

He raced up the stairs behind her, making his way outside. He noticed more guards than on a usual morning but thought little of it because the tribes were known for their less-than-civilized habits. They traveled along the concourse and stopped at the overlook where the sun usually hung below the horizon of the floating city, thus illuminating the world, but with no sun in the sky, the twin moons were still visible at the northwestern end of the city.

Tak had brought sweet buns and shared a few with him while the sun crested the eastern wall. The dragon, Ula, with her golden scales sparkling in the morning sun, flew to the Everset Gate and ignited the brazier, opening the way for people to enter the city and bringing to life the constructs that patrolled the market and keep.

"Why are the tribes meeting now?" Ahkarad asked.

"They want your mother to send soldiers to the border, as they fear Empryss will cross the Eversong Veil and break their treaty," Tak said.

"Maybe she should. It would show them we aren't afraid."

Tak smiled at him and gently patted his head. "That could be seen as an act of aggression, and your mother must think of peace. No matter how you see the conflict, she must find the best path for our people, and it's not always the one everyone agrees with."

Ahkarad frowned at the thought of peaceful negotiations and pulled the wooden practice sword from his bag, swinging it about, attacking invisible enemies. After a short bout, his fun ended abruptly by Tak caught the tip with her hand and softly lifted it from his hands.

"Do you think your teacher will be okay with another missed lesson? The old Dwarf will have your head if we are late, and I wouldn't want to explain that to your mother," Tak said. She pushed it back into his bag and placed the strap back over his shoulder. "If we are late, he might force you to spar with Sasha again, and I know how much you love that."

He stuck out his tongue and pinched his nose. "Fine, if we must, but only because it is better than listening to his lectures."

They traveled the military quarter and passed the soldiers getting suited up. In the distance, the ships were holding far out in the harbor, and storm clouds were coming from the east—not impossible but uncommon for the spring. They carried on and found themselves at the gate with Tak in the rear, a hand pressed against the middle of his back and another on the door handle.

"We must do this so that we can grow, young one. I looked after your grandfather and father, now you. The grumpy Dwarf is waiting." She simultaneously opened the door and pushed him inside, closing the door behind him before he could turn around and sneer at her.

The young Wolvar Sasha practiced her footwork in the arena. Her brown-and-black fur stood out among her people, and the missing chunk of her right ear made Ahkarad feel uneasy, for it was a sign of nobility, the clipping of the ears of those from certain noble houses. Among the Wolvar, they considered her to be small. As a Wolvar being about the size of a human child, it was a challenge for her in combat, but she was more than a match for Ahkarad most days. Ahkarad felt Usuara's eyes on him the moment he entered.

"Yer late. I should guess one of the noble blood

would forget tactfulness. Now that yer here, sweep the barracks hall. A bit dirty these days."

Ahkarad tossed the broom back at him and walked toward the gate.

"What is this? Son of the Warrior Queen is a child still? Sasha, will ya sweep the hall?" he asked.

"Yes sir!" she said, yelling loud enough to be heard on the busy streets outside the walls. She raced inside and jumped straight to work.

Usuara watched while Ahkarad sat on a bench. His eyes were fixed on the soldiers training. They were fit and capable of acrobatic feats, and Ahkarad found himself lost in daydreams of himself being as skilled when Usuara sat beside him. He sneered at the white-bearded Dwarf and moved a few seats over. Usuara's hands were blackened from years of working the forge, and his face bore enough wrinkles to be mistaken for an old leather bag left in the sun for a year.

"Ahkarad, when will ya take this seriously? A prince could be called to stand for his people, and if ya were called today, it would be yer end and theirs. How can I help ya understand these things? Must ya ignore duty and forsake tradition?" Usuara asked.

"What tradition? Learn to fight from a Dwarf? And training beside a Wolvar pup is an insult. I should be training with those of my people, great Ualeon warriors with the greatest of strength. Not some exiled blacksmith claiming to be a master."

Usuara knocked him from the bench. He landed in the dirt and looked up at the old Dwarf with a white-hot rage in his eyes. Usuara kicked him until he climbed to his feet.

The old Dwarf tossed an iron sword on the

ground beside him. "Fight Sasha, and if ya win, I will meet yer demands, and ya can train with whomever ya like. If she wins, ya have to run laps around the concourse until dinner."

Ahkarad bit his tongue and charged at the barrack's steps. Sasha, still sweeping, turned around to a quick swing from Ahkarad, but moving quicker than him, she dodged it effortlessly. She used the broomstick to whack his head and knocked him on his backside. This bought her the time she needed to get a real weapon before he could recover.

She met his halfhearted attacks and put him on his back foot. She returned with a flourish and cut his cheek, leaving a few drops of blood to trickle down his chin. He went at her again, each heavy blow missing its mark, meeting the dirt or being deflected into the air. He wore down quickly, unlike his opponent; she offered no signs of slowing down. His feet were sluggish, and with uneven steps, his heavy swings left him gasping for air. She put the blade to his chin and lifted his head slightly.

"Do you yield?" she asked.

He growled and lashed at her again. With renewed vigor, he pursued her and gave his best effort. Her speed kept him on his back foot. He took another glancing blow above his eye, leaving a small scratch, cutting away a bit of his eyebrow. Their brief fight came to an end with him crawling away on hand and knee.

She approached again and asked once more. "Do you surrender?" She rolled him over and placed a foot on his chest. His arms were too heavy to fight back. He felt the tip of her blade press against his throat.

Gasping for air, he looked to Usuara. "I—"

Before he could surrender, the ground shook with such force that Usuara and Sasha nearly ended up on the ground with him. His knees became weak, and an unease stirred in the pit of his stomach as Usuara ran to the gate to assess the situation. Tak stepped through and whispered into his ear before returning to the concourse. Usuara sauntered toward them and parsed his lips. After a prolonged silence he gave a pat to both of their backs.

"I'll be expecting those laps tomorrow, princeling. Ya both remain here. Tak will come for ya when it is time. Sasha, good work," he said.

He quickly slipped out the door and followed behind a company of soldiers moving toward the market square.

After he left, Ahkarad turned to Sasha. With a twitch of his head, he pointed to their hiding spot, and she followed him to the outer city wall. They ditched the dull iron weapons and climbed over the ledges until they were looking down on the bay. A dozen ships were just outside of the bay, holding until the winds moved in their favor, pushing them along to their next destination. The strict rules for traveling the seas were enforced by the consortium and would lead to harsh negotiations if any were to be broken without just cause.

He sat with his feet hanging over the side, but Sasha, being shorter by a fair amount, her feet only stuck out and couldn't hang over the side.

"Do you always have to show off in front of him? He already thinks I'm a spoiled brat without much promise," Ahkarad said.

She smiled and pushed against his shoulder. It

barely moved his much larger frame, but that didn't change her intent. He responded by giving her a side-eyed glance.

"But you are! It's not like you get out of bed on time any day of the week," she said.

"Yes, someone of my station is afforded such luxuries." He tugged at his tunic. "What about yourself? Do you have the joy of waking to a servant preparing your attire for the day?"

She smiled at him and climbed onto the railing. Her small stature made it easier for her to balance on the narrow planks of wood. Ahkarad remained on the wall, watching her walk effortlessly across to the other side.

"I did when I was little. In Aud Nua. I don't miss the servants, but I miss the people that loved my parents. They were nice, and my parents considered all our people family; our door was always open to them." She watched the tower guards rushing toward their posts and the glinting light from the ships below. "Have you ever cared for anyone but yourself?" she asked.

He rolled his eyes to her question and followed the seagulls with a finger and noticed they were all flying away from the city. A loud moaning rumbled through the air, and a painful screech caused them to cover their ears. Ula came up from beneath the city, arrows and harpoons protruding from her body. Her bloodied claws grabbed on to the walls, digging into the stones and ripping loose chunks of cobblestone. Digging deep, she roared and pulsed with magic. Revitalizing her battered body, she broke free of the chains that were latched to her with harpoons. Free of their grasp, she crawled over the walls into the courtyard and collapsed.

Ahkarad and Sasha raced to the gate to see if they could aid Ula, but they were met with a rumbling and calls for cover.

The ground quaked as fireballs rained down on the concourse, setting fire to the market and residential districts. Cries for aid echoed through the streets, and soldiers rushed to the outer defenses. The warning bells rang out, but the barrier remained down; there was nothing to protect the city from attack. More explosions filled the city, with smoke and ash billowing through the streets.

Ahkarad watched for the glow of the Everset Spire, but nothing happened. The vibrant color remained hollow, and without light, the series of gems that would glow blue and green were a dull gray. Tak stepped through the gate and helped them over the rubble piled at the barracks entrance. She knelt to look them in the eye. "Go to the Bridgeway! Usuara will watch after you." She grabbed their hands and led them toward the undercroft.

Ahkarad stopped and pulled back. "Bridgeway? That is the portcullis to escape the city. Why would we leave? Mother would have your head should she hear your words." He wrenched his hand free and ran through the doors to the concourse. Tak and Sasha did not follow, leaving him to navigate the city alone. His eyes steered away from the people staggering about and the cries of those mourning their fallen loved ones. Burned bodies littered the rubble, and guards attempted to rescue those with a chance of surviving.

He came across Ula on the ground. She had

changed to take the form of a human woman, blood seeping from several wounds along her body. Bits of flesh were missing, and blood soaked her clothes as she struggled to her feet.

"Princeling, I must reach your mother. Will you guide me?" she asked.

Blackened striated lines snaked their way up her neck, spreading in places like a spider's web, weakening her and blackening her eyes. Now blinded, she clutched on to his arm, holding tight. The tremble in her hands made him fearful for his mother and friends.

"I must reach the lady! She must leave before the huntress arrives!" she said.

"Who must leave? Mother? Ula, what do you mean?" he asked.

She remained silent and leaned against him. Her posture slumped lower and lower as they neared the Everset Spire. The streets cleared, and most were already fleeing the city. With a strong jolt, the ground shifted, making the path an incline, but they pressed on. She began coughing and could no longer walk, so she resorted to crawling as they reached the enormous wooden doors to the Spire.

A woman with silver hair and golden eyes, matching what Ahkarad heard of the elves, stood at the Everset Gate. Her silver hair flowed with the rushing current of magic seeping from the Everset Gate. More flaming meteors crashed down across the city, but amid the chaos, she spotted Ula and raced to her side. Tending to her wounds, the elven woman smiled at Ahkarad and focused on the dragon.

"Lady, the huntress has come. We must find allies elsewhere. I-I'm sorry," Ula said.

The woman opened a small gateway of arcane magic, and a man with pale skin and light-blue hair stepped through. He took Ula's arm and helped her through the portal. Her eyes lit up as she looked behind Ahkarad. He turned to see his mother rushing toward them. Though weakened, Ula managed to regain her composure at the sight of Ahkarad's mother.

The queen grabbed Ahkarad and pushed him into the hands of the guards. "Take him to Usuara! I'll—"

The Everset Gate opened, and Ualeon tribesmen poured through, cutting down any that stood in their way. Wearing the mark of the hunt, they were relentless and bloodthirsty. Ahkarad's mother cut down any that came near, but with each passing moment, more flooded in.

The elven woman grabbed her shoulder and looked at Ahkarad. "Massa, my queen! Get him to safety. I will buy your people time."

"No, this is my city, and I will not abandon her. Mel, the council must survive. Go! You will have the aid you seek," Massa said.

The woman refused and formed a barrier around the Everset Spire. She rose to the sky and leveled off the city, buying time for Massa to grab Ahkarad's shoulder and lead him from the square. Soldiers were clashing around every corner, and with no option, she fought any that crossed their path.

One of the tribesmen lunged at her and landed a spear in her side, cutting a deep wound above her hip. She held out her hand, and a flaming sword appeared. With a single swipe, their attacker fell to the ground, but he did not bleed nor burn. Instead, the life drained from his body. He shriveled up like a piece of old rotted fruit. The blade burned brighter until she let go, and it vanished before it could hit the ground.

"You were supposed to leave with Tak and Usuara. Why did you come back?"

Frightened, he hugged her side and dared not look at their surroundings. Fire raged through the streets, and each step brought them closer to an eerie silence. Everyone had fled the city, and they were alone. Tribesmen pounced on any that still moved, cutting the throats of any wounded that still drew breath.

Ahkarad and his mother crossed the Bridgeway but were blocked from their exit to the undercroft. She pulled him close and smiled. The pain from her injury and the situation wore heavy on her face, but she kept a positive tone.

"We must reach the keep, Ahkarad. Do you understand me? Whether I'm with you or not, you must reach Usuara. Do you understand?" she said.

Trembling, he gave an uneasy nod as tears welled in his eyes. "What is happening?" he asked.

She kissed his forehead and rested her chin against the top of his head. While she squeezed, he felt tears land on his head. "Time to go. Stay behind me, and do what I say."

She stood and stuffed a piece of cloth up the side of her armor to stem some of the bleeding. One hand gripped his, and the other held out a sword. They traveled through the alleys until they reached the keep, which was closed off by tribesmen and oathsworn zealots. They would need to find a path through to his chamber. More were entering behind them. With their only escape slowly being closed off, she sprang into action, pushing Ahkarad down behind a pile of rubble.

She cut through the first she came to. An arrow dug into her armor but didn't find flesh. She cut down the next with a slash, cutting his sword in half and gashing his face, and she used the broken tip as a throwing knife and hurled it through one of the archers. More flooded the courtyard, and she cut them down, taking a slash to her back and being run through by a spear. She broke the handle and fought on.

The city shifted again, causing some of the invaders to fall over the side into the bay and others to lose their footing. She used this to her advantage and cut down the few that remained between her and the keep.

Ahkarad ran to her side and helped her to the doors, but they were blocked by the remnants of a crumbled tower. Behind them were more tribesmen. She pushed him down behind her and cut down any that got within arm's reach. She took an arrow to the chest, and it found its mark and dug deep. The ragged gasps for air showed her failing strength, but she defended Ahkarad; on one knee, she fought to keep them at bay.

She turned to him, and through shallow breaths, she smiled. "I love you, son, remember that. Do not forget your duty."

She stood and reached to the sky. "Mothers, honor our bargain." She reached out to him, and he felt everything fade, like he drifted off to sleep. Her skin wore away like dust blown about on a strong wind, and her eyes grew dark. Arrows struck her back, but she smiled at him. "Goodbye, little one."

He blinked and found himself sitting on the shore of Haberndis, a small island across the bay from his home. Netoma crashed into the sea. The shockwave sent tall waves across the bay and caused the ground to shake. The boats reached the docks, and Usuara raced up to him. Ahkarad could not hear his words, and his eyes were fixed on the pile rubble that once floated in the sky. He felt nothing other than a cold empty feeling that wore thin against his heavy thoughts.

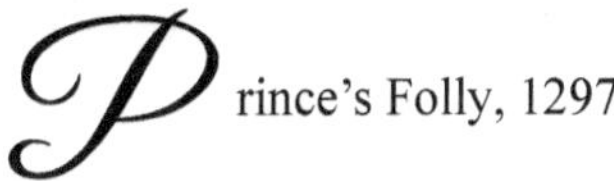

rince's Folly, 1297

SUNLIGHT PEEKING OVER THE HORIZON FORCED Ahkarad's eyes open. Cold iron against his skin sent goose bumps across his body, and the awful taste of stale beer and vomit hung in his mouth. The aroma of urine and sea air crawled up his nose, a stark reminder of the night before and his habitual bad decisions. His hands failed to work properly because he remained extremely intoxicated. The eleven years of waiting on the island of Haberndis wore down all the Ualeon refugees, more so to Ahkarad than most. What started as a small village with a single dock when they arrived became a moderately large town, and over the years, some of the Ualeon sought a life elsewhere and abandoned the hope of their king taking up the mantle.

Finally able to move, he stretched and swung back and forth until he reached the bars to the cage next to his and grabbed the pipe from his recently deceased cellmate. Being placed in a gibbet became such a common occurrence they built an additional cage just for him. Using matches from his inner pocket, he lit the pipe and took a long drag, billowing smoke from his nose and mouth after each pull.

His feet were numb, and seagulls started their morning calls while drifting on the warm currents of sea air. He surveyed the nearby market like he did every other morning and smiled at the angered looks he received from his people. Some would even spit or throw rocks at him when they passed.

Usuara came as he did every morning, standing below him with crossed arms and a frown. "Are ya ready for the magistrate?" he asked.

Ahkarad ignored him and carried on with his drunken stupor. After a bit of silence from both men he started singing, "Wake up, fair mothers, and prepare your sons. Hide your children, the day has come. With sunless volleys, the world is gone. Through Light's victory, the mothers have won."

Usuara sat back on a bench and watched as Ahkarad soiled himself again, urine dripping down his leg and leaving a pool below his cage. The assault on the senses forced Usuara to cover his mouth and nose. The sight of this caused Ahkarad to laugh, but his amusement faded quickly when a man wearing an elegant outfit, polished shoes, and a well-crafted silk robe walked cautiously toward him. As he approached, other unlucky prisoners let out whistles and called for his attention, but he made a line for Ahkarad's cage. In Ahkarad's mind, he looked exceptionally weak for a human, and he laughed at the thought of some well-to-do noble trying to convince him of some grandiose plan or scheme.

"Ahkarad Dres," the man said. His gentle tone carried the weight of nobility. "I am Andros Venae, and I have come to offer you a place at my table—absolution, as some might see it."

He ignored the man and started singing from his cage, "Bring down the harbor of mist, take us from your loving home. Fear not the wayward son, fear not, for the mothers won." He coughed through another drag from the stolen pipe.

"Ahkarad, I knew your mother. Would you offer me the same kindness she did many years ago, or would you rather your legacy be swinging in a cage as a drunkard?" Andros asked.

Ahkarad's eyes narrowed on the man. "Why would I care? What can you offer that I haven't already given away?"

"Because no one is beyond saving, even someone as blind and selfish as you. Again, I offer a chance to be more than a fool sitting in his filth."

"Do you know the origin of the Windsong?" Ahkarad asked.

Andros shook his head and waved for the magistrate's men to come over and lower Ahkarad's cage. The whining of the chains and screeching of gears forced him to wait until it came to rest in the muck that filled the streets.

"When Nyasom came and graced my ancestors with his wondrous presence, he chose to tell us of the doom our people would face. What did they do? Nothing. They did not plan, nor did they ask for guidance. They drank and sang their worries away, and the way I see it—*hic!*—I'm living up to those expectations."

He pulled a flask from a secret pocket and took a long swig. "Wake, fair mothers, and prepare your—"

A man standing atop his cage tilted it over, causing it to crash into the ground. Mud with an awful mixture of wet earth and refuse silenced his abhorrent singing voice. They rolled it over and pulled him from the opening, dragging his limp body to be seen by the magistrate.

His head bobbed about, but it was too heavy to lift in his current state. He wanted to struggle, but the alcohol and being stuffed in a cage that wasn't designed for comfort caused his body to struggle with himself rather than the men carrying him. They plopped him down and tied his chains around a hitching post alongside the horses. One of the men doused him in water with buckets until the dirt washed away and the smell weakened enough for their eyes to stop watering.

On the boardwalk, a modestly dressed man wearing farm clothes and tattered old boots waited. He carried the Holy Book of the Divine, and concern wore heavy over his eyes.

"How many times must they drag you before me, young man?" Magistrate Yunis asked.

"Until you've had enough, I guess," Ahkarad said.

His words were slurred, and he stared at the planks of wood because lifting his head proved a greater challenge than he anticipated. His current level of sobriety did not aid matters.

"No soul is a lost cause, no matter how many fights or drunken rampages you are jailed for. I will hold true to my word and keep hope that you will find the light, but your actions warrant punishment. Andros?" Magistrate Yunis asked.

"Yes sir?"

"By the right of my station, I remand him to your custody, and should he commit such an act again, my hand will be forced. Do you know what comes next, Ahkarad?" he asked.

"You hang me, and I'm done with all of you?" Ahkarad asked.

Yunis grabbed him by the chin and lifted his head to look in his eyes as they spoke. "Your life might not mean anything to you, and given your actions, I have little to argue with, but look at what you have done to your own people. They deserve a king, not a boy chasing death at the bottom of a bottle."

He dropped Ahkarad's head, and his face planted in the mud once more. Ahkarad responded with a chuckle before pissing himself again.

"The next time you are dragged before me, I will be forced to send you below. Sixty years of hard labor. Ahkarad, please, do what's best for your people." Yunis slammed his gavel on the banister and returned the simple wooden hammer to his pocket.

He climbed onto a wagon and drove toward the fields, leaving Andros and Ahkarad to their business.

"Wake, fair mothers, and prepare your sons. Hide your children, the day has come," Ahkarad resumed. "With sunless volleys, the world has gone. Through Light's victory, the mothers have won."

Andros ordered his guards to haul Ahkarad to the estate on the hill overlooking the town. Before leaving, they pilfered his pockets and removed the three flasks and two pipes he had stashed in different places—and even a knife tied to his leg.

"Today, I feel the heir to house Dres might find himself," Andros said, walking beside the horse carrying a tied-up Ahkarad. "Or tomorrow. I am a patient man, and you are a drunkard. Only one of us will enjoy the afternoon sun." Reaching the outer gates, Andros popped the strap, and Ahkarad flopped onto the ground. "Will you speak now, or will this take a bit more effort?"

Ahkarad spat on the man's robe and took a drunken swing at him but missed his mark and landed in the dirt.

"I see. Work it is," Andros said.

Andros guided him to a rock wall just off the main house. A pickaxe and wheelbarrow sat by the section being excavated. Andros motioned for Ahkarad and shoved the pick in his hands.

"You will dig. And when you are sober enough to talk or wish to rest, I will be right here enjoying a glass of wine."

He sat and watched as Ahkarad hammered away at the wall. He did not speak, only tore piece by piece until his arms were too heavy to lift and the sun sank low on the horizon. He sat in the grass and watched Andros smiling back at him. Ahkarad huffed. With chains on his wrists and ankles, he could go no farther than Andros intended from the anchor in the center of the lawn he was bound to.

As time went on, flickering lights rose from the ground and bobbed in the light of the full twin moons, each holding one end of the sky and drowning out the faint bit of sunlight remaining before night overtook the day. Andros still sat just out of range of Ahkarad's reach, eating a meal of pheasant and roasted potatoes, the smell of which taunted Ahkarad and caused his stomach to rumble. His pride forced him to ignore the need for food, and he drew his focus to the ships drifting across the sea.

"Would you like a bite? Or will you pretend food wouldn't ease that fiery hunger gnawing at your stomach?" Andros asked.

Ahkarad grumbled and turned away, stabbing the pickaxe into his chains in a futile attempt at breaking free. Each swing glanced off and caused no visible damage to the links. He swung again and again to no end. Eventually, he threw the pick and pulled on the chains. Even the strength of such a mighty Ualeon proved feeble, and the anchor held. Each time he fought, it wore his body down, and before long, he slumped over, holding his swirling head in his hands.

"You haven't been sober in so long. I remember those days. Would be best if you ate something, or had a bit of water," Andros said.

"When I get free, I'll tear your body limb from limb. And when I'm through, this place will be a pile of rubble," Ahkarad said.

Andros laughed and carried a plate of food to him, standing within reach of Ahkarad's hands. He placed the food on the ground at his feet and turned to leave. Ahkarad sprang forth and placed the chain around his neck and yanked, but Andros didn't budge. He turned and used a scepter from within his robe to strike Ahkarad's chest. He swung again and launched him into the pile of rocks and held it over Ahkarad's face.

"Do you never tire of being tossed about? All those bar fights and reckless tussles with the locals, and still you act like you have some skill. I have fought warriors with such ferocity that your childish thrashing would be swatted away like an unruly pup," Andros said. Andros stowed the scepter and offered a hand to Ahkarad. "Will you learn from my example, or should I put you back in that cage and try again tomorrow?"

With his pride wounded, Ahkarad accepted his hand but struck Andros's chin with a closed fist. With a loud crack, Ahkarad's hand stopped like he'd struck a piece of solid iron, sending pain rippling up his arm.

"Oh dear. I will send for the healer. What part of being a magister do you not understand? Protective spells last for a very long time, and without training, breaching such spells is impossible." He snapped a finger, and the chains vanished; even the bindings on his wrists and ankles were gone. "It is refreshing to find one so naive as yourself. Come along. I will have food brought to you while we wait on the healer."

The plate from earlier vanished, along with the bottle of wine. Even the rock wall vanished into the air. Before him, there was now an open lawn with housing for servants.

"You're an illusionist?" Ahkarad asked.

Andros laughed and snapped his fingers, and a cat appeared on the floor. "That is an illusion. This, on the other hand . . ." He slammed his hands together and pulled them apart, revealing strings of purple and blue light. Each time he pulled against one, the room would change. The chairs and tables—even the windows and doors—changed, until he forced both hands back together and the room returned to normal.

"I am second only to Omvena, Headmaster to the Magisterium. Some call him Carsis. Through the great seal, we can manipulate anything in the physical world. Healers do much the same by mending flesh but are limited by the nature of their magic."

An old man bearing the marks of the northern tribes carried a plate of food and placed it on the table. The servants bore tribal markings and tattoos and scars matching those of a criminal background. Even his maid was a Sethyn. Her scales were scarred, and she was missing a large portion of her tail, but she gently applied a salve to his hand before wrapping it with a splint.

"Tomorrow, it will be as good as new. Are you willing to speak now, or should I return to a more focused set of bindings?" Andros asked.

Ahkarad, still stuffing his face with one hand, paused. "Speak your mind. Not like I have any other choice."

"I want to offer you a place here. That is, until you no longer require caging every night. I will provide clothes, food, and a place to sleep."

Through a full mouth, Ahkarad asked, "What do you gain from such an arrangement?"

Andros walked to a bookshelf and retrieved a journal with a simple leather binding and a neatly tied bow. He flipped through until he reached the final page. A note from Queen Massa, his mother. Ahkarad recognized the handwriting and ran his fingers over the words.

"She was a dear friend. I would have been there, but I was detained with an important matter in Iskal. When I learned of her fate . . ." He closed the journal, tied the laces back, and gently placed it back on the shelf. His voice cracked slightly, but he regained composure and carried on, "It pained me greatly. She would never forgive me if I allowed the most important thing in her life to be another laborer toiling away in the mines because no one cared enough to save him."

Ahkarad swallowed the last bit of food and looked over Andros's face. He didn't appear to be lying, and what could a man with nothing lose? He could feel the bones in his hand shifting, the pain of which caused him to wince. "Is there a catch? Or is that all?"

"Oh, Ahkarad. Some may want to be at your side —a king would be invaluable as an ally—but I am not a lord and do not need such things to make my worth. I ask that you only see my actions and judge whether I am worth listening to," Andros said.

He waved Ahkarad to the stairs and led him to a room. Runes were carved into the floor at each doorway, and there was a glowing light at its center. A change of clothes lay on the bed, waiting for him.

"I will ask that you bathe before bed. In the morning, we will see what worth is in my actions." Andros took a few steps and turned to Ahkarad, who was still removing his filthy clothes. "And, from before, the Windsong was written because no one can change fate, and it would seem your people knew that better than Emual and Nyasom. Even the greatest of things must end, and they were willing to accept that. Get some rest, and tomorrow, we will start our work."

A Bottle of Sand

Morning came, and Ahkarad sat staring at the sunrise. To his right were the runes over his doorway and a prison to hold him from more bad decisions. They were detailed and held the hum of magic within them. The day before, he did not know what he could trust, so he waited patiently for Andros to gather him. When the sun slipped through the blinds, he heard Andros greeting the servants, and it oddly sounded as though they were joining him for breakfast.

After the aroma of bacon and the sweet smell of blueberry muffins tugged at his stomach, he got the nerve to cross the rune and risk the punishment. He stopped at the threshold and took an uneasy step across. The rune did nothing. It still held the same low hum of magic, but he remained unharmed. Laughing to himself, he turned, only to be facing Andros wearing an apron and holding a plate of food.

"Breakfast, sir. Are you alright?" he asked.

Disheveled, Ahkarad tip-toed out of his room. He glanced around and took the plate from Andros's hand. "I thought the door was a trap or some barrier designed to keep me inside."

Andros laughed. "No. When I removed your chains, it would have been a harsh thing to keep you imprisoned. So, if you wish to leave, then do so." He walked down the stairs. "But eat first. You will need your strength for the walk back to town."

Ahkarad followed Andros to the dining hall and found the servants eating, with him serving their food. Ahkarad took a seat and watched as Andros filled glasses and made sure their needs were met.

"A lord that serves his servants?" Ahkarad asked.

The servants laughed and whispered among themselves. One whispered into Andros's ear, causing him to laugh uncontrollably.

"Yes. Would you not do the same for someone that tends to your needs? They care for my every whim, and that can be a hard task at the best of times, so every morning, I tend to theirs."

He filled a cup with juice and appeared beside Ahkarad to take his empty plate. "Could also be that I have always been a magister and only became a lord because it was pushed on me." He appeared by another servant to fill her glass with milk. "Who knows? But they are worth my effort, and you will learn the worth of a life in time."

With breakfast winding down, the staff started their day and went about their tasks. Ahkarad watched Andros eat his food after making sure all were served before him.

"What is it, Ahkarad? You seem as though someone stabbed you in your sleep."

"You are like no noble I have met, tending to your staff and caring for the lives of criminals. Why are you not dining with lords and rubbing elbows at banquets?" Ahkarad asked.

"To be honest, that bores me. Anly, my oldest son, prefers that life, yet he still cares for the people of the northern valleys. He is the lord now, and I am a simple man making his way through the world. Given where you were in your youth, I would think this lifestyle would suit you?"

Ahkarad slid his empty cup aside and stared at the bottle of wine just out of reach. "If I said yes, would that change anything?"

"No. I will still place as much effort in you as an old friend put in me, damned fool he may have been, but he saw what did not. Your clothes are waiting upstairs. We will be waiting by the carriage, when you are ready, of course," Andros said.

Ahkarad found his garments lying on the bed: pants, a shirt of fine silk, and a robe of delicate fur. Each piece was made with care, expertly sewn with golden thread, and his shoes were polished to a mirror shine. The feeling of such soft material at his fingertips reminded him of what he used to wear. In a box to the side sat an old pair of work clothes, ragged and rough but clean. Made of whatever rags were on hand and with many loose threads, it offered more utility, even if it was a bit unkempt and poor.

As the fine silk drew across his skin, it became clear he could not wear such things. He grabbed the tattered rags from the box and left the expensive clothing behind, resting folded neatly on the bed. Out the window, he could see a well-dressed Andros waiting by the carriage and offering carrots to the horses. When coming down the stairs, he saw the bottle of wine still resting on the table. The desire tugged at his mind, so he filled a flask with enough to sip on and slipped out the door.

"About time. Would seem our day will be a bit more complicated. Our presence has been requested at the harbor on a matter of utmost importance."

They climbed in, and the carriage bounced along the dirt road toward town. Inside, Ahkarad watched the shore through the trees and shrubs along the road. He felt the flask pressing against his chest. He desperately wanted to take a sip, but he knew it would require a moment when Andros was preoccupied.

"Not sure why you chose rags over such finery, but who am I to judge?" Andros said.

Sweat formed on Ahkarad's brow, and he could taste the sweet notes of grape on his lips. He felt the need to ease the racing thoughts and horrific images flashing in his mind. More beads of sweat formed on his forehead, and his eyes darted back and forth. Memories of burning bodies and the screams of children buried in rubble crawled back in. His heart began pounding in his chest, and the ringing in his ear echoed the drums of war.

He reached for his pocket and the only relief he knew, when a hand clutched his wrist.

"Do you want to talk about it? I know it can be difficult to fight a war no one can see. Let me help you." Andros changed seats and put an arm around Ahkarad. "It will be a while longer before we reach the harbor, and we both have time. Tell me, what weighs so heavily on your mind?"

Ahkarad felt uncomfortable. His emotions were

never of much concern, but Andros cared, the first to care. Pulled back to the moment, he smiled, took a handkerchief from his pocket, and wiped the sweat away. "You worry too much. I'm fine."

He returned to watching the shore, and Andros let him be and returned to his seat. Through the window, trees turned to buildings, and they were now within the harbor. Ahkarad saw this from afar each morning when he woke. Never being too interested, he kept to the tavern and inn.

Shouting intensified, and soon, the angry mob could be heard lashing out at something, but from his angle, it remained unclear what caused such a commotion. They exited the carriage to Yunis holding nearly the entire city at bay. Behind him was a group of Sethyn refugees. Like many of the people, they were displaced by the conflict in the west and sought a safe haven.

"Everyone, return to your homes!" Yunis said, but yelling over the crowd of angry villagers got him nowhere and only seemed to force him back farther, almost shoving him into the water.

Ahkarad watched Andros move out of sight. The illusionist took a pendant from his pocket and held it aloft. With a few words, a storm cloud formed above the group of people, and he let a shower of torrential rain pelt them. He snapped the fingers on his other hand, and thunder tore through the air around them, sounding as though it cracked the very earth beneath their feet. This caused the crowd to disperse in a panic and return to their homes and businesses.

"Now, let's see to our new arrivals, shall we?" Andros said.

They reached the small raft of broken planks and

sticks—anything they could cobble together quickly to escape the fighting. Before them stood a woman and six children, none old enough to care for themselves other than the middle-aged woman. From Ahkarad's perspective, they weren't worth the effort.

"Welcome. It has come to my attention that you would like to join our community. As a start, could you share your name?" Andros asked.

"Meteri. They are hungry. Could you spare some food?" she asked.

Andros whistled to his assistant and pointed her to the town. "My companion will return shortly. What brings you to our shore—other than the obvious, of course?"

"Our home was burned. I helped as many as I could, but few survived," she said.

The children huddled closer, avoiding eye contact and shying away from Ahkarad as he came closer.

"Do you mind?" she said in a forceful tone to Ahkarad. Pulling back, she looked to Andros. "Sorry, I mean no disrespect, but they fear the horned one. He shares the same look as those that burned our homes and murdered our kin."

Andros brushed Ahkarad's shoulder, and with a tilt of his head, he motioned him back. "You aren't from High Rock, are you?" he asked.

She became fidgety and glared at him. "Correct, but it was their home. I do not seek shelter, only to aid them. Will you help them?" She stepped out from the group and up to Andros. "I am an alchemist, trained—"

Andros cut her off and put an arm around her shoulder. "Yes, I am quite aware of who you are.

Once you have eaten, and they are ready, you and I will have a proper conversation."

She held a look of unease and smiled when looking back at the children. The assistant returned with food and carted them off to the estate. He held them outside and allowed them the freedom to roam without supervision.

Ahkarad stood in the doorway, holding a hand over his jacket pocket and imagining the comfort a single sip would bring. The thought of such a thing became just as intoxicating as the wine at that moment, and he scanned for suspecting eyes. Alone, he slipped behind the servants' building and pulled the flask from his pocket. His hand trembled as he turned the cap and raised it to his lips.

"Shame can make us do horrible things," Meteri said.

Before the taste hit his lips, he lowered the flask and found her sitting tucked away in a corner with her back to the wall. Dried tears left her fur matted, and her plate of food remained full; she hadn't eaten a bite.

"I just needed to take a sip. Nothing shameful in that. What about you, huddled away from your kin?" Ahkarad asked, his voice wavering. He tucked the flask back into his pocket.

She smiled at him and climbed to her feet, sliding her back up the wall. "I spent days on a raft bringing those children here. I needed a moment to myself, but you, the tremors and the sweat on your brow tells me."

"Nothing, I'm fine, really. Just trying to avoid upsetting the little ones." He gave a pat to the flask now back in his pocket. "I'll leave you to it." Before he could walk away, she put a hand on his forearm.

"Andros, he has faults, and a kind heart is one of his most glaring." She peeked at the children sleeping in the sun. Her green eyes narrowed to slits, sparking fear in him, but he pushed it aside to sate his curiosity. "Are you another of his lost causes? A king lost in a bottle?"

He stepped back. "How do you know I'm a king?"

She smiled at him—inviting and warm and nothing like what he heard of their kind. He'd heard what monsters the Sethyn were, but he felt intrigued by her. His desire to drink faded, but his heart still raced. She resembled what Ula looked like in human form, except for scales covering her whole body.

"The horns. Tales recount the exploits of a gold-horned Ualeon king. I would like to hear your story," she said.

"Another time. I must return before he sends a search party, you know, his faults and all," Ahkarad said.

She didn't wait for him to move and pulled him in for a kiss, but he shrugged her off and left her in the shadows behind the building. He found another secluded place where he could get a little taste of relief. Tucked away within a small storeroom, he pulled the flask from his pocket and raised it to his lips. The door opened, and Meteri stood with a devilish look in her eye. She stepped inside and turned the lock with a fire deep within her eyes. Ahakrad felt concerned, short-lived as it may have been. She swatted the flask away and knocked him off the stool he sat on.

She didn't speak and grabbed him, digging her claws into his back and kissing him. The passion burned hot; biting, clawing, and passionate kissing led to a moment of bliss for them both. He'd never experienced the love of a woman of any kind, but Meteri showed her experience and extracted as much pleasure as possible. Using their clothes as a pillow, she climbed on top of him and performed acts he only fantasized about. Their blissful time kept them locked away for almost an hour, and she clawed his body bad enough to draw blood. When the fires cooled and the passion reduced to a low simmer, she lay with her head against his chest and dug the tip of her claw into his skin, just enough to cause discomfort but not enough to leave a scar.

"I could get used to this. Hoping you don't have a lady in your life. Or two?" she asked.

"Burned too many bridges for anyone to take an interest. Guess you had me pegged; I am a bit of a lost cause." He grabbed her hand and held it over his heart. "How exactly do you know Andros?"

"Ha, how do I know him? My father trained alongside him. Both took separate paths. Andros became what you see today, and my father became our village seer and served his people," she said.

"Do they keep in touch?" he asked.

She scooted up and kissed him. "The rebels came a few years ago and asked for my father, Aka. When he greeted them, they forced him to the ground and removed his head. I was gathering herbs, and upon my return, I found my village burning and my family slain. They moved from village to village like this until my people were nearly wiped out." She slid her hand down and lifted the flask. Giving the cap a sniff, she giggled. "Oh, Andros, never change."

She turned it upside down and poured its contents onto the floor beside them. Ahkarad cupped his hands, but sand poured from its spout. He panicked and became visibly ill, his hands shook, and his mind clouded.

"Why? Why would you do that? I needed just a sip. I just needed one sip." Tremors spread down his arms to his fingers, and he lay face down on the ground, "I don't want to remember . . ." He looked up to the rack and saw a bottle of cooking wine and pulled it down. Popping the cork, he placed it to his lips, but she held the bottom and forced it down.

"If you take a sip, it will end badly for you. You are in the house of a very devious man. Why not put it away and enjoy each other's company? Maybe it will help with the memories that trouble you?"

He could smell the sweet aroma and the taste so close, he felt the rush without having a sip. Behind her, the visage of his mother formed. She lay on the cold ground covered in blood. She reached for him, and with outstretched hands, she beckoned for him to rescue her. The whisper returned, "Payment is due."

He closed his eyes as her voice became louder. "Please, please save me," he whimpered.

The reverberations of her voice were deafening until Meteri pulled the bottle away, and it shattered against the wall. She kissed him again and pulled his head against her chest.

"Believe me when I say Andros has placed a spell on you. Every bottle you touch will be filled with sand. Try them, or you could follow me, and I can help you forget what haunts you. Your choice, Ahkarad, king of nothing."

She pulled his tunic over her naked body and left carrying her clothes under her arm, leaving him in the storeroom and making her way to the bedrooms above. Halfway up the stairs, she glared at him through the door and looked up the stairs and back to him. Giving a devious smile, she spun around and left up the stairs. He pulled his pants on and chased up the stairs after her, leaving the flask and bottles of wine on the floor.

CHAPTER 27

S teward of Bosa, 1308

ENDLESS WAVES ROLLED OVER ONE AFTER THE OTHER. The shore had become a peaceful place for Ahkarad to think. In the years since he sobered up, he'd developed a love for the calming monotony of waves rolling in each evening. A lone set of steps meandered up the shore behind him, and Ahkarad moved over to allow Andros to sit. They would both sit for hours watching the sunset and stars claim the night sky. Without saying a word, Ahkarad picked up a smoothed stone and skipped it across the water, breaking the waves with each hop. He picked up another and didn't acknowledge Andros sitting beside him, just kept his focus on the hills barely visible across the sea. His horns had changed color and were a symbol of his coming of age, still bearing the golden tips from his youth but cracked about midway up and missing chunks toward the top.

Andros joined in skipping rocks, tossing a few

before turning his focus back. "I had forgotten how peaceful life could be." He patted Ahkarad's shoulder. "When I was a boy, we spent our evenings on this beach, skipping rocks and daydreaming about the lands beyond. Seems like a lifetime ago, and, even now, I have trouble remembering their names. They have since moved on or perished to the harshness of the land."

He gripped the cane sitting between them. The crystal handle at the top glistened with the glow of arcane energy.

"Will you listen to reason today, or am I to hear more of your attempts to forfeit your kingdom. Your people will not accept such a thing," Andros said.

Ahkarad stood and hurled another stone with an arc. It splashed in the distance, and he grabbed another.

"I just want to live. No kingdom. Andros"—he threw the next stone—"haven't I caused my people enough pain? We have no kingdom, no throne, and I am no king. What is there to forfeit?" He smiled at Andros, warm and peaceful but carrying a bit of reverence, something he had been without since birth yet came into with age. "If I hold on, they all suffer. I must go my own way, make my path. You once offered to rule in my stead. Did you mean that?"

"Ahkarad, do you hear yourself? Does your lineage not matter? And what of your people? I cannot abandon the people of Lonstap either. If this were a real offer, I would reject it outright and have the healers check your head for serious wounds. We can work together and find aid, build an army and retake—"

"Retake what? A mountain of rubble where my

mother's remains lay buried? The people turned on their queen and sank their shining star to the bottom of the sea. No, I want a life free of it. I want to blend into the crowd and be another of my people. What life would it be for them to think I want that role? Andros, being king isn't what I want, not now."

Andros reached up with his cane and tapped the gold-tipped horns on Ahkarad's head. "Those will never allow you to blend in. Ahkarad, I would gladly advise you on where to go next, but I will not watch my friend give away his legacy. I will not stand by as you throw away your responsibility."

Ahkarad shook his head and walked farther up the beach. The tide would soon return, but for now, he admired stars sparkling off the wet rocks. The moons would crest the horizon soon and block out the beauty of a clear night sky. He picked up a few rocks and tossed them out far enough that he could not see the ripples of their landing.

"Why did you pull me from that cage?" Ahkarad asked.

"I saw a young man, the same as I was. One with a great burden but without focus, a ship lost in a cloudy sea. I never wanted to command the vessel, I only wished to be a guide to bring you home."

They walked the narrow path under the cliffs and, in the distance, several Tahnroha—great whales— sang their song as they passed through the shallows. Covered in flakes of Ahn, the passing of the great beasts left behind natural glowstones. Their glimmering light shined through the waves and appeared to be a mirror image of the sky above.

Ahkarad followed their movement until they sank into the depths, and he returned to tossing more rocks into the water. He looked off to the horizon. The water lapping at his toes held a familiar chill, and he could almost smell the seasons changing on the winds rolling across the bay from Tania. The bells rang out, a warning of the coming tide, and the lighthouse sparked, shining beams of light into the surrounding sea.

"The water will rise soon. Don't you think we should make our way back?" Andros asked.

"No, we have a few moments yet. That was my home. Years ago, Netoma could be seen from this point. I came here long before that day. Yunis invited my mother in thanks for her aid in Haberndis's feud with the Order. I stood there and watched my city float on the horizon, thinking of all that would be mine, but now it's just another hill fading at the water's edge."

"Do you truly wish to be rid of your legacy? Do you not care for the plight of your people? More importantly, what would Sasha and Usuara say to this?" Andros asked.

"Andros, be honest. I'm no king. and of my people, none remain that followed her. Would you have me cut a bloody path across the kingdom and forsake the honored deeds of the tribes? No, I'll not spill their blood. As my only act as King of Tania, I declare Andros Venae Steward of Bosa until myself or a proper heir returns to claim her."

Ahkarad sat patiently as the water rose a little with each passing moment. The caress of Andros's hand slipped around his arm, and he heard the calm, yet frustrated tone in his voice. "Do you hear yourself. If I were to accept, it would start a war—a bloody one—and what end would that serve?" He pressed his head against Ahkarad's shoulder and let out a sigh. "When have I ever talked you out of a bad decision?"

Ahkarad smiled and faced him. "There was this time involving a cage and a lot of whiskey." They shared a laugh before making their way to the path back to his estate. Ahkarad paused at the hill to look at the silhouette of Netoma through the light of the two moons. The feelings of doubt crawled back in as his mother's words echoed in his ear, but they faded quickly as Andros gave another tug on his arm, bringing him back to the moment.

"We all have ghosts. Dinner should be waiting. Best not to let it get cold," Andros said.

The city grew over time and became a bustling port for all traveling the region. The trade routes reopened, and the waterways were flooded with travelers and adventure-seekers alike. The modest estate of Andros more resembled a castle than a small estate. Ahkarad called this place home, yet he longed to journey to a land far away. His wardrobe had changed over time and resembled that of his youth, consisting of fine fur and silk. Ornate jewels and precious metals were used as simple decorations, and his room was decorated with such finery that he often avoided his bed and slept on a cot in a spare room off his wing of the house.

The dining hall smelled of roast boar and duck, while other decadent foods were carted out. They could choose anything among the lavishly prepared meal. Ahkarad tore loose a piece of meat and grabbed a few rolls before carrying his food outside to eat under the stars.

His priceless dining utensils and gold-trimmed

goblet were a stark contrast to the wooden table the servants used for their meals. Splintered and cracked, the wood had sat outside in the elements for decades, yet it held together. He pulled a small book from the inner pocket of his shirt and flipped to the most recently folded corner.

Engrossed, he flipped through while eating and hardly looked up other than to greet the passing servants. He poured water into an old mug he left sitting upside down on the bricks beside the door. After his meal, a maid collected the dining ware and left him to study. At times, Ahkarad would look up at the guards and think about their situation but would return to his book again with little else to add to the matter. Hours rolled by, and, soon, the candles burned out, and the moonlight drowned out the light from the glowstone sconces.

"Will you be sleeping in your room tonight or should I request that your cot be moved out here?" a voice asked.

Ahkarad turned and saw Andros stepping out into the courtyard. He'd changed into his evening attire, prepared for bed.

"I could just as easily sleep without a cot. Those fine linens feel harsh to my skin, but could I ask something?" Ahkarad asked.

"Feel free. Have I ever spurned any of your questions? Even those from your formative years,?" Andros said, snickering.

"If I wanted to join the Legion and be treated as a simple soldier, would you object?" Ahkarad asked.

Andros stepped out and sat down opposite of him and ran his hand over the table, small pieces of wood catching slightly against his skin. "I will need to have a new table crafted. This one has seen its use. But to what you asked, I would plead that my friend reconsider. I am not like the other nobles of Empryss. They will see a savage beast and not the man you truly are."

Ahkarad shifted his weight and pulled something from his pocket, sliding a requisition sheet across the table. "All I need to do is turn this in, and I'm on my way. Would be a great help if you would put in a word. I've thought about this, and after all the pain and all the heartbreak I've caused my people, they do not deserve me as a king. There is no other path. I cannot stay here, nor can I return to the lands of my ancestors."

Andros took Ahkarad's hand and looked into his eyes. "You were never one to take advice, but tonight, think about this. I'll sign it, but know this is a mistake to me." He squeezed Ahkarad's hand and closed his eyes. "If only I could understand what truly pains you. Do not remain closed off forever, old friend." He patted Ahkarad's cheek and signed the paper. "Goodnight. Maybe in the morning, you will rethink this. Or not. But either way, sleep well."

He walked back into the hall, turning and gripping the ornate gold handle while standing halfway inside. "Promise me one thing: do not forget all that you have become over these past few years. It would be a shame for you to abandon the honest sweet man you've grown into."

Ahkarad gave a nod and returned to his book. Andros shut the door, and a silence fell over the lawn. The servants were in bed, and Andros would have his nightcap. Ahkarad heard a person whistling outside the walls. He stepped through the side gate and found Sasha sitting just off the road.

He sat beside her and put an arm over her shoulder, but she pulled away, putting a bit of distance between them. Her cold response revealed that she already knew. Placing both hands on his knees, he took a deep breath and waited for her to speak.

"Usuara said you plan on giving up the kingdom? That you want to join the Legion and walk away from who you are! Like when you claimed Meteri could be trusted, that it was love? How did that turn out?" Sasha asked.

He smiled and tried again to hug her, but she resisted, forcing him to face her. The fury of such a small person was cute to most, but Ahkarad knew better than to trifle with her when she retained a foul mood.

"It was love, but not every relationship ends with old age and rocking chairs." He put a hand on her knee. "I never wanted to rule, I just wanted the decadence and perks. I never cared for my people, and now, when I want to give them a future—hope— it is seen as a slight," Ahkarad said.

She slapped him, dragging her claws across his cheek and leaving four bloody streaks on his face.

He did not flinch and maintained eye contact with her. "Why does it matter to you? Why do you care if I—"

"Why does it matter?! You're leaving me!" Tears ran down her face, collecting on her chin and dripping from her fur. "No matter how much I needed you, it was him. You chose him over us, him over your people, and now you act like the only thing left behind is useless stones and worthless memories." She slapped him again. "Did I ever matter?"

He grabbed her shoulders, pulling her to his chest. She fought, but he overpowered her and held her tightly. "I'm not leaving you. I will always be there for you. Sasha?" He knelt and looked her in the eyes. "I will always be there for you. Don't forget that."

Gritting her teeth, she sneered at him.

He pulled her against his chest again. "Maybe you are right. Maybe I couldn't see what was in front of me for those years, but right now, you do matter, and no matter what you think, you—and even the old man—matter to me."

Her eyes softened. "Why give away who you are?" Her voice cracked, and she let her arms slip around his waist and pressed her ear to his chest. "She wouldn't have wanted you to abandon everything. *I* don't want you to abandon everything."

He took a deep breath. "Sasha, I can't remain in that shadow forever, but it's time for me to move on, to start a new chapter."

"We could run away. We could sneak onto one of the ships leaving for Oncier tonight, and from there, we could travel to Iskal or Mourningstar. Or we could . . . we could . . . do anything! Please, Ahkarad, can it go back to when it was just us watching the seasons change from the eastern walls?" she asked.

"And what then? We just keep moving? Restless spirits traveling the land without a home? What of Usuara, and what about your dreams of being a member of the Royal Watch? I think we both need to grow up, and, in that, accept our place in the world," he said.

She pushed off him and stormed back toward town, but the pitter-patter of her feet halted when he grabbed the back of her shirt. She struggled against him briefly but gave in and sat in the middle of the dirt path.

"Why does everything have to change? I miss my home, the songs, and the dancing, but most of all, I miss the warmth. Even within Netoma, I was cold, and here, I am freezing. Is it my fault that you want to leave?" she asked.

Ahkarad sat beside her and sighed. The aroma of burned wood filled the air around the city. Fireplaces being lit meant over the coming weeks, the first frost and snow would arrive like clockwork. Ships floating on the bay were small specs in the moonlight, drifting into port before leaving again and vanishing over the horizon to Oncier or Sarntheris. He placed his coat—large enough to be a blanket for her—over her shoulders, but she shrugged it off.

"Did any of it matter? Did you ever feel the way I did?" she asked.

He draped it back over her and kissed her forehead, drying her tears with a cloth napkin he pulled from his pocket. "We both know the answer to that. I was wrong for the way I treated you, and you know I would take it back if I could."

She slapped his hand away and growled at him. Without words, she slung the coat at his feet and walked away, tossing a sealed note back to him. Before he could collect it and speak, she vanished into the night.

Wiping the dust from his pants, he walked the winding path back to the estate and slipped back in the side gate, waving to the guards playing their card games in the tower. He sat on the bench once more, holding the note upright and turning it on its ends while staring at his name scribbled on the outside. He felt an unnatural chill slip through, and with it, the glowstones were drained of their magic. Even the moonlight pulled back at the presence he felt. He placed the note on the table and looked at the guards still laughing at their game, but he could not hear their words, only the calm whisper of a person outside the gate.

A Wolvar woman. At first, he thought it to be Sasha returned, but as he neared the gate, he noticed the frail, old woman more closely. She was missing fur in patches, and she hunched over while walking the path between the city and the cemetery. She looked at him, and through milky-white eyes she smiled and waved at him, her eyes focused on something over his shoulder. He turned to see what her eyes were fixated on, but she, too, vanished. All that remained of his visitor rolled on the breeze as a whisper on the wind—too distorted to make out, broken up with laughter. He slipped inside and made his way to the cot, placing the note in his jacket pocket before turning in for the night.

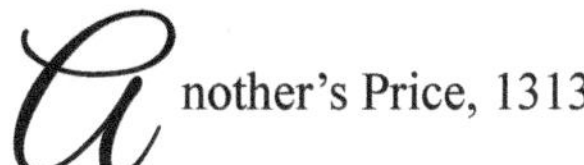

nother's Price, 1313

AHKARAD SAT BY THE CAMPFIRE. HIS UNIT CAMPED on the edge of Empryss lands, waiting for the order to be given and for their march to begin. Thousands would march down the hills into the valley. Weeks of travel brought the main force of the Empryss Legion to the border of Tania, facing only token forces of rebels leading up to their current position. Lonstap held strategic significance as the convergence point for the Legion forces and would be the first true conflict of the war.

He spent hours staring into the crackling flames, watching the flickering embers fade into ash and flutter back down to the ground. Turning his knife into a log at his feet, Ahkarad felt the warmth of a spring breeze at his back. His mind drifted to moments before he left the city. Usuara and Andros bid him farewell, but Sasha didn't bother coming or sending word. They hadn't spoken in years, only exchanging glances if they crossed paths. On the breeze, he heard a whisper, but he blocked it out and focused on carving a hole into the log.

"Must've been something, huh? Come on, big guy, tell me, was she that good in bed?"

Narothen took the seat beside him, feet kicked up and his eyes fixed on the sky. He was unremarkable, even for a Narrissian—pale skin and brown hair, and not even incredibly fit, but, nonetheless, they were a part of the same team, and he could not act on the desire to kill him.

"You know, when this war is over, I'm taking over my father's tavern and just drinking myself into a stupor every night."

Ahkarad turned slightly to remove him from his sight.

Narothen chuckled and hopped up. "You are just what we need! Strong, silent, and broody! Or brooding, whichever of those. We should be drinking and having a jolly time. Tomorrow, we charge into thousands of rebels, and if I die, it better not be sober."

Narothen pulled a flask from his pocket and offered Ahkarad a swig, which he rejected, prompting Narothen to drink it all. "Come on, guys, let's get some music going!"

Of the nearly forty men, none reacted to him, and they continued to sift through their things and ready for the coming fight. He tossed another flask into a group of Wolvar soldiers and sat back down. Their grumbling brought a smile to Ahkarad's face.

A faint whisper crawled into Ahkarad's ear, "Son of Netoma. Payment is due." His smile faded, and he looked about for the source, but no one seemed to be fussed about him; after Narothen's outburst, the camp remained silent.

Narothen plopped down beside him and threw an arm over Ahkarad's shoulder. "We can drink, can't we?" He pulled a bottle from his jacket and pulled the cork with his teeth. "If I'm going to die, might as well be drunk, am I right?"

Ahkarad shoved him back and walked up the road toward Lonstap. He watched the city below. With no movement and no lights, it would be a bloody battle with many casualties. He tugged at the necklace Meteri gave him the night she left, made of shards of Catha and black glass, tied with Alarus silk. She left abruptly, leaving only the necklace on the pillow beside him and the memories. A cool breeze rolled in on the starless night, but the aroma of spring flowers and freshly cut timber wafted up from the densely packed forests below.

"Answer the call of your mothers."

He glanced about, again finding no source. It was the voice of a soft-spoken woman, and its origin seemed to be the air around him. Brushing it off, he watched Narothen stumble about, pulling bottles of wine from his jacket—a special magical contraption his father gave him to carry extra supplies, but Narothen only considered how much booze he would need for the journey. Such items were common from the wealthier of Oncier's residents, and Narothen came from a family of nobles.

He approached and sat a bottle beside Ahkarad and crashed into the pile of leaves, his grin growing as he stared at Ahkarad and chugged more wine, spilling more than he drank. "Tell me, if she was so wonderful, and all you ever do is fawn over that necklace, why leave?"

"You're drunk," Ahkarad said.

"Of course, *Dad!* It's what I do. You still didn't answer my—" The wine he drank caught up with him, and he vomited most of the contents of his stomach onto the ground between them. "Sorry about that. Where were we?"

"You were telling me why your father forced you to join the Legion," Ahkarad said.

"The damned fool said I needed to grow up and that drinking was a boy's passion and that I needed to grow up. Ugh. A man was meant to drink and have a good time." He stood up and shouted to his fellow soldiers, "Let's have a party!" He struggled to his feet, pulled two more bottles from the enchanted pocket, and staggered his way to the rest of the unit.

Ahkarad pulled the cork on the bottle and tipped it over, letting sand pour from its spout. "Guess you thought it would be a bit tempting," he thought aloud.

With a laugh, he returned to watching the faint bit of torchlight moving through the streets of Lonstap. From the corner of his eye, he spotted a woman in thin white robes walking at the forest's edge. She held no torch nor glowstone and moved as though her limbs were broken. He looked over his drunken companions and took the chance to inspect more closely. She followed along the tree line, stumbling and falling before gathering herself and continuing ever deeper into the undergrowth.

He shrugged it off and turned to retake his post when the whisper returned, "Payment is due. Make right what is owed."

It came from the direction the woman traveled.

The winds changed to a bitter cold reminder that winter still lingered, and the smell of rotted flesh crept up his nose. His stomach turned, and shivers went down his spine. Looking over the other soldiers, he figured it would be worth investigating and stepped into the forest. They camped too long for his liking, and so, he followed the woman with caution. Perhaps this was a rebel trap of some sort?

Walking over downed trees and thorned bushes, he followed the woman. She faded from sight often, and he caught only glimpses of her white robes through the dense foliage and dim light. Through spiderwebs and vines, he pressed on, making his way to a campsite by the river. The woman sat by an empty fire pit; dead coals and ashes were all that remained, yet she held her hand out, mimicking an effort to warm herself.

"Have a seat. Our visitors will arrive soon," she said.

Looking closer, Ahkarad realized the woman was a Wolvar with pocked skin and missing splotches of fur, the same he had seen before he left to join the Legion. Her ragged cough sent chills down his spine. Her hands trembled, and her withered and gaunt body fought to stay upright. Taken off-guard, Ahkarad didn't notice when an Ualeon woman stepped from the trees until she was next to the old woman. She sat across from her. Her body bore bloody carved runes all over, and her eyes were nothing but burned cavities, empty and sunken. They both motioned for him to take the third seat.

"Do not fear. The mothers will arrive soon. Join us and enjoy the campfire," the Wolvar woman said.

He stepped back toward the forest's edge, grasping for his weapon.

"They come!" the Ualeon woman said.

She rose and held her hand aloft. The runes ignited, causing her body to burst into flames. Seams formed, tearing her flesh and peeling away her skin, oozing magma and burning the ground beneath her feet. The sockets where her eyes sat were now filled with raging white flames, and her horns grew, breaking their caps, leaving a pile of melted scrap at her feet. Each step she took toward Ahkarad burned away the grass and caused steam to rise from the river, boiling its waters and killing the fish near the bank.

The Wolvar woman fell onto the ground, and worms and insects fell from her mouth and nose, devouring what little bit of meat remained on her bones. They tore away loose flesh, and her left eye landed on the grass beside her corpse. With rigid movement and the sound of cracking bones, she rose, her joints and limbs popping in and out of place as she stood.

He pulled the sword from his side and pointed it toward them. His hands were steady, and his eyes were fixed. The Ualeon woman vanished, leaving molten footprints where she walked. The Wolvar lurched forward, her legs wobbling with each step.

"I want nothing to do with your bargain!" he said.

He grit his teeth as he felt a burning sensation run down his back, the feeling of a red-hot piece of iron bearing down on his flesh. The smell of burning skin filled the air around him. He did not flinch, yet the Ualeon woman walked behind him, running her fingers from one shoulder to the other.

"I have rejected you, why do you remain?" he asked.

"Because we aren't here to bargain. your mother took care of that, we are here to make known the price you owe," the Ualeon woman said.

"My mother," he said.

He looked over his shoulder to glare at the Ualeon woman, and his vision flashed back to his childhood. He remembered the statues Kyra and Irath that were placed beside the Everset Gate—it remained true for all Ualeon holds. This woman—this *demon*—was Kyra.

He spun and struck at her, the blade finding its mark and cutting into her flesh. No blood seeped from the wound, only magma and flakes of charred flesh. She laughed and grabbed the blade, and the steel turned red-hot and warped under the intense heat, leaving it a worthless scrap of metal. She let go and walked around behind him again.

The plagued Wolvar reached him and placed a hand on his shoulder guard. The metal rusted, and the leather peeled away, frayed and molded. It fell to the ground, nothing more than a rusted-out piece of metal with a few scraps of leather attached. Her hand came to rest on his hardened chest piece next, and with the slightest touch, she reduced it to little more than a heap of junk.

Ahkarad growled and lashed out at the Wolvar woman. If the fiery deity behind him was Kyra, then this must be Irath standing before him. She bared her teeth in a warped smile.

"Weapons and armor are worthless against decay. One of our faithful need not hide behind such useless means," Irath said. "Hold out your hand, son of

Netoma. A gift we offer. One given to our champion."

He tried to step away, only to be blocked by Kyra. She grabbed his wrist, and the act seared the flesh. His hand opened, and a flaming sword appeared. Its hilt dug into his skin, and the pain brought him to his knees. Letting go, his hand opened, and the weapon vanished, leaving Kyra's seared handprint on his wrist and the marking of hunger tattooed on his palm.

"It will answer your call, feeding on any you cut down," Kyra said.

Ahkarad looked up to them. "And if I refuse to use it? If I refuse its call? What then? Am I damned either way?"

"Haha! What interesting things mortals think. Call upon our aid, and your soul is ours," Irath said.

"Wait, what is the blade? Why call me your champion? Is my soul not already damned?" he asked.

Kyra walked to him as her feet and hands were burning away. The nub below her wrist brushed his arm. "Your bloodline owes a price, and through this blade, we shall collect. Should you want our aid, it will cost you more than a few souls of fallen soldiers and bandits. In time, we shall see if you can avoid such things."

Irath crumbled to the ground. Insects devoured her body, leaving the broken body rotting in the dirt. Kyra smiled. "Love can cause even the most noble to abandon their convictions. See you soon, son of Netoma."

Flames engulfed her body and burned it to be little more than a pile of ash and bone.

Out of instinct, he placed his right hand on the

corpse of Irath. His eyes turned black, and he found himself standing in a crowd of people within Lonstap. He looked at the world through the Wolvar woman's eyes. They were chanting words he could not understand while painting her skin.

The Ualeon woman lay on a table beside her. They mutilated her body, cutting her insides out after runes were carved into her flesh. Once prepared, they were sent into the woods. During this, both walked past an army greater than reports indicated, and they were preparing for an assault of their own. Trebuchets and other artillery were aimed at the hills, and thousands of tribesmen were slowly climbing the ledges on either side.

He let go of the body and climbed to his feet. The singing from camp fell silent, and he felt the same feeling: an emptiness in the pit of his stomach, followed by the realization that they were soon to spring their trap. With everyone asleep, his unit would be the first hit. He raced through the underbrush, snagging himself on vines and limbs. He stumbled up the hill, clawing at the dirt with his hands, fighting to reach his unit.

Reaching for his weapon, he grabbed at nothing, forgetting his sword had become a pile of useless metal on the riverbank. He looked to his left hand at the scar and tattoo and felt the familiar urge—a thirst, a hunger that would not be sated any other way. He pushed it down and burst through the trees to find tribesmen preparing to attack.

Taking a sword from one of the racks, he launched into an attack, cutting down a few of the ambushers and waking a few of his companions. As people around camp woke, they scrambled to the horn. Ahkarad lost the sword and used one of Narothen's bottles to strike one of the attackers and render them unconscious.

Taking their weapon, he lunged at another and stabbed them through the chest. Hundreds were pouring into their camp, and he would need to wake the whole army before they were overrun and thousands were slaughtered in their sleep. One of the attackers tackled him, making him lose his weapon. This was a battle of might, and he lacked the strength needed to overpower his foe.

"It hungers," Irath's voice whispered into his ear.

He held the rebel's blade at bay. The sharp edge cut into his hands, but he stopped it from puncturing his exposed chest. He was pushing back against the blade when a lute crashed against his attacker's head.

Narothen stumbled over and helped him up. "They broke my bottle." He held a broken wine bottle with sand falling from what remained.

"Shame. We need to sound the alarm," Ahkarad said.

"Right, that would get us more wine," Narothen said.

Ahkarad took the lute from his hand and smacked him over the head with it. "Sorry, but you are more useful unconscious."

He took the weapon from a fallen soldier and cut his path to the peak. A dozen rebels were in pursuit. He reached the horn and sounded the alarm. Fires lit across the hills as reinforcements rushed toward Ahkarad's unit.

argains and Debts

DAY TWO OF THE LIBERATION OF LONSTAP marshaled bloodied battles that continued across several miles of forest. Ahkarad followed the instructions of commander Thadis, but every attempt to take the outer wall failed, and the trenches were filled with the bodies of dead or dying Legion soldiers.

Ahkarad found himself stuck against the wall with his drunken friend Narothen—who was surprisingly still conscious, but he worked diligently to remedy the situation. With the sun yet to rise, the agonized cries of his fellow soldiers masked Narothen's belligerent swearing and random outbursts. Ahkarad reached over and snatched the bottle from his hand and quickly handed it back.

"Maybe that will suit you better!" Ahkarad said.

Narothen raised the bottle, and sand poured into his mouth. His coughing caused the guards patrolling outside the wall to take notice and inspect the area. Ahkarad covered Narothen's mouth and pulled him down against a pile of bodies. Ahkarad's gloves remained on, but he felt an overwhelming presence of tortured souls. From thin air, he heard the voice of Kyra.

"They would taste so much better. Cut them down. Feed our hunger. Know our strength."

His glove became engulfed in flames, and in an attempt to stop the noticeable light just outside the wall, he shoved his hand into the pile of bodies and touched the deceased soldier he lay against with his bare hand. Without warning, his mind returned to the moment of the assault.

Legion forces nearly a thousand strong were cut down as they crashed against the city walls. Soldiers were falling right and left, and he carried one end of a ladder. As they reached their stopping point and raised it, an arrow cut through his neck from above. Another through his collar, and as he fell back, another landed firmly in his chest. Rain fell as soldiers sloshed in the muck. Bodies were dropping, and the call for retreat rang out over the battlefield. He tried to follow his fellow soldiers, but he couldn't move. His last breaths were slowed by blood filling his lungs. He felt the cold fear rush in as the man's life faded.

Ahkarad snapped out of it and pulled away, bumping into one of the rebels patrolling the body piles. He let go of Narothen's mouth, and he popped up covered in blood and swinging his fists violently.

"Damn you, Ahkarad, stop ruining my alcohol," Narothen said.

Another voice drifted on the breeze. Irath spoke to him while the rebels readied their weapons.

"We only want what's best for you. Don't allow pride to be your end."

He reached for his sword, grabbing nothing but an empty scabbard. He took the only thing he could find, which happened to be a bottle Narothen had pulled from his jacket. Scrambling, he snatched the bottle from Narothen's hands and smacked the nearest rebel over the head. The bottle didn't break, but the blow did knock the man off his feet. Ahkarad took his sword and swung it at them, but the weapon turned to sand, and his opponent's blade gashed his shoulder.

"You have such power, but you avoid our aid. Drink of our strength. Imagine what is possible with the gods on your side," the mothers said in unison.

Narothen took another bottle from his special bag. The cork popped, and he licked his lips. He raised it to his mouth, but Ahkarad snatched it and shattered it over the head of another rebel. Sand scattered into the air in a blinding spray. An arrow landed at his feet. He looked up to see another flying at his face. It turned into flower petals when it touched his skin. His heart skipped a beat, and he gasped for air.

"We will not interfere again. Either accept your role, or we will find another," the mothers said, became agitated.

He grabbed the intact bottle from Narothen and smacked the attacker with it. "I'll not bargain with the likes of you."

Laughter rang out, followed by a burst of lightning that rippled across the sky, and in the clouds, Kyra's face formed among the ominous electric discharge. "This is not a bargain! That will come later. This is your duty, King of Netoma."

Thunder shook the ground, and another blinding flash tore across the sky. In his hand, the blade formed. He could feel its hunger; it craved battle and longed to have its flames quenched in blood. A rebel reached him and ran a spear through Ahkarad's side, missing any vital organs, but the pain racked his body. Through the excruciating pain, he snapped the spear handle and jabbed the jagged end into the man's neck, leaving him in a pool of blood and muddy water.

He let go of the blade, and it vanished. "I will not forsake my soul for your lies."

An arrow pierced his shoulder, and another grazed his leg. Narothen found a bottle of whiskey in his pocket and enjoyed the aroma. Taking a sip, he smiled, and then an arrow shattered the bottle, spilling it all over his clothes. He pressed his fingers in the soaked cloth and sucked what he could from his skin.

"Every soul will give you strength. Ahkarad, honor your mother's bargain! Yours has yet to be struck. Or would you rather die than take what is rightfully yours?"

He took cover, dragging Narothen behind a pillar of darkened stone. He pulled the arrows from his skin. They hadn't gone deep but caused plenty of damage to the surrounding flesh. He used a bundle of cloth sitting in the mud to stem the bleeding from his side wound. At the tree line, the Legion forces waited. They held their position and waited for dawn to advance on the walls.

Ahkarad heard another set of feet sloshing through the muck and lunged out, grabbing another rebel. He came around the collapsed tent and was met with Ahkarad using an arrowhead as a knife. Slitting the rebel's throat and reaching for their weapons, he heard a woman's voice struggling against the blood filling her airway. He removed the mask, expecting a vile creature, but was met with a human woman's face, little more than a farmer using poorly maintained weapons and wearing flimsy armor made of assorted pieces thrown together haphazardly. Her weapon turned to water when he tried to lift it.

"You don't offer another option?" Ahkarad asked the air around him.

Taken off-guard, another attacker tackled him to the ground. His opponent missed a few close strikes, but he managed to catch Ahkarad with an elbow and dazed him. Regaining his footing, Ahkarad saw the man's sword too late. It dug into his side and went clean through his stomach. He grabbed the human man by the neck and used a loose brick to crush his skull. He crawled to Narothen, losing blood, and he leaned beside the drunkard and watched as he downed a full bottle of whiskey and fell over into a puddle of murky water.

"Your wounds are nothing that cannot be fixed by sating our hunger," Irath said. One of the corpse's necks snapped around and looked at him as Irath took control of its body. "Resist if you must, but you only delay what is to come. Either you will die, or you will allow the hunger to heal your wounds." The body decayed and rotted before his eyes, turned to dust and spreading across the mixed pile of bodies.

He tore a piece from his tunic, wrapped it around

his shoulder, and did his best to pack the area around the sword. Stumbling to his feet, he grabbed Narothen by the ankle and dragged him back toward the trees. Between the rain and lightning, he could hardly see while moving through the open field. In the confusion, an Ualeon brute charged at him. Seeing this, Ahkarad braced and met a predictable result, being thrown from his feet and landing in the mud. The brute's hands pulled him to his feet, and he took a punch to the face and then his stomach.

Ahkarad fell to a knee and caught an uppercut, landing him on his back again. Still impaled by a sword, Ahkarad knew the fight needed to end soon. The brute threw him into another pile of bodies. Thinking quickly, he pulled the sword free and felt the wound open and gush blood. When yanked from his feet, he jabbed the weapon into the brute's eye.

Exhausted, he collapsed and tried to drag himself back to Narothen. "I won't bargain. Not for my life or anyone else's." His arms were too weak to crawl any farther, and his legs could no longer push him along.

His head landed in the mud, and he rested while soldiers on both sides shouted across the field at each other. He could see Narothen's head sinking toward a puddle of water, his nose coming close to submerging. Ahkarad grabbed Narothen's leg and pulled him just enough for him to no longer be at risk of drowning.

He slipped in and out for a few minutes but managed to grab ahold of Narothen's foot and pull him into cover. The piled logs gave cover from the arrows but would offer no safety if a patrol wandered close.

Narothen woke and looked about. "What did I

miss?" He opened the pocket, and Ahkarad punched him, dazing him. "What was that for?"

"Couldn't say for sure. Felt right, I guess. Now, how about we figure a way out of this?" He pulled a field dressing kit from his small pack. The bandages were soggy and covered in mud, and the remnants of the healing elixir lay broken at the bottom. He tried to climb to his feet, but he'd lost too much blood and stumbled back.

"You're right, I have been a bit too drunk. Tell you what . . ." He sat there blankly staring at Ahkarad while he fought to stand. "Tell me . . . What? Umm . . ." Narothen said.

"Tell me what already?" Ahkarad asked.

Narothen blinked. "Tell what? Not sure I know what you're talking about."

Ahkarad shoved him and watched after each strike of lightning and what each pulse revealed. "Alright, when the rain picks up, we—" He turned to find Narothen passed out with another empty bottle in his hand. "I should just kill you. No, okay, Ahkarad, looks like we are doing this on our own." He pulled Narothen close, and with the storm picking up, he prepared to make his move.

Morning came, and the sky lightened. The rebels advanced on the Legion forces, and Ahkarad tucked Narothen into a gap between stumps and covered him in branches and leaves. Both forces were closing in on Ahkarad's position. He broke a tree limb and waited until an Ualeon soldier reached him. He impaled the first one to reach him, and he took their weapon. He stood over Narothen and cut down a few more before he was surrounded.

"You're a fool. Accept it. There is another. Maybe she would take our bargain," Irath said.

Everything became still. He looked at Narothen and back at the Legion forces falling to the arrows raining down on them from the fort. "What do you mean another? My mother had no other children."

"A fool to the end. The Ualeon aren't the only ones that carry our favor. Imagine a world where a child such as yourself was our only choice," Irath growled.

The harsh, dry voice of Kyra tore into his ear, "To think a Wolvar would be our champion, even one so strong as her."

Rebels were closing in with weapons ready. His hand burned, and he felt the toll his injuries took. With an arcing slash, he took down another attacker and took their spear, throwing it into the next soldier to step up. He refused to go down, cutting his way through any who came near.

Blood trickled down his leg and pooled in his boots. He felt drained, and the insatiable hunger of the blade called. He felt desperate, but not enough to use their gifts. The Legion made a push, and behind him echoed the familiar voice of Usuara, who fought to reach Ahkarad. A group of soldiers charged down the middle of the field, springing the trap laid by the forces of Lonstap. They became hemmed in and were slowly being cut down.

His blood loss caught up with him, and Ahkarad fell to his knees.

Usuara reached him and put his arms around him. "No, boy, ya can't be goin' like this. I've come I shoulda come, shoulda come sooner. Ya goin' to be alright."

Ahkarad reached up to Usuara's face. "You were right, old man. You were right." As the light faded, Ahkarad saw the enemy forces collapsing in on them, and the mothers called to him in the darkness.

"Maybe he would accept a bargain. Either of them would do; they just need the right push."

Ahkarad's eyes opened, and in his hand, the blade formed.

CHAPTER 30

t War's End, 1333

USUARA SHUFFLED UP THE WEATHERED STONE PATH IN the dim light. Bits and pieces of the old structure were missing or scattered about the fields from centuries of neglect and harsh conditions on the northern coast. In the shadow of the crumbled Olian fort, Ahkarad leaned against the outer wall overlooking the city of Maknora.

The people below were gathering firewood and preparing for a feast, often erupting in song and playing music while preparing for the revelry. Even the soldiers across the battlements were cheering and drinking, but Ahkarad sat along the crumbled wall and smoked his ivory pipe, staring out onto the waves rolling along the orange-and-pink light of the setting sun. Each drag bathed his face and broken horns with red light.

Usuara sat beside the dwindling fire, tossed a few moss-covered logs in, and turned the coals about.

"Seems those folks had got the news a little late. Or ya think they have been preparin' all week?"

Ahkarad shrugged and tossed a letter onto the ground beside the old Dwarf. It bore the seal of the High Arch, and it thanked him for his service, offered modest pay, and freed him from service. He leaned back and propped his feet up on the broken archway. "Guess twenty years was good enough. But you didn't travel from Oncier to make small talk. Being so many years have passed since Lonstap, must be something important." He turned and locked eyes with Usuara.

"Aye, it's Sasha. She's run into a . . . umm. A snag. I figured that gift of yers would offer the aid she needs," Usuara said.

Ahkarad shrugged and turned over his pipe, knocking loose the bits of used tobacco. "She doesn't know you came?" He cleaned it with his finger and placed it into his pocket. "Sly old man. You know she'll have your head for trying to push us back together."

Usuara leaned into the light. His skin remained stained black all these years later, and Ahkarad laughed at Usuara using a piece of scrap metal to stoke the fire. Tossing it down, he pulled a pouch of dried meat from his pocket. Stuffing a bit in his mouth, he offered some to Ahkarad, and with his rejection, he tucked it away.

"Not sure she knows how to ask. Besides, this isn't a problem more guards could fix. Would ya do it for an old man regrettin' a decision he made in haste?" Usuara asked.

Ahkarad stood and walked over to the fire. Leaving the note in Usuara's hand, he walked to the crumbled entrance. "I'll think on it. Many things for me to do. Never thought I'd live to see the war end, not to mention me leaving the Legion. And on that, sleep well, old friend. I'll find you in Oncier with my answer."

He pulled his coat up and lifted the collar to block the harsh winds rolling in off the bay.

"Where will ya go? Not like the world's changed much since ya been gone," Usuara said.

"Maybe I'll visit the last home of the paladins or visit your home of Iskal. Not like I have anything keeping me in one place," he said.

Ahkarad walked down the path. Snow covered the short brown grass and concealed the stepping stones from view. Finding his way to the broken shore, he leaned against a crumbled section of a once proud tower. Many centuries ago, this would have been the entrance to the city of Istala, the domain of the Dwarven king, Bayrn. Over time, it became a crumbled shard of road leading into the ocean. Beneath the waves, the glowstones lining the city streets were still visible, glinting like stars in the depths.

Music filled the air, and under cloudy skies, snow fell. People were celebrating the twenty-year war coming to an end, but for Ahkarad, it drew a close to what he knew. A new path forward brought fear but gave him something he longed for, and the idea of venturing into the unknown and being away from the killing brought a sense of ease.

Watching the villagers dancing warmed his heart, and smelling the food cooking over the blazing bonfires brought a smile to his face at the peaceful nature of the people. He enjoyed a small nap, letting the soft, cold kiss of snow caress his skin. Waves crashing sent water rushing up the rocks, nearly reaching him. As twenty years of carnage and pain came to an end, he was at peace with his life, and there he sat at the farthest point north and west without needing a boat.

He reached into his pocket and pulled out a charm, Meteri's necklace. The silk necklace had long since broken, becoming little more than a trinket. He ran his finger across it as he looked over the water. Turbulent seas marked the foul weather ahead. The cold, howling wind cut through his thin clothing and brought a bit of discomfort, but he shrugged it off and watched an old Wolvar woman walk away from town.

Her white robe stuck out in the dark but blended in with the freshly fallen snow. Knowing what came next, he followed her until she reached the brazier at the base of the broken statues of the twin mothers. Taking a deep breath, he joined her and helped light the candles. With her advanced age, it took Ahkarad's help to raise the oil lantern and place it above the altar. After completing her task, she turned to him and smiled.

"They have sent word. A man searches for a way to close the door. This goes against the mothers' interests and must be answered. You are to find and silence this person. There is no name. Only a place. Oncier."

"And if I refuse to answer, say I wished to no longer have their favor?" he asked.

She began walking away when his words gave her pause. "Only a fool would say such things aloud." She waved a hand, and Ahkarad fell to his knees.

Another rune was seared into his flesh, leaving a fresh wound on his chest. "You have a way of angering Kyra. They will call upon you once you have reached the city." She turned and walked back toward the town, with expedience to her steps, and without stopping, she called back to him, "One final order, a girl from the south will cross your path. End her. Do not hesitate. Her life is meaningless and should not be allowed to interfere with our plans. Understood?"

"Yes, Speaker. I understand." He fervently rubbed the burning patch of skin. It turned cold to the touch but felt to be on fire from the inside. The sensation faded, but the mark remained, leaving the Ualeon word for "Obedience" etched into his skin.

After a few hours of watching the waves, he walked into town. Making his way to the barracks, he passed an old Ualeon woman. She took a long look at him and stepped into his path.

"Can it be? Has fate cursed me to not truly recognize you?" she asked.

Ahkarad looked over her face and saw nothing, just another Ualeon woman. "Can I help you?" he asked.

She caressed his cheek and smiled. Tears welled in her eyes, and her hands started to tremble. "Ahkarad? Can it be you? After all these years, can it be?" Her hand ran up his broken horns. "What has happened to my sweet prince?"

He stepped back and grasped her wrists. "Do I know you?" he asked.

"I followed you every morning, and I watched after you as a boy. Do you not remember your own people?" she asked in return.

He looked into her eyes, and through the cataracts, he saw the woman who had snuck him sweet rolls in his youth. Tak. Time did not offer her an easy path. She was missing most of her teeth, and burns covered the left side of her body. No longer did she have the ceremonial garb and weapons of the Queen's Guard. Instead, she wore old maid garments and hobbled on a flimsy cane.

"Where have you been?" she asked.

"Doing what I must, as we all have. How did you end up here?" he asked.

He noticed her eyes had drifted to the fresh marking on his chest, and he pulled the tunic over and buttoned the top to conceal it. With concerned eyes, she looked him over.

"May your mother's fate not be your own. We waited for you, Ahkarad. We waited by the sea. But you never came, and one day, we lost hope that you would come. Can you forgive an old woman for failing to have faith?" She fell to her knees and kissed his feet, and others joined her. People surrounded him, praising his return, but he felt discomfort at how they viewed him and pulled away.

"Please, I'm not the man you wished me to be. Our kingdom is a part of Empryss now, and we are no longer ruled by our own kings," he said.

She stood and cupped his hands. "*You* are our king. Paper and lines drawn by the nobles cannot take it, and their words will never claim what blood gave you."

The people dispersed and left the street empty, with but a few dimmed fire pits and the remnants of their revelries littered around the town square. Soldiers and merchants were passed out around the tables and benches. She still stood, holding his hands and looking into his eyes.

"I know it isn't much"—she placed a few gold coins into his hand and folded his fingers over—"but your mother would have scolded me for not giving you something for your journey. Be good, last son of Netoma. May you find your way home someday." She let go and joined an elderly man traveling toward their home.

After they ducked inside, he returned to the path through the city. He flipped each coin over the other, end over end, until he came to the largest of the smoldering bonfires. He pulled a letter from Anly out of his inner pocket.

"Dear Ahkarad,

I hope this letter finds you well. My father Andros fell ill in early spring. It was my hope to reach you sooner, but with the war reaching its height, I was unable to send a single communication, and it would seem fate decided we would not get a chance to speak until now. Father took a turn, and he passed peacefully at home. The old man never knew how to leave a stone unturned or a person forgotten, requesting that I leave you the deed to his estate on Haberndis Island, which, as the steward of his estate, I will gladly honor and will make arrangements that staff remain indefinitely. It is yours, should you wish to claim it. May the end of the war and this new chapter find you well, and, as Father would say, "Do not send your regards, only honor your word."

Yours truly, Anly."

He folded the paper and tucked it away in his vest pocket. He felt heavier having read it again, and he tossed the request from Sasha into the fire. He watched the embers flicker into the sky before tugging at his chest piece and making his way toward the barracks for his last night with the soldiers he served with.

"Goodbye, old friend. May the beyond give you peace," he said under his breath as he stepped out of the light and into the shadows at the edge of town.

CHAPTER 31

S teward of House Dres

AHKARAD STEPPED OFF THE BOAT TO THE FAMILIAR sight of a larger-than-normal gibbet swinging outside the city jail. It brought a smile to his face and caused him to chuckle. He tugged at the worn pack over his left shoulder and walked into the town square. Everything had changed. The Ualeon and Wolvar were gone, and it was now a bustling city filled with humans and Dwarves. It had grown beyond a refuge for the less than fortunate. At the very center of town stood two statues. One was of Yunis, former magistrate and caretaker of those in need, and Andros, watcher and protector of the island.

He looked over the crude statue of his former mentor and watched people ignore their existence. Everyone needed to be somewhere, and history they often held less important than the present for those around the market. Cloth was draped between the statues, and people covered the brass plaques stating their accomplishments and noting their importance to the people of Haberndis.

A poorly dressed fruit merchant with dirt under his nails and bags under his eyes blocked the notation of what Andros meant to the formation of the city with his belongings. Ahkarad took a deep breath and walked on, passing what were once rows of crude sheds where his people had lived in the days after Netoma's fall. Now there were rows of beautiful homes of fine wood and stone.

Only the wealthy could live in such luxury, and listening to their gossip, he overheard their petitions to the magistrate about taking the Venae Estate in the absence of its steward.

"I hear a beast of a man was given right over the grounds," the noblewoman said.

"No, I heard Anly gave it to his father's mistress. To keep her silent. Magistrate Parno, would you let such vile things happen—"

Ahkarad stepped in. "That would be awful, allowing such filth in this city. Almost makes me wonder about the future of such a place." He grinned at the nobles, particularly, one man named Parno, a magistrate upon whose chest was the emblem of a Legion captain. Taking Parno's arm, he led the man away from the crowd. "Andros left the estate to me, and I would appreciate it if we could keep from having any issues. I don't think Anly would take kindly to his father's dying wish being walked all over."

He gave a soft slap to the magistrate's cheek and stepped back onto the path toward the estate. As he walked away, he heard the gasps from the nobles and shouting about the unruly behavior of such a beastly person. Hearing such things gave him a chuckle.

The miles dragged on, and soon, he could see the gates and hear the staff shouting inside. The same guards who watched the walls greeted him when he entered.

Standing near the back gate, he watched the staff fervently cleaning and preparing a meal. It neared evening, and they were yet to finish supper. Most were still trying to clean and were still half-dressed in their work attire.

Smiling, he walked to the old bench where he'd spent most of his nights reading and watching the stars and ran his finger along a name carved on the seat. He stopped one of the ladies and asked, "What is the rush? Not like anyone special is coming."

She smiled and ran to the kitchen and started shouting that he arrived and to have everything on the table soon. He wore a perplexed look, and he plopped down on the bench.

A voice from the gate caught his attention. "What would he say? It's a matter of seeing everything in the proper light?" Meteri stood against the wall, an old scar running down her right temple to her jaw. Spots where a few scales were missing caught his eye. "They're afraid. The nobles have been calling for the place to be sold off, the greedy bunch," she said.

"Spoke with the magistrate. Feels like we reached an . . . agreement." Ahkarad offered her a seat across from him. "Join me for dinner?"

The staff brought out several plates of steamed food. Rare delicacies from across the kingdom and meals crafted to his preference were laid out on the table before them. She smiled and waved him off.

"I stopped in to say goodbye to this place. There are a lot of memories, and not one I regret," she said.

Ahkarad stood and followed her to the gate.

She stepped away and turned from his gaze. "Sorry, but I really should be going. Some of us are better if we keep moving, and, in my case, word travels fast enough without gossiping nobles watching my every move."

She stepped close and kissed his cheek. "Take care. If you find yourself in Aud Nua, I'll be at the apothecary's den. Maybe you'll require a special kind of healing if you come through? Goodbye, King of Sand." She stepped out the door.

"I would have followed you." Ahkarad stepped through the gate and into the street behind her. "I would have gone anywhere to be with you."

She stood with her back to him. "I know." She took another step and turned her head to the side. "What would he say? If you had, then you wouldn't be the man you are today." She smiled and gave a wink. "For better or worse, I guess he was right."

Ahkarad's shoulders dropped, and he smiled. "He was full of wise words. If you have need of an old friend, I'll be in Oncier handling a sensitive matter for an old friend."

She continued down the path, tossing her hand up and waving as she blended into the crowd traveling the road.

He stepped back inside, and the staff were waiting patiently by the doors, awaiting his approval and watching his every move. He sat and took a few bites and turned over a glass of wine. Sand poured onto the ground beside him. "Guess there are worse curses out there."

He filled the glass with water and finished his meal. The head of staff, in neatly pressed clothes, stood at his shoulder until he motioned for them to take the plates away. He turned to face the middle-aged, well-groomed Wolvar.

"What's your name?" Ahkarad asked.

"Bola. We are here to serve. Do you need anything, sir?"

Ahkarad shook his head. "How long have you been here?"

"Seven years, sir. Took over from the last steward, yet wasn't given the title." He fidgeted and raised his hand. "Could I speak freely, sir?"

"First of all, only soldiers under me ever called me sir. Second, I'm no better than you. Say what you please, and let what happens happen."

"Thank you, si— Thank you. Without a steward, the nobles can petition the magistrate once you leave. I am just concerned about the future of the estate and those who work here." He swallowed hard and looked ahead, avoiding eye contact with Ahkarad.

"Bola, then you are the steward, enough said. Enjoy laughing at the nobles, I guess."

"Sir— Sorry, Ahkarad. They will only honor a stewardship if you choose someone qualified for the task and do so with the magistrate's blessing."

Ahkarad bit the inside of his cheek. "Tell you what, call for the magistrate first thing. We'll take care of everything." He stood and looked the Wolvar in the eyes while turning the collar of his shirt just a bit off center. "Could I ask you something?"

Bola gave a frightened nod.

"Good. Did you ever meet Andros?"

"No, sir. He moved home before I started here. My father knew him and sent for me when I was old enough to work."

Ahkarad looked at the stairs. "I'll be going to bed now. Make sure the magistrate is here at dawn."

Bola and the other staff gathered the plates and carried them inside.

"Bola."

The Wolvar stopped at the top step. "Yes, sir?"

"Make sure everyone has a good meal. I'm not much of a chef, but I'll cook for myself in the morning."

Ahkarad tossed and turned through the night, finding the soft mattress as uncomfortable as he remembered. Halfway through the night, he carried a blanket and pillow out onto the lawn and finished the night under the stars.

The hard, cold ground offered a familiar comfort, and he enjoyed the ease of watching the shooting stars until his eyes became too heavy and sleep took him.

Morning came, and he was eating a whole roasted chicken with his knife stuck through the carcass when the magistrate pushed his way through the gate. His frilled clothes and oddly colorful hair annoyed Ahkarad. Parno was just as irritating as the previous day, and his voice and general disgust at those beneath him set Ahkarad to be annoyed early on.

"Dear Ahkarad, the nobles would like to know how long it will be before you . . ." his voice faded to a whisper, "decide you're not the estate type."

Ahkarad stood and slung the chicken, the knife still in his hand. "Hmm, I called you here to name a steward, but"—he put the knife to the magistrate's neck and trimmed the Wolvar's fur down to the skin —"it would seem you care more about gold than what's right."

He clasped the nape of Parno's neck and lifted him into the air. "So, I give you two choices." He dropped the knife and held out his hand, and the flaming blade appeared. "One, you honor my wishes and that of the late Andros Venae, or two—" He moved the blade over Parno's fur, causing the ends to smoke and singe. "I can see about a new magistrate. I may not be serving the Legion in a full capacity, but I still know a few names that could cause a serious headache. They would look the other way when it comes to a Wolvar or two going missing."

He opened his hand and let the blade vanish. Parno's body shook, and when Ahkarad put his feet back on the ground, he fainted, falling back into the shrubs.

"Did you kill him?" Bola asked.

"Nope, never that lucky. But be ready to sign your name," Ahkarad said. A smile crept across his face as he slapped Parno with an open hand. "Still with us?"

"Yes, sorry, sir Ahkarad. Uh. Umm, so you are—?"

"Ahkarad Dres, son of Massa. There is enough gold for my steward to keep the estate for the next century, and due to my presence being requested in Oncier, I must travel. Would you be so kind as to recognize Bola as head of estate in my absence? And should I hear that you have allowed the nobles their way?" Flames filled Ahkarad's eyes, and his hands clasped Parno's throat. "I will send you all to the twin mothers. Personally." His hands tightened, and his eyes burned with rage. "Do I make myself clear?"

Parno gave a nod, with his throat closed, and his face turning blue. Ahkarad carried him to the table where a document was prepared for Bola to be named the official steward. Once done, Ahkarad tossed him out the gate, sending him sliding in the dirt.

Ahkarad slammed the gate shut and walked up the stairs to his room. While he was stuffing his things in a satchel, he noticed Bola standing in the doorway.

"What do you need?" Ahkarad asked.

Bola took a breath and stepped into the room, the door closing behind him. "What are your orders for the estate while you're away, sir?"

"Thought I made that clear. Sir isn't my title. Call me Ahkarad, and keep the place clean. Could be months or years before I return. Anly said there was a deep coffer and that a stream of gold would be coming in. Use it well, and should things get thin, seek me in Oncier. I'll be staying with the Royal Watch."

"But, sir—"

"What did I say?"

"My father spoke of you, King of the Ualeon, that one day you would return to Netoma, and it would be risen once more."

Ahkarad smiled and walked Bola out to the front step. "My mother was the queen, but I'm no king. I'm just a man like you. Nothing in this world would change that. And Netoma is gone. Take care, Steward of House Dres. From what I can tell, you'll not let me down."

He tossed a pack over his shoulder and carried a

satchel across his chest. Under the straps rested a shield bearing the crest of the Legion, but he left his uniform to be stored within the estate.

Boarding the ship, he found his seat beside two Sethyn women. Both were setting out for the city of Oncier, and he smiled at their attempts at rounding up their small children scattered across the main hold.

Listening to the harbor master shout about which ship needed to depart and in what order, he opened a letter Narothen sent to him and started leafing through the pages as the ship raised its anchor and moved out to sea.

ABOUT THE AUTHOR

Barry Foster, the youngest of four boys developed a passion for writing at an early age. Using his free time between double shifts and tending to his responsibilities as a father and husband Barry writes stories of fantasy and horror to escape the mundane happenings of normal life.

www.ingramcontent.com/pod-product-compliance
Lightning Source LLC
Chambersburg PA
CBHW071207210726
48293CB00002B/329